The Truth Within the Fog

Julian Mercer

Cedar Hill
— BOOKS —

"Heart of mine so malicious and so full of guile

Give you an inch, and you'll take a mile."

– Bob Dylan

The Fog

Kaya

Just sixteen years old, tight against my side, her petite brown frame touching mine, my hands firmly planted on the wheel of Mom's brand-spankin' new Buick.

We are parked just down the street from her small suburban home.

An early evening mist shrouds the sidewalks and front lawns of the postwar tract surrounding us.

The mist thickens, cloaking the street in a white blanket.

I'm smitten; I admit it.

Fuck, she's the one for me!

I want her.

Her eyes stare out through the glass, out into the gray.

Mine is fixed on her profile.

It's not just that I want Kaya; it's that I want her… and her alone.

It didn't start out that way, but what does that matter?

This is what it became, what it is, and I will not be denied.

Finally, she moves, her head turns.

Our faces touching, Kaya shouts, her voice filling the still small space:

"Okay, I won't!"

"Okay, you won't what?

"Say it!" I demand.

"Okay, I won't see anyone else.

There, I said it!

Isn't that what you wanted?" she sneers and turns away again, distracted.

Kaya concentrates on the fog, trembling.

It thickens with every passing moment, finally encasing the car.

Then she grabs the door handle.

The door swings open without a sound, as if greased by the fog.

She moves fast and smoothly.

Instantaneously, she's over the curb and onto the dew-covered grass.

Gone into the mist.

Justin

It's been twenty years since that foggy evening in the South Bay when Kaya got off my road and traveled down another.

Our paths have never crossed since.

There have been many forks.

Sometimes, you can travel down one road a bit and then double back.

Sometimes you can't.

Some roads cross; most never again intersect; that seems our fate.

Some say that in the end, all roads lead to the same place; perhaps that is where we will again meet.

Who can know these things?

One might as well go where the journey takes you, as I see it.

Hell, half the time, other things—people, circumstances, events—decide which direction you should take.

You can pretend; you can fight it. But you might as well give up.

I did.

I work in the Wells Fargo Building.

Sitting smack on Bunker Hill, it is one of the tallest skyscrapers in downtown Los Angeles.

There's no fuckin' way I wanted to end up here, but I did.

That's just my point!

I have a fancy office on the twenty-third floor and run Piedmont Textiles on the West Coast.

I damn well know that I don't belong in this large office in this fine building, and I certainly shouldn't be running Piedmont, but I do.

Nobody else thinks I should run the place either, but they have to eat, so they come to work.

They have no control; we share the same fate and are 'dealt a hand,' as the old saying goes.

I met my wife twenty years ago, and we wed three years later.

Let me tell you, it's no easy feat to please a woman – or to raise a son, for that matter.

My wife never wanted me to be a businessman; she married a thinker, not a dealmaker.

I think she figures she didn't get what she'd bargained for.

Well, join the club.

Most people don't get what they bargain for; that's how I see it.

Lacy is a woman of style, sophistication, and excellent manners. I, on the other hand, can come off a bit gruff and uncouth.

People get confused when they meet us; we're an odd couple.

I suppose they figure opposites attract or something like that – a simple explanation.

Lacy rarely comes downtown to visit me at the office.

She doesn't like deal-making, and deal-making is my thing.

We live in one of the most exclusive neighborhoods in Los Angeles.

We receive invitations on fine cardstock from rich, connected, and "interesting" people, people with a pot to piss in, people who could do me good, but Lacy can't stand any of them.

She declines most invitations, and if we do accept one, she bitches all the way home about "those people."

I'd tell her,

"Lacy, you sound like Old Bobbie Lee, talking about the Yankees:

'Those people.' He'd called them that."

"Justin, what are you talking about? Just shut up!"

I spend my Saturdays with my son David, and Lacy spends her Saturdays talking to Velma on the phone.

We're not Ozzie and Harriet; it's not a perfect marriage; hell, it seems like I spend half my time in the doghouse.

If it isn't about how I eat or dress, it's about my attention to work.

"Justin, all you care about is making money; it's all you think about. You care more about Piedmont than your own family; you're never home, you've changed!

Where's your humanity? You used to pray and shed tears.

What happened to the humanist?"

She's probably right, but I always fight it off.

"What the fuck?

I'm doing the best I can! I support a kid and a big fuckin' house, and you live in it – that's what happened!"

"You love it! All you want to do is work!" she'd retort.

(Nothing could be farther from the truth. What I do is useless; anybody could do it. I do it to make money.)

Sometimes, she persists.

"What a crybaby! My daddy works a thousand times harder than you and never cries. You cry like a little girl."

Most of the time, I hold my tongue, but sometimes my emotions get the better of me.

"Your daddy, your daddy! He drove the fuckin' company into the ground! If it weren't for me, your whole sorry-ass family would be out on the streets instead of living where they're living right now."

Sometimes, I reckon that none of this struggle with life makes any sense, that it's one big stupid battle… and for what?

I'd rant at anyone who'd listen.

One day, I told Willard, the security guard at Piedmont,

"Ya know, Willard, here we are working our asses off inside this frickin' building, and out on Sixth, I saw this bum harassing pedestrians. He's sitting outside Starbucks, under a frickin' umbrella in the sun, watching the chicks walk by like he's on an island or something. The motherfucker's on vacation! He's doing what I do on vacation: sitting in the sun, watching the girls; and drinking booze from a bag. Come on now, Willard, who has a better life, us or them?"

Willard smiled and said,

"Well, Mr. Larkin, I never thought about it like that."

I'm sure he thinks I'm plum crazy, but I mean it!

All day long in the office, it's the same useless activity.

I waste hours arguing with some slump on Santee Street about a fuckin' shipment date.

Who's the fool, the bum or me?

I have this great office with this massive glass wall – don't get too close to the edge, or you might fall…

I sit behind the conference table (to feel safe), and I can see the futuristic Frank Gehry Disney Concert Hall below.

I eye old brick high-rises with ancient fading script out of the same window.

Off in the distance, I spy Broadway, like a teeming Mexican village, and the Los Angeles River beyond that.

I am living a life, one life; to others, it might look like the perfect life, the rich life, the fancy life, or the good life, but I'm not so sure.

The way I see it, there are so many possibilities and roads to travel, but it seems we just get stuck going down one, and there's no way of escaping.

I try to bring up questions like this with the guys over a Coke and Meyers on a Friday night at McCormick and Schmicks or the Los Angeles Athletic Club, but I never get too far.

Try to talk philosophy with a bunch of half-drunk salespeople on Friday night and see how far you get.

I drive a Jaguar and run around in fancy suits.

Once a year, Lacy drags me down to Brooks Brothers on Seventh and Figueroa to buy them, so her daddy won't be upset if he sees me—he's a sharp dresser and thinks a suit makes a man.

I was going to school in New Orleans when I first met her.

I was awestruck when I first saw her, and twenty years later, her beauty remains untarnished.

Most afternoons, I'd end up in the stacks at Tulane, in a little library facing St. Charles Avenue, which runs in front of Audubon Park.

Back then, it was a small but wonderful place, unused and unappreciated, full of rare and exotic texts.

This diminutive but quaint library overlooked Audubon Park with views of ancient live oaks dripping with Spanish moss.

The Saint Charles streetcar lazily passes on its way somewhere and back, its route determined by a track established by others.

Fated to repeat its voyage (as beautiful as it seems) again and again, never able to break free and find a path of its own making.

Seated on a chair of smooth, faded mahogany, I perused a worn volume of *The Rise and Fall of the Confederacy,* personally signed by Jefferson Davis.

There could be no better place in the entire world, I thought to myself.

Working amongst the stacks, carefully studying each spine as if she were reading the contents of the book itself, she was the essence of Southern beauty, frail and refined.

Her jet-black hair gently fell just below the nape of her neck, and her tight, gaunt features constrained a not-so-subtle sensuality.

Who knows what draws us to people?

In Lacy's case, her physique and feminine ways were a catalyst.

Still, her attention to the texts in the library belied something more: a curiosity about the unknown, new ideas, thoughts, and concepts, a mind curious about all it encountered.

It is my sincerest hope that this yearning for knowledge I observed, as much as my vision of her as a fulfillment of some illusory and mystical vision of the Old South, were the sources of my attraction.

I can't recall much.

Though shy by nature, I resolved to make an introduction, so waiting until Lacy was out of the librarian's line of sight, I approached from behind and said,

"Miss?"

Startled, she quickly turned toward me, our faces but inches apart.

"Yes?" she said.

"How can I help you, Sir?"

"You can have coffee with me when you're off," I replied.

Lacy smiled half-cocked as if she knew what was coming all along.

At liberty to look me over thoroughly as if with permission granted by my words, she saw a man twenty-two years of age, average height, fine black hair, and a slender build, with heavy eyebrows and piercing hazel green eyes.

I wore tan corduroy pants, a tweed sports coat with large brown elbow patches, tan dime loafers, and mismatched socks.

After a thoughtful look that seemed to last far longer than it must have, a grand surprise that changed my life came my way as she said in a soft but clear and strong voice.

"Okay. I'm off in an hour. Can you wait?"

"Absolutely, I can." I said, tasting victory, and returned to my mahogany chair.

Finally, Lacy beckoned me, and I followed her down the long wooden plank stairs that led to St Charles Avenue.

Sheltering oaks canopied the boulevard as the evening light mixed with the whir of the steel streetcar wheels rubbing against ancient tracks buried deep in the green neutral ground.

The hiss of electricity popped and sparked as it coursed through the wires above the trolley tracks, casting a chaotic hum that echoed the sparks I felt between Lacy and me as we walked, our bodies close, almost touching.

"How about the Camilla Grill? Is that okay?" I asked.

"That's perfect and quick; I need to head home soon," Lacy replied.

"Forgive me, but I don't even know your name," I asked.

"Lacy. And yours?" she replied.

"Justin. Justin Larkin," I answered.

"You're not from here. I can tell you are not native New Orleans," Lacy said.

I was unsure if that was a compliment, but I replied.

"California, Los Angeles. I'm here studying at Tulane."

"I knew right away you weren't from here.

California, what a wonderful place! I've never been there, but I know it is!

One day, I'll be there as sure as I am standing right now.

And when I get there, I'm never coming back.

It's not that I haven't traveled; I've been to many places.

Daddy took me to all the capitals of Europe, and we've been to South America and all the islands, but in my own country, I've never left the South.

As far as Daddy is concerned, the United States ends at the Mason-Dixon Line."

Her words fell from delicate lips, so beautifully formed.

The language trickled down like honey. I was enthralled.

While she busily admired California as a place so free and open, I was felled by the mere sound of her voice, the mystery and romanticism it summoned.

Everything I admired about the South was contained in her voice, her words, and her ways.

Why anyone would want to leave a place that gave birth to such beauty bewildered me.

The Camilla Grill was packed, but as luck would have it, there were two seats at the end of the counter. An older Black gentleman, neatly attired in white with a black tie, approached.

"What can I get y'all folks today?" he declared, sporting a counterfeit smile.

"Just coffee chicory. That's all I want. Thank you," said Lacy.

As she turned to me on the counter chair, our shoulders touched for the very first time, sending strange sensations the length of my torso.

"The same for me. Two coffees," I said and smiled.

I'd have matched her order had it been for a cup of mud.

The waiter reached under the counter and pulled up two cups and saucers, the industrial white kind, and placed one in front of me and the other in front of Lacy.

From the same hidden space, he produced a steaming pot of coffee and poured it to where the black just touched the rims.

Lacy picked up her cup, looked kindly at me, and softly said,

"Why did you come down here to study anyway, Mr. Larkin? It's so hot and humid, and California has great universities."

"Call me Justin," I said.

"Oh, sure, thank you, Justin," she replied.

"Yes, that may be so, but there's no culture there.

It's full of nothingness, as if the people look through you as if you're invisible. They don't care," I said.

"Oh, I'd love that. Here, everyone cares; everyone knows or wants to know your business. It's like you're never alone," she said.

Lacy again daintily lifted her cup to her lips.

"Justin, now what are you doing? Are you just looking at me like that? Is there something on my face? You're staring at me so."

Lacy rubbed her face, thinking maybe something was smudged.

Then she pulled a small mirror from her purse and opened it.

"Not at all," I said. "Sorry, I was just looking, noticing how beautiful you were."

"Oh, do tell, but that's a very kind thing to say, and… may I say I find you very handsome yourself," she said.

"But external beauty is a blessing from above, and certainly you've been blessed, but what's inside is even more compelling and important… it was your attentiveness to the books."

I said as I looked at her loveliness.

"The books that you were shelving in the library. That demonstrated that what is on the outside is a mere reflection of a more real something inside. An inner wealth," I continued.

Lacy began to blush.

"I couldn't help but notice it took you several minutes to shelve a single book. It seems you were putting them on the racks with a real reluctance as if you wanted to stop right there and read the entire tome."

Lacy giggled and replied,

"My god, you're very observant. I do love books. Sometimes, I see a title, and I want to pick it up and go outside to sit under a tree and read until the cows come home, but Ms. Trudeau, the librarian, no, she wouldn't have that at all.

The fact is, if it weren't for Doctor Rankin, I wouldn't have this job.

Ms. Trudeau says I'm the slowest assistant she's ever had, and she as much as told me she'd have my head if it weren't for 'certain parties.'

The fact is, I don't give a care what she thinks. Imagine! A librarian who doesn't like books!

It's appalling.

I believe she's simply a file clerk, a slave to the Dewey Decimal System, and she has no regard for what's inside. It's as if the library were just a collection of files in a cabinet."

"I couldn't agree more, I said,

I could never figure it out, but I always disdain librarians. Bookstore owners always impressed me more. It seemed like they loved their collections."

I gave her a long, pensive look, then continued,

"Lacy, I have a confession to make: the real reason I keep coming back to this library… is *you.*""

Lacy blushed.

"This library may be small, with others offering far larger collections, but none of them can compare to the view—of Audubon Park or of *you.*"

"Oh dear," Lacy said, blushing again.

"I've been watching you for weeks, and today, I finally got the courage to speak to you," I said.

"Oh, Justin, you think I didn't notice you? At first, I thought what an odd collection of volumes you left strewn all over the table where you always sit.

Such a random array.

I must confess… At first, they made no sense to me at all, but then, on closer inspection, I had to admit they were well-chosen… indicative of a genuinely thoughtful person.

I checked out the same volumes each evening when you left and spent the entire night poring over them.

I wanted to know who you were, and what better way to find out about a person than through the volumes they choose?

I think I really know you, Justin.

It's such an odd thing, but it's true," Lacy says.

"And what do you know?" I inquired.

"I know you are a lover of history and an admirer of the South, a very unusual thing for a Yankee.

I think even Daddy would approve of that.

You're a romantic, no doubt, a lover of lost causes, perhaps to a fault. I would say you see with your mind, often something that is not there, or something that was there once but that's gone.

I never met anyone like that in my life.

You're a very interesting person,

"I must say, but I also must say it's time to go now. I need to go home."

"Do you live far away?" Kaya asked.

"In the Quarter, on the 1200 block of Bourbon."

And you, Kaya, where do you live?" I asked.

"On Pine Street, a few blocks from here," Kaya answered.

"Can I walk you there?"

"That would be exceedingly kind, thank you. It's just a five-minute walk, right behind Newcomb College. It's such a beautiful night for a walk. I love these balmy nights. Don't you?"

"Yes," I said, nodding in agreement.

Little did I know that our walk down this boulevard would completely alter my life.

This stroll down a tiny path between two Southern Colleges, this chance meeting among texts I had come so long and far to touch, would determine the rest of my days on this earth.

Like the chance combination of millions upon millions of atoms, time, and circumstance.

Was it chaos or destiny that put Lacy and me together in this place and time?

This was truly a question for the ages; in any case, there's no doubt that our meeting would alter the universe's life, the chaos of creation, replication, and destruction, the fusing of atoms that could not be torn asunder.

We left the Grill, which sits along Carrollton near the levee and walked back up St. Charles towards Pine Street and her home.

Staring at the streetlights, I was overcome with a feeling of warmth and satiety—not an overwhelming passion or lust, not excitement or exhilaration, but rather a sense of calm.

Lacy extended her right arm, and I held her close as we strolled down the deserted streets.

Streetlights reflected bright yellow on the cracked sidewalks; an occasional roach ambled by as we reached Pine Street.

Tall trees formed a canopy over the tiny road.

Cars were parked on both sides, creating a narrow path. It's a wonder anything could pass at all.

In the center of the block was a bright white house of sufficient but unimpressive scale, with a proper porch supported by two white columns.

Sitting on the porch, as if in a portrait, were a graying white man and woman occupying ancient but pristine rocking chairs, rocking one forward and one back, opposite but in harmony.

Staring wide-eyed at Pine Street bathed in twilight, they watched intently as we approached.

"Evening, Ms. Rankin, Professor. Beautiful evening," Lacy said and smiled.

"Yes indeed," replied the Professor.

"Yes, indeed," echoed his wife.

Lacy spoke up again.

"Ms. Rankin, Professor, this is Justin Larkin. He's a graduate student at Tulane and just visiting for a little while."

Turning to me, Lacy continued,

"Professor Rankin teaches at Tulane in the History Department."

"Evening, Professor,"

I said with as much respect and admiration as I could muster, and I meant it.

The old professor looked my way and spoke.

"Well, young man, what are you studying?"

"Philosophy. Existential philosophy, mainly Sartre, Camus, and Heidegger," I replied.

To assuage any concern on his part regarding our intentions, Lacy added,

"Not to worry, Doctor Rankin. Justin is going to visit with me for a few minutes. He wants to pick up a book of poems."

Lacy grabbed my hand firmly and led me away from the house, sensing I was about to launch into a long dialog with the professor. She was right.

"Y'all have a nice evening," she declared.

"Y'all have a pleasant evening, too, and Lacy, my Dear, I'll be around if you need anything, Lacy, anything at all," Dr. Rankin said.

"I'll be just fine. Y'all rest now. Good Evening," she said.

Lacy led me around the porch to a gate off the levee side of the house. This gate led to a small backyard of lush elephant ears and greenish-blue Bermuda grass surrounded by a faded silver hurricane fence, adding an air of seclusion to the yard.

A tiny wood-slat cottage covered in faded whitewash was parked inside this space like an overgrown dollhouse.

We went up the three steps and inside, and she quietly shut the door.

Then she said softly,

"Justin, they watch out for me. They know my family in Charleston. Jeff Rankin taught my father when he was at Tulane, if you can believe it."

"I can believe it," I said.

"He's a sweet old man but overprotective," Lacy added.

I couldn't take this talking anymore, and neither could Lacy.

All I could see in my mind's eye was her slender ass, her striking face, that gorgeous body with luscious breasts.

I wanted to see and touch those things, and it was clear that Lacy had exactly the same idea about me.

So, on this hot summer night, in that little back cottage, with the sounds of the locusts in the background, we fell into a Southern embrace.

Exhausted, we lay naked in her single bed, our bodies compressed into this small space, not cramped but rather cozy and warm.

I gazed at her subtle form, even more beautiful and perfect than I had imagined.

The songs of the locust and the scent of honeysuckle permeated the room.

All we lacked was a thunderstorm to cool us; the breeze from the open window was non-existent.

Even then, I found fault in the perfect.

That was a long time ago.

Over twenty years have passed, but I will never forget that evening, nor should I.

Yet, until this moment, I had hardly thought about the first time Lacy and I met and how we were immediately attracted to each other.

Lacy knew I was a graduate student at Tulane; heck, I handed her my Tulane ID at least three times when checking out books.

She probably figured I'd be around a while.

Yet, unknown to Lacy, there was an issue with my academic status. I was pretty sure this would be my first and last semester, and they would toss me out.

But if Lacy had known this detail, I might not have been where I was at that moment, which was a good place, so I didn't mention it.

As we lay in her bed, I was sure Professor Rankin would have me checked out in the morning.

Later that day, he would call Lacy's father, his former student, and inform him that Lacy was hanging out with a degenerate from California, not a scholar.

Two hours passed, and the lights were still bright in the Rankin house.

Lacy whispered,

"Justin, you'd better leave now and make some noise so they know you're leaving."

I smiled with total understanding, pecked her on the cheek, and said,

"I'll call you in the morning."

Descending the three steps, I walked out the side gate and gave it a good slam so the old professor would be sure to hear me leave.

Then I headed up Pine Street to St Charles, took the Trolley to Canal Street, and hoofed the mile or so to the 1200 block of Bourbon and my little second-story slave quarter apartment.

The next day, the phone rang. It was Lacy, and I was ready for the hammer to drop.

It had been a great night, and she was sweet, but the way I looked at it, I wouldn't be seeing Lacy again.

I richly deserved my fate. I should have been honest with her in the first place.

Lacy said,

"Justin, Professor Rankin told my daddy that there had been an incident at the university involving you and a young female adjunct professor from Paris."

"Yes," I said.

"There was an incident, and I'm probably not going to be able to return to Tulane after this semester."

She didn't seem too upset, and that surprised me a bit.

She asked me to stop by later in the afternoon. I wasn't sure what she would say, but I owed her an explanation.

In any event, I wanted to see her again.

When I arrived at the house on Pine Street, Lacy appeared at the side gate, directed me to the Rankin Porch, and sat me down on a hanging swing between the rocking chairs and the window from which Dr. Rankin peered.

"Justin, whatever happened, I don't care to know," she said in a voice that echoed along the wooden porch.

She held me tight as we sat side by side, spooning and sparking in plain view of Old Doc Rankin.

Things were developing fast, and I felt I could not control the situation.

Lacy was obviously serious about what happened the previous night, and while it seemed spontaneous enough, I couldn't banish the thought that it was somehow a planned event.

Lacy admitted she had read everything I read that summer, and those books pretty much told my tale.

She may have known me better than I knew myself.

Upon reflection, it may well have been a case of the hunter being hunted.

A flash of dread overcame me and softened into a vague ennui, quickly disappearing: why worry?

I was returning to California at the end of the semester, and I figured this girl would not follow me there.

Over the next couple of months, Lacy and I were constantly together; the truth is, she couldn't get enough of me, and somehow, other women got the scent – they always do, feast or famine if you ask me.

There were a couple of other affairs, but Lacy took up most of my time.

I frequently stopped by her cottage to "read poetry."

Dr. Rankin took to letting his dog, Eve, run free in the yard, a mean, scruffy-looking German Shepard that barked furiously each time I approached. I'm sure that bastard left him in the yard to fuck with me.

Lacy had no control over that dog, and Doc Rankin would have to come out and get him and bring him into the big house before I could leave the cottage.

He would grab Eve by the scruff of the neck and yank her into the house.

"Come on, Eve! Eve, come,"

he'd say as he pulled that mean bitch into the house, all the while barking up a storm, showing her evil and deadly teeth.

That was one fucked up dog.

As soon as I entered Lacy's' cottage, that fuckin' dog would be back in the yard, hollering its ass off.

When I was ready to leave, Lacy would have to walk out there and get Doc Rankin to take the dog into the house so I could escape.

A couple of times, that fucker let the dog go, faking like he thought I was gone, and I had to jump the fence to avoid her gnawing on my ass.

I could see the son of a bitch, Rankin, smirking in the background.

"Sorry about that," he'd say with a smile.

That was one evil son of a bitch, it turned out.

Unlike my time with Eve, my relationship with Lacy was supremely calm.

We were constantly on the phone, yet I can recollect little of what we spoke about.

Mostly I just talked, and she'd listen as if she was soaking up whatever I knew, sucking it out of me.

On the weekends, we'd take pleasant walks around the yacht harbor out by Lake Pontchartrain, and on Sunday afternoons, we'd go to City Park.

She'd pack the most beautiful lunches in a fine wicker basket with all fine utensils, napkins, and such.

Yes, just like in the movies.

I couldn't take her to dinner or restaurants; I had no money and mainly lived on BLTs, which my friend Tom taught me to cook.

I could tell you the recipe, but you can figure it out.

Lacy never complained.

I recall our first actual dinner date: I took her to the Church's Chicken near the quarter.

It was in a black neighborhood off Elysian Fields opposite the Winn Dixie Supermarket.

I reckon we were the first white folks there in quite a while, or ever.

I pulled the Nissan through the drive-thru, and the Black girl working there looked at us as if we were aliens.

I wasn't from around there and had no idea this was a black drive-thru.

Lacy must have known, but she didn't say a thing—she had that much class.

As we pulled out of the drive-thru and up Elysian Fields, I said, "Lacy, it was a bit scary there; I guess white people don't go there much."

"It's fine, just fine," she said.

"Well, I guess we can't eat here; why don't we just go over to my place in the quarter and eat the chicken?"

"Sure," she replied,

and I continued up Elysian Fields to the quarter and found a place to park the Nissan off Governor Nichols.

As I recall, it was a calm night.

The air was still warm as we walked the few blocks to my apartment, the streetlamps glimmering yellow. There was no traffic noise to interrupt our stroll.

That end of the quarter was quiet and still at night—a holdover from some old, serene town in rural France.

I turned the key, which opened the large wooden door guarding the entrance to the garden and the big house.

The house was separated from Bourbon Street by a massive cement wall topped with shards of colored cut glass.

Closing the big door tight, we walked through the sparsely lit atrium entry to a small garden in the rear.

The cement wall on our left was bordered by massive green trees that overhung the small garden.

On the right, one story high, was a wooden staircase covered by an enclosed hall—the entrance to the old slave quarters, now an apartment for white folks.

We went up the staircase; Lacy patiently waited in front of the door as I worked the key back and forth until the old lock clicked, and the door squeaked open.

My apartment was small.

It consisted of a main room that couldn't have been much bigger than six by six feet and contained little more than a small sofa that converted into a bed at night.

Directly in front of the bed was a small kitchen, and down a hallway to the right of the kitchen was a bathroom.

It was cozy, with solid walls and storm windows opening to the wooden balcony overlooking the garden.

I also had an aluminum metal rocking chair that creaked against the green wood floorboards.

I was convinced Lacy would be thrilled by this place's quaintness, especially since she was so fond of her cottage uptown.

Instead, as I opened the door, she shrieked.

"I am not going in there!"

Surprised, I replied, "Why not? What's wrong?"

"Justin, this place is filthy; there is no way I am going in! And how can you live like this?"

Sure, there were books all over the place and a little desk with my Olympic Manual Typewriter, some paper on the desk, more books piled on the sofa, and the kitchen had a few dishes in the sink, but I was a <u>student</u> and a bachelor, it wasn't like roaches were crawling around or anything (maybe a few).

Christ, there were even a couple of pictures on the wall!

Lacy stood at the door, craning her head toward the little kitchenette and the sofa.

"Do you have a broom?" she asked.

"Yes," I replied,

At this point, Lacy entered with extreme trepidation, on tiptoes as if to limit contact with whatever filth so offended her.

I ran into the kitchen to retrieve the broom and handed it to her.

She commenced to sweep without comment, her rapid and sustained motions driven as if by some spirit.

"Justin, do you have a vacuum?"

"No, but John Aldridge does. He lives around the corner on St. Anne. He'll loan it to me, I'm sure."

"Well, get it now; I'll get started here."

"Um… Okay, I'll be right back."

Lacy didn't respond; she just continued sweeping.

I ran the block to St. Anne and sprinted up the twenty stairs leading to John's large and airy apartment on the corner of St. Anne and Bourbon, pounding on his front door.

John answered, and before he could say one word, I said,

"John, let me borrow your vacuum!"

"Sure, let me get it for you. Do you want to come in?"

"No, I am kinda in a rush; I'll explain later. I need the vacuum."

John turned as I waited impatiently at the front door.

Finally, he returned with the machine, which I thrust over my shoulder like a bazooka and held tightly with both hands.

"Thanks, man; I'll bring it back tomorrow with some Chili Con Queso. I have Campbell's Cheese Soup and chips; you have Jalapenos, right?"

I said on the run.

"Yes, I do. You are truly a gentleman and a scholar,"

John called after me in his drawling Texas accent.

I hauled my load down the stairwell, three steps at a time, sweating, grunting, and worried that Lacy would leave.

Two Black guys approached as I hit St. Anne and was about to turn onto Bourbon.

One had a newsboy's cap turned sideways out of Bowery Boys, and the other was a nondescript guy with a dark face above rumpled clothes.

They approached quickly, from out of nowhere. There I was with this load on my back. The guy with the newsboy hat said,

"Give me your money."

Not menacing, not angry, just direct.

In an instant, the dark-faced guy had his hands in my pockets and was pulling out whatever he could get.

There I was, with this stupid, blunt object on my shoulder, and I did nothing.

I thought to myself, if I take a swing with John's vacuum—there are two of them—they may take it and beat me to a pulp with the thing, but in a flash, they were gone anyway, and with the twenty bucks that were in my right front pocket, and there I stood in the middle of St. Anne Street with a vacuum on my back and my pockets vacuumed.

I was more surprised than upset.

It happened so fast, but I had bigger fish to fry.

I had to get back to Lacy. It was better not to mention this incident; there was no telling how she'd take it.

In my absence, Lacy cleaned the room, rearranged the furniture, and organized my papers.

It looked fabulous.

"Justin, plug in the vacuum and let me make a pass," she said as I entered the room.

"Jeez, Lacy, you didn't have to do this; this place never looked this good!"

Lacy stopped in her tracks and looked at me.

"Just please keep it this way. If I ever see it like it was when I come over, I won't enter, I swear."

"Not to worry, Lacy, you can count on me."

That was a lie.

Lacy stopped by many times, and it took more effort each time to cajole her to enter.

At that point, she would commence cleaning, and I'd have to hightail it to St. Anne to get the vacuum.

John finally offered to sell me the contraption for ten dollars, as he was tired of loaning it to me. I took him up on the offer.

Lacy stayed that night, and when I awoke, the table was set, and a vase with flowers was arranged on its top.

On the stove, there was a breakfast of hot grits, biscuits in the oven, bacon, and eggs frying in my cast iron skillet, and the ancient percolator I bought at the flea market was singing a lovely tune.

Coffee and bacon scents wafted throughout the small space; it smelled like a home.

"Where did you get this stuff?" I asked.

"I took a walk in the morning and found a cute little store a few blocks down, and I got everything," Lacy said.

Somehow, Lacy found two plates with the same pattern.

They sat on the table with napkins folded underneath, and the eggs, bacon, and grits were all in separate bowls.

She even bought matching coffee cups, and this little cow was filled with half and half.

When you lifted the cow with a tiny handle, the half-and-half came out of its mouth.

Lacy picked it up and poured the thick white mixture into my cup.

"Isn't this adorable?" she exclaimed.

"Yes, Lacy, it's wonderful."

To say I was impressed would be an understatement: memories of that breakfast linger to this day.

"What a wonderful breakfast."

I looked up and kissed her on the cheek.

"This is beautiful; thank you so much."

"I'm glad you like it. Now eat before it gets cold."

A few weeks later, Lacy called and told me she was going home to visit her parents in Charleston.

She asked me to come along.

I'd never been there before and jumped at the chance.

The family house was on King Street.

Charleston

As we exited the baggage claim, there they stood: Mr. and Mrs. Watson Wilkins craning their necks in every direction, searching high and searching low for their dear daughter; naturally, they were concerned:

I could only imagine what Dr. Rankin had told them about me. I'm sure apprehension was written all over their faces (as well as mine).

Mr. Wilkins stood a good six feet tall, quite the Beau Brummell, dressed in a fine-tailored gray suit, while Mrs. Wilkins was small in stature, five feet, if that.

Wilkins reminded me of my Hungarian grandfather, a throwback to an age and time when refinement and grace were de rigueur for the business class.

It was a warm day in Charleston, South Carolina, but there was a breeze.

Already, I was feeling a bit out of place; these were people of airs.

Yet the pieces of the puzzle were starting to fit clearly; a woman with Lacy's grace, style, and breeding wouldn't ordinarily be working in the stacks at Tulane or, for that matter, living in a tiny cottage in Uptown New Orleans with no air-conditioning.

She was from a family of wealth and status; this was becoming perfectly clear.

Approaching Lacy's parents, my nervousness grew as I wondered what they would think of me.

Was Daddy going to pull out a gun and perform some Dixie honor killing?

This was the old South, what the fuck did I know?

Walking down a long concourse to the terminal entrance, we passed a bar, an arcade, and several gift stores.

Face to face with Mr. and Mrs. Wilkins, I extended my hand. Mr. Wilkins reached for it.

Expecting the worst,

I said, "Hello, Mr. Wilkins, Mrs. Wilkins. I'm Justin Larkin."

Mrs. Wilkins replied,

"Welcome to Charleston, my dear. Lacy speaks highly of you. I'm so delighted you could make it. She claims you're a brilliant philosopher and from California to boot.

Lacy loves California, though she's never set foot there.

Dear Lacy, she's always bringing home new and unique people."

I could only imagine the background they received from Doc Rankin and what she meant by unique, but she greeted me kindly.

Mercifully, Mr. Wilkins chimed in,

"Grace, come on now! Let the boy get acclimated."

"Yes, Dear," she said.

"Certainly, it's just that it's so nice to see my little darling home after such a long while."

Lacy stood back, then moved nearer to her mother, who continued,

"Lacy, dear, Velma can't wait to see you, and naturally, your sisters will be passing by. We'll have a wonderful evening, finally all together again, the whole family."

"Mother, it's only been six months! I've only been away six months," Lacy exclaimed with evident frustration.

"Six months is an eternity, dear, for a mother away from her daughter. You'll understand one day when you have children of your own," Grace countered.

On hearing that, Lacy turned her nose up and looked at me for relief.

Mr. Wilkins put his arm around my back and, looking at his wife, said,

"Mother, leave the kids be; they're tired."

Looking behind him, he continued,

"Mr. Larkin, let Davis here, get your bags."

A Black Fellow in a chauffeur's uniform stood a good ten feet behind us, so far removed that I figured he was on his own.

On cue, he came forward and grabbed our overnight bags.

Mrs. Wilkins looked at Lacy and spoke,

"Is that all you brought, Dear?"

"Mom, we're only staying two nights!"

"Oh, Justin – may I call you Justin?" she asked.

"Of course," I replied.

Looking my way, Mrs. Wilkins continued,

"Lacy, she's such a minimalist. I do declare, you'd think she was a Buddhist the way she carries herself."

Lacy ignored the remark and said,

"Daddy, I had no idea you had a driver! When did this happen? You love to drive; how come you have a driver now?"

Lacy then turned to the driver and added,

"Hello, Mr. Davis, no offense. I just never thought Daddy would get a driver."

Davis bent his head and doffed his cap.

"Hello, Miss Lacy. I'm pleased to meet you," he said, continuing his task.

Mr. Wilkins walked closer to Lacy and whispered, so I could also hear:

"Lacy, I do like to drive, but this is business, a tax thing. Either I have a driver, or the money goes to the government, and you know how I detest the government. Especially the Democrats. Having a driver actually makes me money."

Talking as much to me as to Lacy, Mr. Wilkins continued,

"I'm a businessman, and when it comes to money, I'll do what I have to do. That's what a businessman does; we have responsibilities."

Mr. Wilkins looked at me shrewdly.

"Larkin, you're not a Democrat, are you? We can't have any Democrats dating a Wilkins woman, no sir. Well, if you were a

Democrat, it wouldn't matter. It's a free country, son. Stand up for what you believe!"

"Sir, I am a Democrat."

"Daddy, forget the politics. Just tell me—did you hire Mr. Davis or not?"

Lacy asked, her tone cut through the air with urgency.

"Well, Lacy, the Piedmont Board…"

Wilkins paused, glanced at me, and continued,

"…of which I happen to be chairman, decided I either needed to hire a driver or buy a plane."

He paused again, turning to Davis.

"And since Davis here can't fly worth a damn, I settled for an automobile."

Davis smiled.

"Now, Mr. Wilkins, I can't fly—I never had a lesson in my life, no. But if you want me to fly, I will; now we might be meetin' the Lord Jesus the very next day if I do, but I'll try if you want me to."

We all laughed and commenced walking, me next to Mr. Wilkins, Lacy trailing behind with her mother, the two barely speaking. Wilkins patted me on the back as we walked down the long corridor leading out of the airport.

"So, son, you're from California. Well, now, that ain't so bad— not bad at all. President Reagan hails from California; if you ask me, he's the best thing to happen to this country in my entire lifetime. Mark my words, he'll go down as the greatest president since Thomas

Jefferson—maybe even better. And Richard Nixon? Now, he was from California, too, and I don't care what they say. He was a good man. I voted for him twice. There's got to be something in the water out there to breed such fine men—damn fine men.

It pleases me to no end that Yankee with a drawl, Carter, lost the Palmetto State. And if it weren't for the nigra vote, it would've been a landslide. Why nigras would vote for that slave-holding son of a bitch is beyond me."

Lacy sped up her pace, reaching us, and said.

"Now, Daddy, please, no more politics; if I hear Ronald Reagan's name one more time, I am going just to keel over."

Thankfully (as it appeared to me Lacy and her daddy were about to tangle), we exited the airport into the noonday sun.

Directly in front of us was a black Town Car guarded by two members of Charleston's Finest.

"Damn, Mr. Wilkins, it looks like you're getting a ticket; I'm so sorry if we caused you any problem; we should have just taken a cab. I guess we're lucky they didn't tow it away."

Wilkins looked at me cock eyed and said,

"My word, what are you talking about, son? We were picking you up, and the policemen were watching our car for us; this ain't New York City; you're in the South, and people have manners here."

Then, Wilkins whirled to face his daughter,

"See, honey, your friend here, Justin, is telling the truth: in New York City, those Yankees would have your car in some impound yard before you could blink an eye; it's what I've been telling you all along."

"Oh, Daddy, you know as well as I that anyone else parking here would be towed away lickety-split. And Daddy Justin is from California, not New York City."

Looking at me, Lacy continued,

" Justin, they know it's daddy's car, and they wouldn't dare touch it; he has special privileges down here. It's not fair. That's why I hate this place."

"Now, Lacy, what do you mean you hate this place? It's your home; how can you say such a thing? And I know Justin is from California; I was just talking about how they act in New York. Now Justin, you've been to New York, haven't you?"

"Yes, Sir, I have; I was there once," I replied.

"Well, am I right or not? Would they tow your car away at the airport at the drop of a hat?"

"Yes, Sir, I imagine they would; I am pretty sure they would."

Mr. Wilkins, vindicated, looked at Lacy and said,

"See there, honey. I was right. Justin here just confirmed it."

I could see that Lacy was about to tear into her Daddy, but Davis picked up on it and said,

"Y'all folks get in the car now; it's so awful hot for y'all white folks; I left the air conditioner on so y'all could cool off and be most comfortable inside the automobile."

Believe it or not, the officer opened the door for us, and Lacy and her mom got in the back, and Mr. Wilkins and I sat in the front next to Davis.

It was clear that Wilkins was upset with Lacy's remarks, but he held his tongue and sat silently on the ride to their house.

It was like a tomb in there: Lacy and Mrs. Wilkins said nigh a word on the drive.

All I could think about was what I was getting into here; the tension was palpable.

No wonder Lacy brought me along.

The Wilkins house was on King Street in the heart of Old Charleston.

A vast iron gate opened onto a circular drive, which led to the house, which was bordered by bountiful gardens on both sides.

Farther on, we passed a lushly camouflaged swimming pool tiled in a mosaic blue-green.

Two Black men toiled in the calm and quiet gardens on King Street.

Outside the gates, the city teemed with traffic, noise, and confusion.

Beyond the majestic entryway, there was no evidence of the outside world; it was a serene and private place.

Like New Orleans, Charleston reeked of history and tradition, but whereas New Orleans seemed to have a muck growing just above the surface, Charleston seemed bathed in a gentle and cleansing breeze.

The Wilkins Estate boasted an immense front porch with massive columns supporting a high and vaulted frame.

Many rattan chairs with plump cushions sat neatly arranged on the green lawn, beckoning one and all.

One could not help but imagine the gentry of Old Charleston looking towards Charleston Bay, talking business, discussing shipments of rice or cotton, or even the war against the Yankee invaders.

Davis pulled the ultra-long black Lincoln Town Car into the midst of this calm and tranquil place and cut off the engine as we came to a full stop.

Davis quickly opened the door and exited,

Mr. Wilkins followed him out.

Then, Davis ran around and opened the passenger doors;

Lacy, Mrs. Wilkins, and I got out.

All along, Davis doffing his cap with a slight bow.

Immediately, a woman attired in a muumuu of many colors appeared from the house portal as if tossed out the front door.

She had a pretty face and long black dreadlocks that fell over dark ebony skin as she ran across the large portico that surrounded the house and down the steps toward the circular drive and the parked Town Car, her ample breasts bouncing like honeydew melons, screaming.

"Lacy, goddammit, why'd you stay away so long?"

"Velma!" Lacy shouted,

The two women grabbed each other, hugging and twirling around like little children on some school playground.

They flattened the neatly arranged flowerbeds the two black gardeners were tending.

They extricated themselves quickly, lest they be overtaken by the wailing and swirling duality of rapidly moving womanhood.

Mr. and Mrs. Wilkins and I just stood our ground.

The gardeners in their green uniforms with names neatly sewn on their breast pockets watched in awe, as did Davis, standing on the driver's side of the Lincoln, leaning against the door.

When the twirling concluded, the women walked into the house arm in arm and disappeared, leaving the audience in silence and wonder.

"Wow, who was that?" I said, figuring it was a friend or something.

Unlike the other Black people, she was not in a uniform.

Lacy had mentioned she was looking forward to seeing her friend.

Mr. Wilkins replied,

"That's Velma; they're like sisters. The fact is that Lacy is much closer to Velma than she is to her own sisters; it's a shame.

Velma's mama worked here until she got old and died.

Velma has been coming here since she was three.

She and Lacy were the cutest things running around this very yard. Seems like yesterday."

His voice trailed off as if he were in a daydream.

Then he roused himself and continued.

"Velma was a sickly child. She was born with sickle cell anemia and was in the hospital a lot.

Lacy took it really hard when Velma got sick.

Whenever Velma ended up in the hospital, Lacy stayed with her day and night; she wouldn't leave the hospital 'til Velma was better," he moaned.

"The fact of the matter is that Velma is one reason Lacy was in New Orleans; she couldn't stand to see Velma suffer.

You know Lacy was at Clemson, right?

She told you that?"

"No, sir," I responded.

Mrs. Wilkins left us and entered the house.

Wilkins and I remained in the garden with the two gardeners.

Drawn to a large fountain with Seraphim surrounded by chairs with beautiful plump pillows, I sat down, and Wilkins followed suit.

"Good choice. This is a wonderful place to sit," declared Wilkins.

"What a beautiful garden, Mr. Wilkins, very serene."

"Yes, true enough, but as I was saying about Velma, last year was very bad for her. Lacy started visiting her at the hospital. She stayed there night after night and slept on a little cot right beside Velma's hospital bed.

Lacy's sisters and her boyfriend, a Doctor at the hospital, put a lot of pressure on Lacy to return to school and lead a normal life.

Instead of listening to reason, Lacy began to question God as Velma's illness continued.

We called on the Reverend Darby to speak to her in a vain attempt to reason with her and get her to stay in school.

Lacy demanded answers.

She couldn't understand why Velma had to suffer.

Reverend Darby told her the story of Job, the suffering servant of God, but that wasn't good enough for Lacy.

She told the good Reverend to leave; she said she would never go to church again and would leave Charleston for California."

Shock and despair twisted his visage merely from recalling the event; one could only imagine the pain at the time.

"Son," he continued,

"We Wilkins have a long history in South Carolina. In Charleston, it's hard to be a Wilkins. Charleston is really a very small town.

At that time, in particular, my baby Lacy was under a great deal of stress.

I came to understand her desire to leave was serious and would not abate.

We agreed that a change of scenery might do her good, so we suggested Savannah.

Lacy would have none of it; we finally settled on New Orleans.

Lacy reluctantly agreed.

Charleston is bad enough with its libertine element; we would have much preferred Savannah.

As you are well aware, New Orleans is a hotbed of sin and inequity, and it's full of Catholics, but at least it's in the South.

Fortunately, residing there was Professor Rankin, who was my counselor at Tulane. You met Doctor Rankin, I understand?"

"Yes," I replied, figuring, here it comes, but Wilkins continued.

"We've remained friends throughout the years. Dr. Rankin is a Christian of the highest order; I knew he would watch out for Lacy.

We accepted the fact that she couldn't be around Velma when she was sick; there was no way around it- at least for now.

She wouldn't eat; she was as skinny as a stick.

Mother always said,

'Lacy has a sorrowful heart.' It's true; she does. Velma recovered in time; one day, she turned up as if out of nowhere, and we were glad she was home. She has her room here; she's free to come and go as she pleases."

"So, Velma lives here all the time, does she?" I asked.

"No," Mr. Wilkins replied,

"Mama Geraldine has a small house in town and left it to Velma when she passed on.

Velma stays here most of the time and helps with things."

"So, Mr. Wilkins, do you know where her house is?" I asked.

Wilkins looked at me and shrugged.

"No, why should I? Velma is a worker, a diligent one.

She never stops working. We don't want her to work so hard, but she insists.

I tell her,

'Put that broom down; you don't need to do that. You don't want to wake up those sickle cells! I am getting too old to carry you down these stairs!'

The fact is, I haven't carried her down in years, but I did many times when she was little. She would writhe in terrible pain.

When it first came upon her, she would just stay in her room, and we would wait.

Sometimes, the crisis would pass, and sometimes, it wouldn't.

She stayed in bed until she could stand it no longer; then, she would begin to moan and scream, and we would know.

Lacy would run into our bedroom and scream,

'Daddy, daddy, come quick, Velma's sick.'

Then I would grab her up as if she were my own, and we would all jump in the car and take her to the hospital.

As soon as they saw us coming, the doctors would prepare a drip and get right to her.

We would stay a little while to make sure she'd be okay, but Lacy would stay as long as she could.

Sometimes, it would be days before she'd come home, eat a bit of food, get a bit of sleep, and then go right back to the hospital to be near Velma.

The doctors and nurses would watch out for her.

Can you imagine a little girl, nine or ten years old, sleeping at the hospital to be next to her friend?

We tried as we could but couldn't get Lacy home until Velma was better.

School or no school, when that girl has a notion, there is no way to change it.

She's like her grandfather Hiram, my daddy, hardheaded as they come.

After Velma was released, we wouldn't see her for a good while.

She would go home to live at Mama Geraldine's.

Then, one day, when she felt good enough, her mama would bring her back here as if nothing had happened.

Lacy insisted she stay with us, and we never objected.

If we suggested she was better off living with her mama, Lacy would go into such a crying jag that we'd have no choice but to let her stay.

Besides, we all loved Velma like our own.

What a curse this ailment is!

Why the good Lord would pass it on to a good girl like Velma is a mystery to me, but who am I to question his ways?

God willing, there must be a purpose; when it is his will, his right hand will reveal a cure."

I was not sure why he was telling me all this. I figured he just liked to talk, and he went on,

"Now, with all the girls gone—Lacy in New Orleans, Jade and Ashley married—Velma is the only one we have left.

When Velma leaves here, it's like we've all gone into a dark hole, a fog, a mist, somewhere we don't know, where we can't see."

Wilkins lost himself in thought for a bit, then perked up and continued.

"Velma is in charge of the house; that is when she's feeling well.

She's a family member, and though she's black as night, the help swears she's my baby girl.

One day, I heard them joshing with her.

'Velma, I know, Mr. Wilkins, your daddy. He don't look like you, but he's your daddy.'

She just looked at them and turned her head a bit, the way she always does, and said,

'If you say so.'

"It was the cutest thing," he mused.

The Wilkins

I guess Wilkins got tired of talking, so he stopped suddenly and stared at the fountain, lost in some trance.

Perhaps he was thinking about Lacy, their little spat at the airport, or maybe Velma running around the yard.

Who knows?

It didn't disturb me in the least; it was truly pleasant to be in this garden surrounded by immense trees, the sounds of the water gurgling from the fountain, birds flying overhead, the faint scent of salt wafting through my nostrils, a cool ocean breeze whipping at my face.

I was glad to be here, away from New Orleans and the oppressive heat, if only temporarily.

As suddenly as he had stopped talking, Wilkins got up and, without a word, walked through the garden and up towards the mansion, its long white steps buried under an immense porch leading to a vast foyer.

A white spiral staircase extended up the center of the house.

I followed in his footsteps, entering the grand salon, until he walked past the stairs, upon which I alighted, hearing Lacy above.

I stopped halfway up the staircase, Lacy and Velma looking down at me. Out of earshot of her daddy,

Lacy whispered, "Justin, those bitches won't come! Don't fret; you're not missing a damn thing,"

The two of them looked at each other and giggled, then continued climbing the stairs till they were out of sight.

I had figured she meant her sisters.

I was hoping she was wrong. I really was hoping her sisters would show up. I wanted to see them, and I figured they'd be pleasing to the eye.

Mr. Wilkins, seeing me standing alone and somewhat out of place, shouted up,

"Hey, Justin, let the girls go on up now. Come with me into the library; I have some fine brandy there; you like brandy, don't you?"

"Yes, Sir," I replied.

"And a nice cigar; you like cigars, don't you?"

"I'll try one; all I ever smoked are tiparillos, the menthol ones. I never had a good cigar, but I'll try one."

"Justin, it's like Thomas Jefferson said, 'A woman is a woman, but a good cigar is a smoke.'"

"Very Funny, that one. Really is. But wasn't it Freud who said that Sigmund Freud?"

Wilkins turned and looked a bit perturbed at my insolence.

"No matter, whoever said it was right, as wonderful and as necessary as women are, there is no doubt they are perplexing, and a good cigar is a simple and singular pleasure, and without bite, I might add."

"Agreed, but naturally, your kind wife and Lacy are excluded," I replied.

"Touché!" replied Wilkins, leading me into the library.

As impressive as the gardens were, the library was even more spectacular.

A huge, high vaulted ceiling surrounded exquisite, polished wood paneling and bookcases filled with gilt and leather volumes on all sides.

The floor sported matching and detailed parquet, and the entry was accented with wooden pocket doors, which Mr. Wilkins slid shut tightly as we entered.

On the opposite side was a bay window with a dazzling view of the gardens, complete with a cozy alcove covered with large, overstuffed cushions.

Late afternoon light streamed through the bay window, warming the room and filling it with a dim hue, adding to an already sedate and relaxing atmosphere.

The shelves brimmed with extraordinary volumes of every sort, neatly arranged by topic.

An intriguing series of volumes on the Civil War grabbed my eye.

I drifted away from Wilkins, my attention drawn to the striking collection before me.

Suddenly, his voice echoed through the cavernous space, breaking the quiet.

"Justin, do you like books?"

"Oh yes, sir."

"Well, son, to tell you the truth, I couldn't care less about books. No book ever put any food on my table. The old ones were my father's and his father's before that, and so on.

There would be a lot more, but we lost a great deal during the War Between the States.

Of course, new ones come in from book clubs and such all the time, but I don't waste much time on books.

Lacy loves books, and a lot of these are hers.

I read the Charleston Post each morning and, of course, the Wall Street Journal. I get what I need there. You see, I'm a businessman. We run a mill, which has been in the family since the 1850s. It keeps me very busy.

But that run may soon end.

I can see our business ending in my lifetime with nothing to pass on to the girls," he said.

"Why is that, Mr. Wilkins?"

"Well, you see, I have three daughters.

Lacy, you know, but the two others, Ashley and Jade, should've been here by now.

Those two girls are married to doctors, and they want nothing to do with the mill.

I love those girls so much, but this business is too rough for women, and their husbands have no time.

Lacy has no interest in business, none at all. She likes pretty things, but I could never perk her interest – she's plum disinterested.

And then there are the Chinese."

"The Chinese?"

"Yes, our American companies sell them looms, enabling them to produce textiles for a fraction of what it costs us.

As God is my witness, it won't be long before all our mills are shut tight.

We're shooting ourselves in the foot.

All these foolish people care about is cheap goods. They can't think beyond the moment. Soon enough, it won't matter how cheap things are—they won't have jobs, and without jobs, they won't have a red cent to buy anything."

At that very moment, Mrs. Wilkins pulled open the doors and announced,

"Ashley and Jade are here! Y'all, come on out. We are going to have supper together for once. Lacy and Velma are on their way down."

Mr. Wilkins and I exited the library, crossed into a huge parlor, and stepped into the dining room, dominated by its large chandelier and black and white marble floor.

The chandelier reflected rainbow colors onto a fine linen brocade covering a Louis the XIV table.

Several large picture windows with intricate moldings provided excellent views of the garden and the Seraphim fountain.

Lacy and Velma, seeing Ashley, Jade, and their husbands had entered, strode down the stairs like they were on their high horses, and we all met in a congregation at the base: Ashley, Jade, and the husbands, Velma, Lacy, Mr. Wilkins and me; Mrs. Wilkins must have been in the kitchen.

Ashley and Jade crowded around Lacy, their doctor husbands at their sides.

Mr. Wilkins exclaimed,

"Excuse me, y'all, I am gonna ask Mama if everything is alright. Y'all kids do what y'all do, but don't go anywhere too far; your mama's been waiting too long for this day, and you know how she is about starting on time."

With that, Mr. Wilkins took his leave through a large entryway and disappeared.

Oddly, Ashley grabbed me by the shoulders as if to push me aside for a better view of Lacy.

Lacy moved forward to dislodge her, and both sisters had their hands on me (one pushing and one pulling).

It was as if I were a piece of unwanted furniture.

Then Ashley spoke,

"Lacy, now you… you look great—a bit pale, but great. Nothing could change you, Lacy, nothing at all! Jade, don't we have the most beautiful sister in Charleston?" Ashley asked rhetorically.

Jade immediately replied,

"Oh yes, we do, we surely do. And Lacy, your Doctor, Glenn Wilson, has been calling for you like crazy. He's a resident now. He's so worried about you in New Orleans with the high crime and all.

He asks about you all the time. I would say he's madly in love with you, but everyone's known that since high school. He'll never get over you, never. Just imagine all three of us together, all married to doctors! Wouldn't that be grand?"

If that wasn't enough, Jade and Ashley looked at me and giggled.

Can you imagine that?

I knew those ditsy bitches fully realized I was there while they were saying that stuff.

Lacy, a girl of taste and refinement, didn't bat an eyelash.

What'd they think; I was a fuckin' fag?

Lacy looked at me. I swear she was worried that I would tear into those haughty wenches, and believe me, I was close.

"Jade, Ashley," she said,

"Let me introduce you to my new good friend from New Orleans. He's visiting with us. Mr. Justin Larkin. He's a philosophy graduate student at Tulane University, working on a doctorate. This is his first visit to Charleston."

Lacy stopped and looked at me affectionately. Then she added,

"I sincerely hope there will be many more visits."

Ashley and Jade gave me a quick gander, and then Ashley spoke

"Oh yes, is this the young man? Daddy told us about him and the… the unfortunate incident at Tulane."

They looked at me and snickered; their husbands looked at me and scowled.

Their expressions cracked me up.

I knew I should have been humiliated, but I wasn't.

In fact, it took all my effort not to break out in laughter and curse them out.

I looked over at Lacy and saw in her eyes that she knew I was about to lose it, one way or another.

"Justin, come into the dining room and sit beside me."

Lacy grabbed me by the arm and led me through the foyer into the dining room off the entry, with Velma, Jade, Ashley, and their husbands at my tail.

An intricate crystal chandelier hung over a table covered with a graceful white tablecloth set with fine silver and elegant China bordered with black and gold trim.

While I couldn't see it, I imagined the table was fine mahogany with delicate inlay.

It had to be.

The room was surrounded by full-length windows on either side, which overlooked the garden and the pool.

"This room is amazing. Each room in this house is more beautiful than before; I can't wait to see the upstairs."

I said, and we all found our seats around the dining room table.

Lacy looked at me with disapproval, the sisters sneered, and the doctors scowled.

"Well, Mister Larkin, you won't be seeing that area of the mansion as it is reserved for family. You will be sleeping in the guest cottage by the pool; I am sure you will find it far superior to your accommodations on Bourbon Street," Ashley sarcastically replied.

"Oh really? Well, that will be fine; I look forward to it."

Ashley continued,

"Yes, given the circumstances, that's the best we can offer."

Upon hearing that, Lacy abruptly stood up; I could tell she'd had just about enough.

She gazed directly at her sisters and, without batting an eye, said,

"Ashley, Jade, c'est suffit."

Velma, who had been standing by, unacknowledged by Ashley or Jade, took a seat on the opposite side of Lacy, our backs to the window (much to my chagrin, I would have much preferred looking at the garden than those bitches).

Ashley Jade and their husbands faced us and the garden view.

Mr. Wilkins returned and sat next to me at the head of the table.

Mrs. Wilkins entered, seated at the opposite end of the table closest to the kitchen door.

Looking from Mrs. to Mr. Wilkins, I said,

"Mr. and Mrs. Wilkins, I just want to thank you for welcoming me to your home. Lacy is a woman of grace, style, and intelligence, and it makes perfect sense that she comes from such a fine and refined family as this. "

"That's very kind of you, Mr. Larkin, very kind," Mr. Wilkins replied.

I went on,

"Sir, but I have one question for you. Please excuse my curious nature, but I could not help but notice eleven settings and only ten of us. Is there another guest?"

"Very observant you are, Mr. Larkin, a superior quality, I might add. Yes, one more person is coming, one more," Wilkins replied, to which Ashley exclaimed:

"Daddy, is it absolutely necessary? Do we have to wait? It's always the same: they're never on time; why do we have to do this anyway?"

"Ashley, if I've explained it once, I've explained it a thousand times; furthermore, now is not the time to rehash this, especially in front of Lacy's Friend."

Ashley frowned.

Her cut features and fine figure were highlighted by a chic and tasteful black gown, which was couture by some New York designer, I'm sure.

A simple gold chain fell to her neckline, and a huge rock encased in white gold stood up from a finger.

Her husband next to her wore high-tone kakis, obnoxious white buff deck shoes, and that ubiquitous Blue Dress Shirt (the kind with the Polo Player Logo), his collar wide open.

Jade was in a stunning red dress that accentuated awesome curves, blond hair framing a model's face.

She was short like her mother but a hell of a package.

I knew Lacy's sisters would be hot.

Jade's husband wore a black suit with a designer cravat.

Lacy told me he was a pediatrician, but he looked more like a mortician if you ask me.

A few minutes passed.

Lacy engaged Velma to her right as Mr. and Mrs. Wilkins spoke with servants who filled our glasses with red wine and brought a tray of delicate crystal glasses filled with lemon-infused water.

Ashley and Jade switched chairs to commiserate, leaving the doctors to chat.

Lacy and Velma were ever deeper into their chatter, allowing me to observe the surroundings, including a tired-looking black man who came in the front door wearing a pair of stained and faded coveralls.

Wilkins beckoned him with a raised hand, which he noticed, and then sauntered towards the dining table and sat between Velma and Mrs. Wilkins, whereupon Wilkins stood up at the head of the table and spoke.

"Y'all raise your glass now, you too, Raaf – y'all, Raaf is our special guest tonight, and Justin graces our table from New Orleans. Raff has been with Piedmont for 25 years."

"Justin," he said, looking my way,

"Mr. Larkin, we invite one of my workers to each dinner we have.

I am sure it is a blessing to share with the poor, as the saying goes in the good book somewhere. The Lord blesses those who share their blessings, right, Raaf?

Raaf looked out of place, uncomfortable, like he'd rather be anywhere else, but on hearing Wilkins, he raised his head and said,

"Yes sir, Mr. Wilkins, that's right, you're right there, and y'all know your daddy, Mr. Wilkins, he's a good man and a hardworking man, not afraid to do anything we do at the mill, that's why we all love him so, and y'all girls have a wonderful daddy, thank y'all for this fine dinner."

Lacy smiled at Raaf; Jade, Ashley, and the doctors kept their eyes on Mr. Wilkins.

"Now y'all, we're going to praise our Lord and Savior Jesus Christ, who drank wine on his last supper, so sure enough, it's okay for us to drink the stuff."

Everyone chuckled, and Wilkins continued,

"Let's bow our heads."

Everyone bowed their heads at this point, and Wilkins began his prayer.

"Now all praises to our lord and master, Jesus Christ, for creating this fruit of the vine, and this is particularly good stuff, that our lord placed in California, Justin's home State, and also thank you, lord, for Raaf for working so hard at Piedmont all these years, and to all the others who have labored to bring us the blessing we share today, Amen.

Now that being said, I ask all y'all to raise your glasses high and give thanks and praises to him who created it all and blessed us with the bounty, in the name of the Father, Son, and Holy Ghost; Amen, Amen, Amen."

Everyone drank except Raaf, who put down his glass. I suspect I was the only one who noticed.

"That was a beautiful prayer, Daddy, lovely." Lacy declared.

"Why, thank you, Lacy. Now, y'all eat up."

With that, the servants entered and placed slices of roast beef, gravy, spears of asparagus in white sauce, a tossed salad of endive and other leaves I had never seen before, plus huge baked potatoes served off a rolling cart with butter, sour cream, and chives in silver bowls.

This was a meal fit for a King, and I dug in with gusto.

Jade, who was barely picking at her plate and seated directly across from me, spoke up,

"Now, Mr. Larkin, do tell, I have a friend at Newcomb, and they heard the same horrible rumor my sister Ashley spoke about you and that French Professor, Levy. Now, that's a Jewish name, am I right? We have loads of Levy's in Charleston, and they're Jewish. Was Professor Levy Jewish?"

She giggled, only stopping when her husband broke in,

"Come on, Jade, you know very well it is a Jewish name. My medical partner is Gerald Levy, and he is Jewish. Levy is a Jewish name."

Lacy had her mouth open; I guess she wanted to see where this went because she managed to keep any sound from coming out.

"I suppose it is," I said.

"But I never really asked. She was a professor, and her religious background never arose. She was teaching Philosophy. I don't know what you heard, but in any case, she left the country before I met your sister."

"Is that so?" Jade replied and went back to her dinner.

"Come on, Larkin," doctor husband #1 said.

"Listen, let's get this out on the table; we have some concerns here."

Mr. Wilkins cut him off, saying,

"Neal, listen. We do have concerns, but this is not the time and place."

Doctor Neal replied,

"All due respect, Sir, this is a serious matter, and what better time to discuss it than when we are all together over a fine meal that Mrs. Wilkins prepared?"

He said, nodding to Mrs. Wilkins, who I could bet my bottom dollar didn't cook one item.

"Yes, Daddy, this is not the time and place," Lacy said, looking at her father.

Wilkins looked at Lacy and then at Neal, clearly considering both sides.

Then, after some deep reflection, face to face with Solomon's sincerity, he spoke,

"Now, it is true we are all family here, except Mr. Larkin. Raaf has been with me longer than you, dear Lacy, and he is in the Piedmont Family like one of us."

Wilkins stopped and seemed to ponder a bit more. All eyes were on him now as he continued, clearly enjoying the rapt attention. Then he turned his gaze to Neal.

"Son, perhaps you are right; maybe it is a good time, but please treat Mr. Larkin respectfully: he is a guest."

Dr. Neal replied, "Naturally, Mr. Wilkins, naturally."

Now, Dr. Neal directed his attention at me,

"Mr. Larkin, let me be frank: we have some concerns as a family. First, let me tell you we know all the intimate details of your affair or whatever they call it in California."

At this, Wilkins interjected like a Judge cautioning an attorney,

"Manners, Neal, manners."

Dr. Neal looked over and said,

"Yes, yes," and continued.

"Sir, we know you had an affair with this Jewish Woman and further created a scene in a classroom at Tulane University. Dean Bougiere told Jefferson that this was the most outlandish and despicable act he knew of in his thirty years at the institution.

Naturally, we are concerned when a family member is even remotely associated with such a scandal. Mr. Larkin, you might not be aware of this fact, but Tulane is considered the 'Harvard of the South.'"

"Who is Jefferson?" I asked.

Jade's husband stood up and answered,

"I am Dr. Jefferson Larson. I will have you know I attended Tulane Medical School, and your behavior was a disgrace to the institution, the South, and our family."

"Listen, Dr. Larson," I replied,

"I am sure that incident at Tulane was no reflection on the Wilkins Family whatsoever. It was a personal matter between Dr. Levy and me. Further, at this time, I was not acquainted with Lacy. There is no connection whatsoever. I am sure some personal matters in your life should be private, no?

Honestly, why you are bringing this up is a mystery to me."

At this, Ashley blurted out,

"It matters a lot to us! Lacy is our sister; she brought you here, Justin, if that's your name. As a family, we don't think you are the kind of person Lacy should socialize with. She has been under a lot of stress lately, and Dr. Rankin informs us you are taking advantage of her in the same way you caused that poor Jewish Girl's problems. What is wrong with you anyway?"

Lacy, who had been listening all along, raised herself carefully from the table and turned to Mr. Wilkins.

"Daddy? Are you going to put up with this, letting them talk this way? Justin is our guest; you know nothing about him, and he is a wonderful person."

Wilkins, stone-faced, said,

"Lacy, sit down now. This is a family: would it be better if we did not express our concerns?"

Then, looking over at me, he said,

"Y'all, I spent some time speaking with Mr. Larkin. He is a reasonable fellow. Son, please don't take this the wrong way. It's just the way we feel. We understand that you are soon returning home to California, and naturally, we don't want Lacy hurt."

Lacy looked at Ashley, Jade, their husbands, and her father and intensely stared at Mrs. Wilkins, who said nothing.

The table was plunged into silence; a full minute or more passed, and finally, Mrs. Wilkins got up and, without a word, retreated towards the kitchen.

Then Lacy stood again and, in a stern and loud voice, declared,

"Thanks, Mother. Thanks a lot. I am sure you are behind this."

She left the dining room, stomping up the staircase.

We all sat silently for a moment, and then Velma got up.

"Excuse me, I am going to check on Lacy," Velma said.

Velma departed, and Wilkins said,

"Oh, she'll be alright, son. She'll be fine in the morning. Lacy always had such a taste of the dramatic."

And so went my introduction to the Wilkins family.

The way I figured it, the two doctors thought I was a complete pervert or perhaps admired my cojones – it was hard to tell; they were such snits.

And as for Lacy's sisters, I understood why Lacy wanted to leave Charleston so much.

Mr. Wilkins seemed like an amicable guy, and Lacy's mother was well-mannered and kind on the surface, but I didn't trust her.

I figured she talked behind my back, and Lacy as much as admitted it.

The next day, we flew back to New Orleans.

Upon our return to New Orleans, Dean Bougiere called me into his office, demanding an accounting of my actions in Professor Levy's Lecture Hall.

Who knows how he learned of the incident? I never asked, yet I understood that it was the talk of the campus.

I sat opposite him on a hard wooden chair, the Dean sitting sternly behind a disheveled desk.

The office had an open window to the campus below.

Cheap pine shelving lined the walls, books stacked this way and that, huge empty spaces between them, as if the world had somehow run out of books.

These voids were stuffed with non-descript statues and silly commendations.

We faced each other, and I tried to mimic his stern demeanor.

Neither he nor I wanted to show our hand by making the first move.

In my gut, I felt there was no way Tulane would allow a student to remain in the graduate program that they figured had had his way with a professor, especially a good-looking one.

Still, there is always hope; I will do my best to preserve my seat.

The Dean continued to eye me.

Each second, his visage became darker and increasingly dour.

He was waiting for me to break, but I would not relent. How could he understand, and how could I explain?

On the other hand, how could he not understand?

He, too, was human, flesh and blood like me.

"Young man, what do you have to say for yourself?"

"Dean, it was a personal matter. I am sure you understand it will never happen again," I replied.

"Is that all you have to say for yourself?" was his retort.

"Yes, Sir," I replied.

What else could I say?

In truth, I had already spoken more than I intended; this was not a time for words but for human understanding.

Yet the silence was becoming uncomfortable, and I was beginning to perspire. I just wanted to leave, to get out of the solemn and sterile space.

Then suddenly, his expression changed.

A smile appeared. Perhaps he understood, I thought.

He continued,

"Well then. Fine, Mr. Larkin, you may leave now."

A smile was now plastered across his face as he arose from behind his desk. I felt his arm upon my back as I turned and left the office.

"Take care, son," he said.

Gently shutting his door, I stood in the hallway, confused and befuddled.

I was sure the Dean now knew what had transpired in Dr. Levy's lecture hall and that it was a matter of the heart.

I didn't know what the Dean felt about it, and I suspect that's just how he wanted it.

The Hands of Others

It was perplexing that the Dean said nothing about the Jergens; perhaps he was just being cagey, but then again, so was I.

That said, even if he had directly asked for an explanation, there was none that I would have supplied.

Perhaps our meeting put an end to the matter.

He did pat me on the back, so surely, he understood.

Maybe I misread him. He had done his duty and put me on notice.

As fate would have it, we crossed paths on campus later that day.

The Dean greeted me with an enormous smile, like an old friend.

"Hello, Justin. I might as well inform you about some new developments in your case; you will find out sooner or later, in any event.

Dr. Levy has decided to return to France. She will remain your instructor for the next few weeks until we can find her a replacement."

He turned away and continued walking, that shit-eating grin wider than ever.

My initial impression of him was right; he was truly a fuckin' asshole; I shivered at the thought.

Was I next?

Naturally, I was sad for Bridgette, regretful that my outburst would have had such an immediate and profound effect on her life.

Indeed, she was partly to blame, of that I am sure.

But it seems my simple outburst was responsible for irrevocably altering our lives' paths.

Why had she been so persistent?

I told her I was not in love with her, but she would not relent.

I did the honorable and honest thing.

Would it have been better if I had misled and lied to continue sleeping with her?

Bridgette was a woman of great passion.

Was it just that she enjoyed sex so much, or was it rather that her love for me drove her to such passionate and complete extremes?

No woman before or since has pleased me so much, who was so free with her body.

With Bridgette, I could empty my mind.

She was clearly a brilliant woman, but reason was not at play with us; neither discussion nor ideas encumbered our pure animal instinct.

She showered me with gifts and affection, and though I was her junior in both years and knowledge, she treated me with the utmost respect, love, and difference.

I was only human. Who could blame me? If I had not been so honest, perhaps this misfortune could have been avoided.

I cared for her, and she treated me kindly.

Did she not deserve the truth?

Would it have been better to mislead her?

The end would have come in due time, but I had to end the charade at the right time; that was honorable.

Hence, I told her that I did not love her.

But there is no compassionate way to say such things.

She immediately clarified that she did not consider our relationship a dalliance.

She was above such things, and I had committed a grave and unforgivable crime.

Like the earth moving on its axis, her reaction was defined and clear: this should not be the course of events, she felt—it could not be.

What was once love and acceptance instantly turned to disdain, caustic, and vile daggers aimed at my psyche.

She didn't argue aloud, but her overwhelming anger was piercing and shrilled stern and stone silence.

I took my punishment in private. I owed her at least that, if not more. I begged her pardon, and in her anger, she warned,

" Ne dis pas un seul mot dans la classe, rester loin de moi."

Taking her advice, I sat in the farthest corner of the lecture hall with Annie, a fellow student and friend.

Annie sat in the extreme rear of the lecture hall, right near the exit.

As a newcomer to the back row, she gave me the aisle seat.

"It's the best seat in the house; you owe me," she said.

Annie had absolute disdain for existentialists.

Here, she could do her nails out of sight of Bridgette while completing the requirement to take a general course in philosophy.

She sat sufficiently far from the lectern to grumble criticism and sarcasm out of earshot of others or Dr. Levy.

When I took my seat, she said.

"What are you sitting here for anyways? I thought you were an existentialist. The class is usually a fuckin' dialogue between you and Dr. Levy.

On the other hand, this is interesting. Do tell?"

"I have my reasons, Annie. Anyways, the class is starting, so shut the fuck up and do your nails."

"Okay, Big Boy, tell me after class."

As the class progressed, this distance seemed insufficient, though as far away from the lectern as possible and still in the hall, Bridgette's anger was unrelenting.

She constantly reached out with oblique comments directed at me.

She scolded ideas and thoughts that, a week before, she had lauded when I expressed them in class.

Moreover, although I did not say one word, it was as if she were commenting on my remarks that instant.

Annie just smiled and jived at me as if this was proof existentialism was without reason, and then she whispered,

"What's going on between you two? She won't lay off."

I ignored Annie's remark, but Bridgette continued until I could no longer contain my anger.

Instinctively, without forethought, I reached for a glass bottle of Pink Jergens Lotion sitting beside Annie and, with all my strength, flung it against the far wall of the lecture hall.

It shattered with a loud crash, splattering gobs and streaks of pinkish goo over the assembled.

Ouro Infirmary

A pall fell over the lecture hall; I was able to slink quickly out the back exit, hoping that perhaps I was invisible and hoping, too, that what had just happened, in a fit of anger, would soon also disappear, fade from my memory, and somehow magically obliterate the memory of all those in the room.

However, in my heart, I knew that this would not happen, that what was, was… and would always be.

In a haze, unable or unwilling to fully comprehend the ramifications of my actions, I commenced a rapid and sustained walk for four miles back to the impound yard under the Claiborne Bridge on the edge of the quarter.

The Nissan had been towed there the night before.

What a fuckin' day- first walking out only to find my car gone again (it had to be at the tow yard) and now this fiasco with Bridgette.

What was to become of me?

On top of it all, the workers at the tow yard had that shit-eating grin on their faces; they remembered me, I am sure.

I was just one more citizen; they were about to fleece to support their parasitic existence.

I slipped the money under the bulletproof glass, and the bitch exchanged it for my keys, a receipt, and a parking ticket.

Growling, I stomped under I-10 to retrieve the Nissan, thinking perhaps there was some good in all this.

At least I was not thinking about Tulane and my future there.

The walk calmed me down a bit. It was good exercise.

There is good in everything; you just have to find it.

As I pulled the car out of the yard and onto Rampart, I swore that this would be the last time I ended up in this godforsaken hellhole underneath the interstate.

The drive to the quarter takes minutes. I quickly found a safe place a few blocks off Bourbon, parked the Nissan, and walked to my apartment on the 1200 Block.

Behind the big, gated door, tall brick walls and green overgrowth surrounded me, and the ancient pavers with blades of grass growing between the cracks calmed and comforted me.

I was away from everything outside the walls—the Tow Yard, Bridgette, Tulane; I couldn't think about these things now.

Small insects crawled along the pavers; they knew nothing of these things.

Numb and immobile, exhausted and dispirited, all I wanted was sleep. I threw myself down on the small spring sofa bed, which comprised thirty percent of the space I called home. The remainder was the diminutive kitchen, desk, and tiny bathroom down a dark, unlit hallway.

Falling into a deep sleep, I awoke the next afternoon to the relentless ringing of the telephone. Annie was on the other end.

"Justin, I'm glad I got you. I am so glad I got you. Are you all right? You shot out of class like a bat out of hell. I hope I didn't upset you. I'm sorry. I was only joking; I meant nothing."

"No, no, you had nothing to do with it. It was Bridgette. She kept giving me hell in front of the class, and I couldn't take it anymore," I said.

"What was that about anyways? Why was she doing that? It was uncalled for," she said.

"It's complicated; there's a bit more than class involved," I admitted.

"Don't worry. Nobody was hurt with the glass shards, but my Jergens was all over the place; you owe me a bottle."

"Great, they'll probably kick me out of Tulane. Shit, I fucked up," I said.

"Why did you do it? What were you thinking?" she asked.

"It's too complicated. What did Levy say when I left?" I inquired.

"It was bizarre. Nobody said anything. It was like it didn't happen. A few students left to clean the lotion off their clothes, but she continued her lecture as if nothing happened. Everyone figures you were sleeping with her; at least, that's what they are saying. Is that what it was? You can tell me."

"I need to think about this. Thanks for calling. Bye." I said.

"Wait," Annie said before I could hang up, and she continued.

"I understand, but that's not why I called. I heard Levy was admitted to Ouro. My roommate has her Sartre class; what a waste.

In any event, it was canceled. A proctor showed up and said she was admitted to Ouro. He was taking donations to send flowers to cheer her up. I thought you would want to know."

"Jeez… Annie, thanks. Listen, I gotta go now. I will see you soon. Bye."

Hanging up the phone, all I could think was,

"What a fuckin' disaster."

Surely, she had attempted suicide, and I was the cause.

Besides losing me, who knows how Tulane would react if they knew about her fraternization with a student?

On top of that, she was French and an existentialist to boot; there could be no other rational conclusion.

She displayed such passion, only to find out my love did not drive it but rather pure lust. She was debauched, disgraced. Such misjudgment on her part; indeed, she tried to take her life and mercifully failed.

I imagined her wrists bandaged, her olive skin, pale as a ghost, and tubes inserted into her tender loins.

Panicked thoughts raced through my mind as I drove to Ouro Infirmary, hysterical at what I might find there.

Totally unconscious of my surroundings, I ran red lights and barely missed hitting pedestrians; so much was I in a state of utter chaos.

Arriving in the halls, as if expected, mumbling names and personages unknown, I was escorted into a small room in a corner of the hospital.

There lay Bridgette, unbandaged and half-dressed, on a hospital bed.

"Bridgette, how are you? Are you okay? I just heard you were in here and rushed right over. What happened?"

"I'm fine. Last night, I had a gastric attack. I am staying at the hospital tonight, and tomorrow, I can return home," she said.

"I was so worried about you. I thought it was worse. I'm so glad. You look fine. There are no tubes in you at all."

"Oui, je suis très bien ce que vous a fait penser que j'allais de se suicider, pas une chance," she said.

"God Forbid," I gently touched her side.

"I'm fine now, really. I was hoping you would come," she said.

"Nothing could keep me away," I added.

Somehow, lying on that bed, Bridgette looked sweeter and more beautiful than ever before, and without thinking, I began to probe the top of her and then the bottom. Bridgette moved in all directions, re-igniting my passion.

That was the very last time I saw Bridgette.

I assume she returned to France.

Bridgette seemed to exist in the here and now, for her knowledge and passion seemed to be one, as did her mind and body.

For me, these things cannot exist in the same space.

The Sandwich

On Saturdays, I'd find my way to Central Grocery in the French Quarter, a block from the Swap Meet.

Old blankets lay on the ground, and funky fruit and vegetable stands extended all the way to the Old Mint Building.

History crumbling behind a solid iron fence.

Someone's tossed-away goods were of scant interest, and I didn't want yellow meat watermelon.

Instead, I was allured by the fragrant aromas of that old Central Grocery, with its wooden floors and shelves covered with strange and exotic concoctions reminiscent of some odd syncretism of European and American Culture.

Within the core of the grocery itself, what most intrigued me was a singular round sandwich, what they called a muffuletta. It was a mammoth loaf generously spread with chopped olives, covered by a brilliant array of luncheon meats and cheeses. I often washed the flavorful things down with Barq's Root Beer.

Grabbing the sandwich, wrapped tightly in white butcher paper, I took a few steps to the little island opposite Central Grocery, which separates Decatur from St. Peters.

At this junction, every car and the people within must travel down St. Peter to the sea and its depths or up Decatur to Esplanade and home, the choice we all must make every minute of our lives until an inevitable end.

Opening the neatly wrapped butcher paper and taking a massive bite of the sandwich, I pulled the tab off the Barq's and thrust it into the can, which was the tradition then.

I took a large bit of the sandwich and one long sip from the can, whence the pleasant taste of the delicacy was replaced with an agonizing, searing burn.

The tinge of the burn persisted, but it was minor; I could almost write it off. I felt okay, but some inner knowledge told me to visit Lacy on Pine Street, so I made the short drive and was fortunate (I think) to find her home.

"Can I rest a while? Somehow, I'm… just tired," I say.

"Sure, lie on the bed, and let me get a blanket to cover you."

Almost instantly, I fall into a deep sleep, and when I awake, I am overcome by the oppressive damp and tropical heat.

Lacy is by my side.

"How long was I resting?"

"A couple of hours," said Lacy.

Sleep is like death, especially during the day, a time and space without knowledge or consciousness.

Usually, I would have asked more questions, needed more details, and couldn't lose the time.

But in this instance, I didn't ask another thing; I was distracted by a fever, overcome by the heat, and oddly without thirst.

Getting up, I lunged for the front door.

"One second. I gotta step outside for a second. I'll be right back," I said.

The warmth of the day surrounded me, then something that had never occurred before or since happened:

A vast, red-black wad of blood pooled in my mouth. I opened my lips, and the globule fell slowly onto the grass near the side of Lacy's cottage.

It sat there like a red bubbling volcanic lake.

Slowly, I took it in. Indeed, I was concerned, but there was no time to think. I needed to act.

Entering the cottage, I told Lacy,

"I'm not feeling well. I spit a bit of blood, and I'm going over to Charity to have it checked out."

A look of puzzlement and concern covered her face.

"Yes, good idea. I'll drive you."

"No, it's fine; I might be there a while. I'll call you later," I said, slamming the door and exiting toward the Nissan parked on quiet little Pine Street.

Naturally, I wanted to get to Charity Hospital as quickly as possible, so I headed to Claiborne instead of taking the more scenic St. Charles Route.

Making a right on Tulane, I turned into an empty parking lot opposite the hospital, paved with millions of loose white oyster shells.

The faded yellow Nissan made little crunching sounds as it crushed whatever unfortunate random abandoned shell got in its way.

Making a circle in the empty lot, the sound of the shells echoed even louder; I pictured hundreds, maybe thousands, dying a brutal death smashed against each other, some continuing to live and others shattered, all accidental, knowing they were all long gone but still picturing it thus.

I was in control or near it, but there was no intention. I was excused by chance, prohibiting the assignment of any personal blame for their death and destruction.

Alas, I would bring the order.

There must be order, I thought, maneuvering the Nissan perfectly perpendicular to the Hospital, ensuring an end to the chaos.

Good fortune assured.

Walking across the street to the enormous gray hospital, I mounted the steps of its imposing entry, imagining in my mind that it was Epidaurus or Delphi.

I entered the rotunda and was received by a woman of middle age and great warmth seated behind a half-moon desk.

"How can we help you?" she asked.

"I spit up some blood," I replied.

"How long ago was it?" she asked.

"Maybe an hour, something like that," I said.

She looked me over a bit.

"May I have your driver's license?"

"Yes, ma'am."

I reached into my wallet, removed my driver's license, and handed it to her.

Oddly enough, she grasped my hand as she acquired the license, holding it tight.

Without thinking, I let my hand remain; it was comforting, as if she were healing me on the spot.

In truth, she seemed to be barely looking at the driver's license.

Something more was happening, I was sure, as she continued to rub her fingers against mine.

In due course, she released my hand and returned the license.

Then, pulling a form from beneath her desk, she commenced to write on it and check off this and that, writing words here and there. After a few minutes, she finished the task and handed me some hospital papers.

"Young man," she said, "You go all the way down that long hall to a room marked one hundred and fifty-six and give them these papers. Follow the yellow line, and good luck to you."

Holding the papers, I gazed back as she focused on me walking away.

On reflection, it seemed odd how she held my hand as if she were searching for something within my veins, but she was only a receptionist, not a seer, so how could that be?

The yellow line was a mere shadow of its former self, and upon the path, I felt the shadows of the crowds that had tread this line before me, removing tiny molecules of paint with each footstep.

They marched, I am sure, in full faith of a good result, with confidence in the knowledge and skills of those who directed them to take this path.

Soon enough, I arrived at a solid wooden door, one hundred and fifty-six imprinted near the top.

Anxiously, I slammed my knuckles hard against it, pulling them away in pain. Then, emerging as if from a hole in a white lab coat, a young Black man with a deadpan look said,

"Yes?"

Typically, I would have engaged him in a tirade about the exact meaning of "Yes" and perhaps a lecture on the importance of clarity in language use.

However, this was no time for such talk; my mission was urgent and personal. Therefore, without discussion and in haste, I handed him the same papers the kind lady gave me at the reception.

Glancing at them, he exclaimed in a rather perfunctory fashion,

"Come on, take that shirt off and stand behind the metal plates."

He entered a solid lead room with a window facing the green X-ray machine bolted tightly to the floor.

Positioning myself between the metal plates, cold like ice against my now bare chest, the plates moved closer and closer as he watched from the safety of his lead-enclosed cubical.

Soon, I was pinned inescapably, trapped, unable to move, encapsulated in a metal prison.

"Hold your breath," he instructed.

I did as he told me, and in seconds, he emerged from behind his protections and declared,

"You can go now; just wait outside. I'll develop the film and bring you the X-ray. It will be about twenty minutes, so please be patient."

Finding a worn wooden chair in the long hospital corridor, I sat and stared into space, thinking nothing in particular.

Soon enough, the technician returned with the X-ray in a large manila envelope. I took it and held it tightly; certainly, it contained the solution to this mystery.

"So, what's the verdict?" I asked.

"You'll have to wait for a doctor to review it. Take it down the hall to a window marked one hundred and thirty-six. The doctor is there, and he will read it and let you know."

There was no longer a line or path to direct me, but even without a line, I found the place behind a Dutch door of the same ancient and graying wood as all the others.

Presently, a handsome woman in a blue hospital outfit popped her head out of the top of the Dutch door.

Without hesitation, I handed her the x-ray.

"Wait here, and I will have the doctor read it," she said.

She departed, and I sat down, spying a gray metal chair with a well-worn cushion against the hospital corridor wall.

In an instant, I was overcome with vertigo so intense that I arose and ambled down the hallway – for what or where, I had no idea. I staggered and rocked down the hallway, zigzag style.

The terminus of the hallway came into view with a large turn to the right, heading back to reception.

Somehow, I needed to get there; I knew that. I had to get back to the woman who held my hand.

Sweating and swerving, I continued about fifteen feet and fell to the tile floor, blood gushing from my mouth and consciousness departing.

For a moment, it was as if I could see and hear again, but then I was out and gone, only to awake in an operating room surrounded by doctors speaking a language I could not understand, perhaps a foreign tongue, on reflection I am not sure, they were working with great intensity.

A fixture hung over my head, radiating a tropical and hellish heat. At the same time, I felt a terrible chill, as if my veins were full of ice.

Yet, in all this chaos and anxiety, I was awed.

Calm and peace overwhelmed me, and then consciousness departed for a second time.

Sometime later, I awoke in a hospital bed in a huge ward filled with rows and rows of empty beds.

I occupied the one nearest the entrance door. It was mystifying that only I and I would be in this vast ward; it was otherwise empty, endless beds and only me occupying a single bed.

How could that be?

And there was Lacy beside me, her hand on my arm, looking like the angel that she is.

She concentrated on my visage.

Lifting my head, her gaze transfixed, I calmly said,

"Lacy, I'm so glad you're here. How did you know where I was?"

"Justin, you told me you were going to Charity; naturally, I called to find out if you were okay. Your friend Dr. Kennedy stopped by yesterday after I arrived. You didn't sleep well at all last night. You were very agitated and yelling. They had to tie your hands down."

Ignoring her speech, I blundered on as she untied my hands from the metal bed rails.

"I must have given your number to the doctors when I was going in and out.

They asked me lots of questions, and they kept asking me if I had been drinking. I kept telling them 'No,' but they kept asking me. I guess people that bleed usually drink?" I said.

Lacy did not respond but gazed at me with affection.

I was overwhelmed with appreciation for her concern and uneasy in my time of need.

A lifetime would be needed to repay this debt.

A Diagnosis of Doubt

The hospital kept me for a few days, I guess, to see if I was okay,

"Hey, Doc, what happened anyway?"

"You were bleeding," he replied.

"I know that, but why, why was I bleeding?" I enquired.

"We're not sure, but you're okay now, so you can go home tomorrow," the doctor proclaimed matter-of-factly without fear of embarrassment.

It was a very unsatisfying response, to say the least; naturally, I was concerned and perplexed. These were medical men, scientific shamans dressed in white smocks, with medallions hanging from their necks, referred to by a fancy appellation.

How could they not know what was wrong?

Was medicine truly a science or mere voodoo?

Was it an art or some religion in which faith was vital for its efficacy?

If so, I was no longer convinced, a believer or a man of that faith.

What I needed was certainty; they gave me none!

Sure, I was delighted they agreed to let me go, but given that they did not know causation, it could happen again.

They had cured nothing, only forestalled the inevitable.

Was I to spend the rest of my life knowing that one day, blood would flow from my mouth?

Would that be my finish? I persisted; this could not be the case!

I demanded a better answer from the surgeon, but he replied with the same song.

"I don't think it was a pop top," the doctor grinned.

"Then what was it?" I asked.

"We're not sure," he replied.

So, I was released in a state of panic and ennui, worried about life and limb.

Given the circumstances, one would imagine that in such a condition, I'd head over to see Lacy and thank her for her kindness and consideration.

Certainly, she'd provide comfort, assailing doubt and confusion.

Yet, to the contrary, the thought of seeing Lacy terrified me more than my fear of bleeding to death.

So, rather than driving over to visit her, I telephoned and said,

"I'm fine, and I'll be heading home to rest. I'll contact you in a few days, so don't worry. I'm fine. Thanks so much for visiting me; you'll never know how much I appreciated it."

And Lacy replied,

"What do you mean, Justin? How could I not have come? I was worried sick. I should come over now. It's really not a problem, but if you want to be alone, I'll understand that, too."

There was silence on the phone. I could feel she wanted to come over, but I would not relent, saying,

"I just want to be alone now, Lacy, please."

"Thanks a lot," I said.

And hung up.

The Fear

Back on Bourbon Street, more bad news awaited me.

A letter from Tulane sat in the mailbox. Not that I didn't expect it, but the letter made it official. They completely cut me off, and my stipend and scholarship were suspended.

The letter stated in part,

"After careful review, the Faculty of the Graduate School of Philosophy at Tulane University has withdrawn your scholarship and stipend for the coming school year. Furthermore, your position as a Graduate Student has been rescinded. We wish you the greatest of success in your future studies."

If there were ever any doubts about my next move, that letter assuaged them. It seems I just wasn't cut out for New Orleans; hell, New Orleans Town never gives a sucker an even break.

One false move, and she'll wash you under. She'll cut you up before she spits you out, so walk the straight and narrow, or something bad's gonna happen.

The fact that my Nissan spent half the time at the police impound under Claiborne Bridge should have been clue enough, but there was more, much more.

Getting kicked out of Tulane and swallowing a Barq's tab top were merely icing on the cake.

Honestly, if it wasn't one thing, it was another. It was as clear as the bell on the top of the Cathedral at Jackson Square that I needed to leave this place and leave it while I was still in one piece. That was the wise thing to do.

At that point, I figured the best way to stay out of trouble until I departed was to just stay in my apartment and out of harm's way. Besides, I was terrified that I was going to spit blood any second, so I wanted to be near a telephone.

I pecked at the typewriter, read this and that; I know I wrote Kaya, the high school crush, the one who jilted me, the one who was on my mind some of the time – I couldn't just let her go.

Sure, there had been others before and after Kaya, but for some reason, she was special, with some connection that she seemed able to break, but the one and only I just couldn't.

I sat and wrote Kaya a note, the details of which I can recall not even one.

I gave the Landlord notice and packed my books and scattered belongings for the return drive home.

The prospect of a two-thousand-mile drive across Louisiana, Texas, New Mexico, Arizona, and California was daunting, to say the least.

What if I started bleeding in the middle of nowhere?

Frozen in this space, unable to act, paralyzed with fear, I could not move.

My final days in New Orleans were encapsulated in my hot, muggy, benign, secure quarters.

Then, the doorbell rang on one of those dark and paranoid days.

I quickly scampered down the stairs, through the courtyard and the long walkway, then ran between the big house and the slave quarters to the enormous wooden door that fronted Bourbon Street to see who it was.

Annie was in a loose-fitting calico dress and standing before the door.

Her breasts jutted out into the calico-like rockets, and she grabbed me, compressing those things against my body.

"Justin, you're okay; I'm so glad you're okay. I heard from James that you were in the hospital. He said he visited you."

"Yes, James came by. It was nice of him, but like the rest of the doctors, they had no idea what happened; they kinda just said it was okay to go, so I'm worried."

Annie looked at me with concern and said,

"After I spoke to James, I called Lacy; she was out of her mind. I told her I would stop by; she was concerned and asked me to tell her how you felt.

Didn't you call her?"

"Come on, Annie, you know how it is; I just don't want to worry her."

"I understand," she replied, but I am unsure she did.

As it was, I was a bit tired of being holed up in the little room, and as afraid as I was of imminent death, with Annie around, I figured if I keeled over, she could at least get me help, so I made a suggestion.

"You want to walk to Café du Monde and get some of that café? I gotta load up. No coffee like that in LA, and I'm going home soon."

"Sure, that'll be nice. Let's go," she agreed.

It was always fun being out with Annie. I was already feeling better and so glad she came. Since we disagreed about everything serious, we could concentrate on lighter things. I could turn my mind off and enjoy, and Annie seemed to be able to do the same.

It seems we both understood that's the way it had to be.

Easy-going Annie, that's what most saw, and most of the time, that is what she was, but there was another side of Annie, a darker side, a side of hopelessness and futility, and I knew that side, too.

Yet, such hopelessness and confusion were the inevitable outcome of her philosophy, and I told her so.

"Listen, Annie, it's that Marxist bullshit that fucks you up. That's why you're depressed. It makes no sense. The whole philosophy is non-functional. It doesn't work, so each time you try to apply it to your life, it fails you, and you're down. You'd be better off as a Buddhist, Confucian, or Jainist. Try Jean-Paul Sartre or Buber, and then you will be happy."

And Annie would reply,

"Justin, you're completely immoral. You have no concern for the struggling masses, and there is so much injustice and corruption in this world. I can't stand it; it must be stopped. So many big corporations exploit people and the environment for their benefit, and there will be no justice until we overturn the oppressors. Justin, 'if you're not part of the solution, you're a part of the problem,' just like Huey P. Newton said."

"Okay, okay, you're right. Let's go get some coffee from the capitalists at Café du Monde, you sweet baby bird," I replied, and she laughed.

What else could I do? She needed tenderness, not disdain. She was a good, if confused, soul.

In truth, I held that her notions were irrational and without hope, naturally leading to desolation. Annie was two people: the serious scholar and the playful nymph. I preferred the nymph and found more reason in her way of life than in her way of thinking.

As we walked, she said,

"I visited my daddy today, and as usual, we fought. All he could talk about was Captain Crunch. What a bore."

"Come on, Annie, your daddy is a great guy. So damn funny."

Annie hated him, yet I found him a gas.

He was full of humor, and even his job was funny: He sold Captain Crunch for a living. His garage was stuffed to the brim with boxes upon boxes of Captain Crunch.

You'd see him on the phone trying to sell that shit. It was a work of art how his words moved pallets of Captain Crunch cereal out the door. Annie detested everything about it, fuming while I smiled as her daddy worked his magic.

"So, what if your daddy sells Captain Crunch? He's paying your way through Tulane and making an honest living, right?" I said.

"No, he's selling garbage to kids, and their company executives are making huge profits, and what do the workers get? Nothing! It's a damn shame. Pure exploitation, that's all it is," she said.

"Okay, even if that's true, Captain Crunch is awesome stuff," I said.

"Okay, Justin, just try living on it and see what happens. It will rot your teeth and drive you to an early death," she said.

"Sure, tell your daddy to give me a supply, and I will," I replied in jest, grabbing her side as we moved up Governor Nicholls towards the French Market.

"When are you leaving for California?" she asked, changing the subject.

"As soon as I feel better, it's a long drive, and I am a bit worried about my illness. I hate to have something go wrong on the road."

"I'll go with you. I can drive, and I've always wanted to see California! I want to head up Salinas Way and work with the Farm Workers' Union. I'd love to come. Do you mind if I come?" she asked.

I had to chuckle like there weren't enough oppressed farm workers in the South, but I kept my thoughts to myself, as having Annie along for the ride would be great.

Besides, Lacy's situation was complicated: she was a great girl, but the notion of settling down didn't sit well with me.

I needed time to think.

Leaving quickly with Annie seemed like a good idea. Not only was she very sympathetic, but she could drive and given my current mental state and fear of imminent death, she was the perfect traveling companion. I wanted out, and she was my ticket.

"Sure, that would be great. You really can come?" I asked.

"Yes, it was on my mind earlier, so I came. I want to go to California; I mentioned it to Lacy, and she thought it would be good if I traveled with you. She thought it would be safer for you. She loves you, Justin. I wanted to check and see if she was good with it."

"And what did Lacy say?" I asked.

"She was fine with it, very supportive, and she felt it would be a lot safer. She just told me: 'Make sure that crazy boy calls me every day at 4 PM. I will be waiting by the telephone.' You're a lucky man; she's a really wonderful person and so beautiful."

To say that I was perplexed would be an understatement. Whereas I was attracted to Annie, Lacy seemed to have no idea and seemed to trust her perfectly.

It was not that Annie was untrustworthy – she was a good and loyal sort – but we had a history of which Lacy seemed oblivious.

I thought women could sense these things, but evidently not.

Or could it be that Lacy loved me so much as to be solely concerned with my welfare and was thus willing to take these risks for my safety?

In any event, Lacy and I never discussed my adventures with Annie; Annie and I were just friends.

Sure, there was a history of some physical contact a couple of times, but we were drunk and having fun—we were buddies, that's the way I saw it. I guess Annie felt the same way.

With Lacy, things were more serious and profound; she was as traditional as they come in many ways.

Discussion of political and social issues was the rule, whereas, with Annie, small talk and horseplay dominated, starting from our first minutes in Louisiana and continuing on our trip through Texas and beyond.

Lacy and I saw the world through similar lenses – a world of chaos and suffering.

We could not ignore it, even in everyday life.

Lacy naturally bonded with ordinary people.

It was not conceptual with Lacy; it was organic.

She was drawn to these people, though she was not from them, and they were drawn to her.

She participated in their suffering. She wanted to be a part of it; there was no theory. Though she was troubled by organized religion like me, she was a true believer in God.

Annie felt for the troubled, sure, but she was not one of them. She assisted them and wanted to help them, but she could not be one with them; in effect, she knew more than them, but Lacy was one of them.

Velma, who worked as a maid like her mother before, was her best friend. There was no gap between them. Lacy detested people of wealth and status; although she had come from that, she was drawn to the lowly. It was not theory; it was nature.

Lacy was integrated with her struggle; Annie was detached and separated, which worked great for me.

We could just have fun. I could not have a serious discussion with her or get upset with her because, unlike Lacy, I did not take her seriously.

So, Annie and I took a trip to California together. Annie put up with my craziness, never criticizing my absurd thoughts and actions.

As we approached a hospital exit, I would spit into a Kleenex.

We kept going if it was clean (and it always was). Lacy would have told me I was ridiculous, overdramatic, and had no idea what actual sickness was. She was harkening back to her youth with Velma and her constant trips to the hospital in crisis.

Perhaps I knew I was a bit psychosomatic, but I could not help it.

Lacy was right, I know, but Annie took my failings in stride without comment; they were irrational, sure, but so was Annie.

It was easier on my mind knowing I did not have to feel guilty about my neurosis.

The farther away from New Orleans we got, the more playful she and I became.

It would start as just a little fun, maybe throwing water across the Nissan's seat. Soon, I would be grabbing and fondling her as we drove.

"Stop, Justin, stop. What would Lacy say? We can't do this, stop."

I knew she didn't really care.

The crazier and more outlandish my actions were, the more she laughed.

I guess we felt the same way.

It didn't start out that way; it never does.

Annie and I were inseparable. Being in LA with Annie was like being on vacation. I can recall no details of that time except that it was blissful and carefree.

Annie planned to head up to Salinas a day or so after we arrived in LA, but a day turned into weeks.

I was broke, but Annie had some money, and we got by.

I would call Lacy every few days and tell her how I was.

I wouldn't mention Annie. There was no need, was there?

Lacy never asked. I believe she assumed she was gone, but that was not the case at all.

On one of these calls, Lacy told me she was coming to LA.

"Justin, I'll be there in forty-eight hours. I'm so excited," she said.

I broke the news to Annie. I really hated to see her go as she packed up and left.

That last night was a real pain in the ass.

I checked out of the cheap motel on Hollywood and Highland that Annie and I called home and checked into the cheapest place I could find – the Hollywood YMCA, a notorious haunt of homosexuals in those days.

The place was okay once you got through fighting off the 40-plus homos who hung out in the lobby looking for young meat.

Trust me: I double-bolted the locks on the door.

I checked out again the following day and loaded up the Nissan for LAX.

Lacy sauntered down the long, tiled corridor of the airport with the grace and style of a supermodel, looking perfect (as usual), not a hair out of place.

On the other hand, I had stained Levis, with long hair dangling down from under a New York Yankees Cap that Annie'd bought me at a swap meet at the Roadium Drive-In near San Pedro during one of our city jaunts.

I looked like shit, and she looked great. I was happy to see her, but a million thoughts were running through my mind.

I could summarize them with "Oh shit."

Now, no doubt I wanted to jump her bones as soon as we got in a room – that was not the problem.

But then what?

I was barely twenty-two, and this was a serious-ass chick with intentions.

I guess I was thinking, my mind spinning a thousand RPM, as I could find little to say as we drove from the airport to Sunset Strip, a great place to view the city.

From the top of the Sunset Strip, the lights reflected somberly on me.

I knew I should be happy, but I was perplexed.

Here was a beautiful, intelligent, kind, wonderful woman who wanted me, but I was not satisfied. With my last ten bucks, I bought two coffees and pastries and set them down in front of Lacy.

"Thank you so much. This place is lovely and look at those city lights—they go on forever and ever. I am so glad to be here; you cannot know. It was all worth it."

Then, Lacy hugged me, sipped her coffee, and gazed at the lights.

"What do you mean, worth it?" I asked.

"Nothing, nothing at all. I'll tell you later, just family, that's all, but it doesn't matter. I am here now and delighted. Thank you, Justin, thank you."

"For what?" I asked.

"What do you mean, 'for what'? For being here. For being… you."

This made nothing easier. My mind continued to spin, but I put it out of my mind as Lacy returned her gaze to the City Lights.

"Lacy, do you have any money?" I asked.

"Yes, Justin. Why?"

"I hate to say it, but I'm broke. Tulane cut me off, as you know. I am sure I can find some work soon, but we will need something to get by in the meantime."

"I have a thousand dollars; it's money I saved from Tulane," she said.

"Great, that will easily cover us till I can get a job."

Lacy opened her purse and handed me a stack of bills. It was a thousand dollars – more money than I ever held at one time. I jammed it into my wallet as fast as I could.

"I'll handle this," I said

"I bet it created a ruckus when you told your family you were coming to see me," I asked.

"It sure did. I told Dr. Rankin I was going home and flew back to Charleston so nobody in New Orleans would know I was here.

When I told Daddy I was going to California, the word got around fast.

Jade and Ashley called and launched into a tirade about you being a pervert, an axe murderer, or something. Jade was sure I would be coming home in a bag.

They told me I was ruining my life and that no Christian in Charleston, except perhaps a low-class, born-again, would have anything to do with me upon my return.

They said that Glen Wilson would have nothing to do with me anymore.

Those were precisely the words they used.

Justin. I hate those bitches.

Mother just cried, and Daddy looked at me somberly and told me I was welcome home anytime.

When the cab picked me up for the airport, Daddy didn't even pay for it.

He looked at me and said,

'Lacy, you're always welcome home if things don't work out. I know you have to go your own way. You're grown up now, but bad decisions have negative consequences. Take care of yourself.'

If he had offered me money, I wouldn't have taken it; I couldn't believe Daddy would do that. It was so sad; he offered me no encouragement at all. The only one who supported me was Velma, who told me to

'Go with your heart.'"

"So, Velma likes me?" I asked.

"I didn't say that, but Velma knows the value of life. She loves me and knows I was unhappy in Charleston and that I have to strike out on my own path.

Justin, I have dreams.

I always knew I would end up in California, maybe Los Angeles or San Francisco. I wanted to be here. But you need to understand something:

I'm not going back if it doesn't work out between us. I'll never go back. Do you understand?

This is my dream, not yours."

Jerry's Motel

I found this dive downtown on Third and Lucas. It didn't look like much, but Lacy didn't complain.

The room was tiny, with a substantial antique radio console jammed against the east wall.

An extensive set of dresser drawers made of beautiful, amber-stained oak with plasticized buttons and ornate knobs backed the west wall.

A colossal brass bed with a grayish-brown patina was at the room's center, leaving little space to maneuver.

Two beat wood chairs with print seat covers sat against a small table near a window facing Lucas.

The kicker was this automatic bed: when we put a dime in the slot on the bedpost, the bed bumped up and down for about ten minutes and then stopped.

The room was on the second floor, with a small door opening to a fragile balcony and only a walkway between rooms.

Jerry's Motel was a U-shaped affair with two stories painted a sad, pale green.

A driveway ran down the center, and a giant neon sign advertising "Jerry's Motel" pointed toward Lucas.

Across the street was a liquor store with various sundries – every sort of "delicacy" one could desire.

I was amazed at what Lacy could do with the fixings she obtained there.

Our routine went pretty fast: Lacy jaywalked Lucas and did the shopping.

Then we took the room's wooden chairs and the small wooden table onto the "balcony" and ate, overlooking Bukowski's Los Angeles.

When we went to sleep at night, Lacy curled her body, and I curled mine.

We fit together perfectly in that automatic bed, like two pieces that fit its frame, as if God had created a puzzle.

Big Hat Man

The thousand bucks that Lacy gave me had to do many things: high on that list? We had to find a place to live.

As nice as Jerry's was for what it was, we couldn't live forever in some two-bit motel on Third and Lucas.

I saw an ad in the Times for a place up on Cahuenga in Hollywood, about six miles from Jerry's, that sounded like an ideal pad. I drove up Franklin while Lacy read the ad aloud for the third time.

"Rustic Hideaway in Canyon near Hollywood for Rent.' It's in the Hollywood Hills; I'm so excited!"

"Yeah, very romantic," I said, nudging her with my right arm.

Lacy smiled as I pulled the Nissan up to the curb, abutting a large brown Craftsman-style home. A cement walkway extended about twenty feet from the curb to an oversized brown door.

We rang the doorbell, and a short man in a safari hat and brown shirt answered. His outfit looked straight out of the Warner Bros. wardrobe department—just like the guy in the Curious George books!

"Follow me, please," he said.

His eyes wrapped around Lacy like a python around its prey. Then he turned and led us up a long white cement driveway into a backyard filled with stunning tropical flowers adjoining a cottage precisely as the advertisement described.

Lacy was astounded and declared,

"So beautiful. It's just like my place on Pine Street, except far more interesting."

The man in the hat looked Lacy up and down and said,

"Yes, it is beautiful, my dear, but not nearly as beautiful as you."

Then he looked my way and said,

"You're a lucky man."

I nodded in agreement, but there was something odd about his admiration.

Certainly, Lacy was a beautiful woman; naturally, men admired her, but somehow, this adoration was disconcerting.

Over the years, Lacy has told me that I'm blind to such advances, somehow indicating that I lack the chivalry required of a gentleman— just one of my many shortcomings.

But in all fairness, in this case, thus far, the evidence was sparse.

Sure, the proprietor seemed eccentric, right out of a Hollywood B-picture.

Still, I felt he was harmless enough, and besides, what more excellent introduction to the oddities of Hollywood could there be than this character?

Big Hat Man invited us to his "office," just a room in the rear of his house.

Leaving the cottage, we followed him around the side of his house, through the front door, and down a long, dark, dank hallway into a room bursting with African Art, knick-knacks, statues, and ivory-carved objects.

Masks and books of every sort covered the four walls.

He produced a rental agreement; we signed and shook hands, fixing the deal.

Then, he led us out the front door and back to our car.

We drove the Nissan through a gate and up the cement driveway to the rear of his house. Big Hat Man met us at the cottage, his hands full of bed sheets and towels.

He handed Lacy the sheets with a smirk.

"Don't worry about washing them before you return them—I'll handle that," he said.

"That's very kind of you, Sir, but we will ensure they are cleaned and pressed before we return them. We will get our own tomorrow first thing," Lacy replied.

Giving her a sly smile, he left us alone in this small, intimate space surrounded by canyons. Its tiny but lush tropical garden framed our new existence.

What more could we ask from a place?

Sure, I was looking forward to sleeping with Lacy each night; I would envision the night throughout the day.

But other things were on my mind, like what was I getting myself into here? There was something serious about this, a feeling of permanence, bafflement, and complexity beyond simple analysis that's incomprehensible even today.

I needed to put any doubts aside, and so I did.

As soon as Big Hat Man left, Lacy closed the blinds and removed her blouse and skirt, revealing her curves. She pulled the clean white sheets tightly across the bed with military precision. I sat in silence as she slipped into the shower as if it were an act of ritual purification prescribed by some unknown and distant source.

A deep calm washed over me as I lay on the newly made bed—the same warmth I felt that first evening with Lacy, walking to her cottage on Pine Street, when everything felt right.

My mind wandered, thinking of absolutely nothing, as if in meditative bliss, without consciousness, knowledge, or any notion of time, ideas, thoughts, or fears.

After her shower, Lacy returned to me as God made her, sweet smelling of perfume and essence.

She lay down next to me on the sheets. Reaching for her perfection, I took hold of her soft, curvaceous body, and then suddenly, without notice, the front door opened and slammed hard against the opposite wall, crashing with violence that could not have been more out of place at that moment.

Startled, we immediately lifted our heads.

Who could be coming in?

There was no doubt, no question: it was Big Hat Man.

He shifted to the right as he entered, his face stern and his eyes focused forward with utter and complete determination. Seeing us there together and with naked torsos, his expression mirrored ours, startled and aghast.

But who was I to read his intentions?

Upon seeing us, he turned and left without uttering a word, as if silence would somehow annul the incident altogether.

"What the hell was he doing here?" asked Lacy, the mood and tempo completely altered.

"Can you believe that?" Lacy said in a voice

"Maybe he thought we left?" I asked.

I thought such an act was unexplainable; therefore, it must have been an accident.

"Justin, our car is parked right in front. How could he think that?" she said.

"Well, Lacy, what do you want to do?" I asked.

"Justin, we can't stay here! This guy is too weird, and he could come in anytime."

Lacy was clearly upset.

In her mind, this was a capital offense. He walked in, and we had to move out. I was thinking about how beautiful a place it was. In all likelihood, the old guy just forgot he rented the cottage or something. There were a million possible explanations; besides, there was the money to consider. We'd given him a month's rent.

How things change in a week. A few days ago, I was with Annie. We would have laughed it off and stayed. But now I was with Lacy, and things were different.

"Sure, Lacy, whatever you want. I'll speak to him in the morning and get the money back."

"I couldn't care less about the money. We're not staying here any longer! There is no way I am staying here; that guy is a creep; who knows what he might do? We have to get out of here right now. It's a shame; it is such a cute place – but not under these circumstances."

"Okay, Lacy, relax. I'll take care of it in the morning."

"No way. We need to leave now. I am not sleeping here. Can I have the keys? I want to pack everything in the car so we can go as soon as we check out."

"Sure, Lacy."

I said, hearing my own voice as if it belonged to someone else. It wasn't that I agreed or even understood—it made no sense to me—but I went along with it anyway. Like a twig caught in the flow of a river, I had no choice—or maybe I lacked the will to fight.

"Just let me get showered and dressed, and I'll put the stuff in the car."

I quickly showered and moved our gear into the car. We both returned to the office and sat on the two chairs in front of Big Hat Man's desk.

"Listen, Sir, Lacy changed her mind; we'll pass on the apartment."

Big Hat Man listened without saying a word. You could tell he wasn't happy, but he could see Lacy's stern expression. I had never seen that expression before.

"You signed an agreement; the best I can do is give back half the rent."

Big Hat Man replied with a stern and confident voice.

"Come on, we've been here less than an hour, and you already walked into our room," I argued with conviction.

He didn't answer, just stared at us with a blank face.

"By rights, I am entitled to a full month," he said, stone-faced.

"Take the money, Justin; let's get out of here," Lacy said.

I reached across the desk, took the money, and handed him the key, and we left without exchanging words.

Sure, I resented returning to Jerry's, but what other choice was there?

On driving back to the motel, Lacy was not upset. She just said,

"I'm so glad to leave. We had to get out. Our home is a private place, you understand."

I didn't then, but it was my first lesson about Lacy and how important home is to her.

She protects it like a mother hen in her nest; there's no getting around that.

We stayed at Jerry's and continued our search for a permanent place to live. Within a week, we found a redwood bungalow in the Echo Park hills, which became our home.

Dogs and cats from the neighborhood scampered onto our shaded wooden porch, and shrouds of flaming red bougainvillea covered the ancient redwoods.

At dusk, the sea breeze blew up the canyon, carrying a calm and pleasant wind that wandered through the house.

Fifteen Feet from Never

I figured everything was all right.

We had a wonderful house, and Lacy was happy.

Lacy was all over the place, arranging things and settling in, making runs to Goodwill for hidden gems.

I was making runs to the hardware store, getting this and that.

One fine day, we were painting the bedroom walls, the scent of fresh paint hanging heavily in the air.

Everything seemed perfect—until it wasn't.

Suddenly, Lacy locked herself in the bathroom. I followed her and waited in the living room opposite the bathroom.

I could hear her moaning and screaming.

Her jagged and raw voice pierced the stillness—all this, out of nowhere.

Her screams and moaning clawed at my chest, each one more disconcerting than the last.

Fear churned in my stomach as my mind raced through possibilities, each one darker than the last.

Were there drugs in there? Aspirin? Something stronger?

Was she going to do herself in?

My heart pounded as I tried to make sense of it all. This was something new—something I had never seen before.

Finally, after what seemed like hours but was maybe thirty minutes, she walked out of the bathroom and into the bedroom, slamming the door behind her. I remained on the sofa, staring at the door and hoping things would calm down.

After about thirty minutes, she walked out of the bedroom composed and wholly dressed, looking great except for the faint tracks of tears on her cheeks.

By her side was her suitcase. She stood erect and said,

"I am leaving."

I looked at her, confused, but her expression was firm and determined. It reminded me of the look she had with the big hat man—there was no room for argument. I just wanted to diffuse the matter.

"Lacy, come on, this is nuts. Put the suitcase down. Let's talk. What is wrong?"

She was stone-faced.

"I am going to call a cab; I want to go home," she said.

Where did this come from? All I could say was,

"No, if you are going, I will take you."

She walked out the front door and down to the car, opened the door, and put her suitcase in. I got on the driver's side, started the car, and took off down the hill. She was stone-faced, quiet, and looked straight ahead.

I said nothing.

We pulled down Echo Park Avenue and headed toward the freeway.

The bright afternoon sun streamed through the windshield, glaringly contrasting the shadow hanging between us.

It felt like we were driving through a tunnel with the echo of the cars hallowing in my ears, but there was no tunnel, only the stillness between us as vast and unyielding as the open road ahead.

I figured I'd drop her off, then maybe head north to see Annie. I have no idea where those thoughts came from, but they were there.

As we pulled into the airport and up to the passenger unloading space, I was perplexed, confused, and somewhat relieved.

Lacy got out of the car, and I opened my door. I grabbed her suitcase and set it at her feet.

We looked at each other, and then she gave me this strange look, her mood shifting for a second.

"You were really going to let me go," she said.

I grabbed her and hugged her, and she let me.

"Of course not. I don't want you to go." What else could I say?

She held me tight, her body trembling slightly as if relieved.

We maintained the embrace, confused by her sudden mood shift; I was trying to understand what had just happened.

Her embrace softened, but the weight of her earlier resolve lingered in the air, leaving me unsure of what to feel.

Then she got back in the car.

If she had walked just fifteen feet through the terminal door, she would have disappeared into nothingness.

Everything would have changed, and the world would have been completely altered, but she did not walk in.

She never pulled that shit again.

Simple Life

The redwood bungalow on the top of the hill was a good and simple place.

Neighbors came and went; dogs and cats wandered the property.

Lacy loved Echo Park and its combination of the inane and the bizarre, a laid-back and unpretentious amalgam of renegade priests, leftie commies, and serious rock and rollers.

Even the Gang Members living at the bottom of the Hill put up with us.

In the end, we were all ExP and lived in relative tranquility.

The hilly geography and relative separation of houses allowed people to do their own thing and not worry about disturbing other neighbors; even the dogs ran free.

Lacy was an instant hit among these folks.

She occasionally brought home refugees from the city, people she met on the street, and people without luck or resources.

She had a knack for finding losers, users, deadbeats, and cheap skates, to whom she would shower generosity without concern for reciprocity.

At Christmastime, she would find some residents of Skid Row and bring them to our small table, putting on a feast as best she could, given my meager income as a graduate student and hers as a clerk at Blue Cross.

Whoever she brought was gracious and thankful and left with a massive package of leftovers.

On our second summer, Lacy came home full of bluster:

"Justin, Justin, I met this man on the street downtown. He was playing the blues guitar. It was amazing. I invited him over. Don't plan anything for Sunday. I will pick him up from his corner, and we can have some people from the street over. It will be great. You're going to love him."

"You invited a bum from Skid Row to play at our house?"

Lacy looked at me in confusion, seemingly unaware of what I said, or perhaps she chose to ignore it. What could I do? This was going to happen.

On Sunday Morning, Lacy arrives with someone in tow who commences to sit on the front porch and starts strumming on the beat-to-shit guitar like some derelict Robert Johnson.

I headed out as fast as my Sunday Drawers would take me and screamed at the fucker,

"Dude, they call this place Echo Park for a reason, your broadcasting to Dodger Stadium; it's Sunday Morning."

Lacy started beaking me for screaming at her honored guest; at the same time, Sophie, this vile and ugly hold-over from the McCarthy Trials (they should've kept her) is already marching up the twenty concrete steps to our high porch like the Wicked Witch of the West.

I figured the shit was gonna hit the fan… instead, it turns out Comrade Sophie loves the guy and walks right into the fricken house past the screen door (ignoring me in my drawers completely) into the kitchen where Lacy is cooking Sunday grits and bacon for our honored guest and gives her a big hug.

"Lacy, Lacy, Lacy, he's marvelous; where did you find him?" she asks.

"Right on skid row, hired him for the day, isn't he talented?" asks Lacy.

"A genius!" replies the commissar.

"Please, y'all, come around. Bring June, anyone you want; it'll be a lot of fun; he needs help; he's homeless; we'll all have a great Sunday and help him out."

Well, you can pretty much figure out what happened next. The entire neighborhood spent the day at our Bungalow; it was a regular fuckin' hootenanny.

Sophie may have been Echo Park's "big macher," but Lacy was the queen, and they loved her, and she loved it.

"See, Justin, I told you this would work out. That was a lot of fun, right?"

The event wasn't bad, but she could have missed it, too, like when she invited her clerical co-workers (also read 'big fat women') from the Blue Cross Office.

It was supposed to be a surprise birthday party for me.

Still, instead of inviting my college chums (whom she felt were pretentious twits), she decided a good birthday surprise would be a collection of overweight file clerks sitting around the front room, like teenagers at a 9th-grade social.

I opened the door and saw these fat fucks sitting around the walls of the front room, and immediately asked Lacy to step out,

"Lacy, I need to talk to you. Can you step outside?"

She looked at me with this sweet face, but I was clearly upset.

"Where did you get this crew?"

"Justin, they had nowhere else to go, and when I mentioned at work it was your birthday and that I was throwing a party, they all wanted to come."

"Look at them, feeding their faces; they don't know me; those fat fucks just wanted free food, and I'm paying for it; they came empty-handed for a feast."

"Come on, it's your birthday, Justin; I just wanted to do something nice."

"I can't believe this; go on in; I will be in after a bit; I need a second to compose myself, "I said.

"Okay, "she replied and closed the door.

I have no idea what she told them, but I just went down the outside stairs, entered the side basement door, and hung out until I could hear no more people stamping on the hardwood floor above.

They left pretty quickly after I departed, as soon as they finished the feast Lacy had prepared. Lacy and I never spoke about this incident. I figured she knew she was out of line; she never did it again.

We have different views of cool, that's all I can say!

Now and then, there was an event at USC where I continued my studies, and she would reluctantly tag along if I insisted, but it was clear she did not want to be around these people, especially in groups.

It's not that she didn't like to dress up; she did but put her in a room with people in suits and gowns for more than ten minutes, and she wanted to jet.

I wanted to schmooze, find out who these people were, and make some connections, but I never really had a chance.

The odd thing is how the high and mighty were attracted to her, not me; she drew them like a magnet.

On one occasion, I actually got her to attend. The husband of a fellow student turned out to be a big-time Hollywood Producer, who offered Lacy a position on the Film Rating Board.

All she would have to do was watch films all day in a fancy screening room and go to lunches, but she would have nothing of it.

"Imagine watching films all day, what a boring job!" she said.

"It's in a beautiful screening room. You'll get wonderful lunches and invitations to all kinds of Hollywood events—you'll be a big shot," I said.

"Oh poo, who wants to do that?"

"You'd rather work at Blue Cross and file shit all day?"

"You've got a point there, but I will not watch films either. I want to open a Flower Shop, and one day I will."

"A flower shop? Why?"

"Just imagine being surrounded by flowers all day long! The beauty, the scent. People coming and going, happier as they leave. And I do love to arrange them. You asked what I wanted to do, and I told you."

About six months later, she was still working at Blue Cross, and another opportunity crossed her path: one of the members of the esteemed Chandler Family, which owned the Los Angeles Times, had a wife at USC with me. He met Lacy at a mixer at the school and offered her a tour of the Times Building.

Lacy was excited; she wanted to see the presses and how the paper was made, so she took him on the tour, but they never made it to the press room.

"You wouldn't believe it. They took me up a private elevator into the most elegant dining room I've ever seen—the China and artwork were exquisite. It was incredible. Then Mr. Chandler took me to this beautiful office. I thought it was his, but he said it was mine. My word!"

"Chandler himself, you're telling me they offered you a job, Chandler offers you a job, the Publisher of the Los Angeles Times, Norman Chandler," I asked.

I told Mr. Chandler I was only a typist at Blue Cross, but he said,

"That's fine. "Oh, Blue Cross, that's excellent training. When can you start?"

"You're going to take it, right?" I asked.

"Oh, my dear, no… what do I know about the Newspaper Business?"

"Lacy, you knew nothing about the Insurance Business, and you work at Blue Cross; it's the same thing – you will learn."

"Oh no, Justin, that place is not for me."

"What do you mean?"

"It's just not for me; I told you I will open a flower shop as soon as we have a little extra money.

Are you hungry?"

That's Lacy: style, elegance, class, but was totally immune to others with the same.

Now, if she finds a bum on the street or some fat fuck hair stylist with not a penny to spare. They come over for dinner.

That's just the way it went. Lacy was at Blue Cross, and I continued my studies at USC. Lacy was biding her time, waiting for us to pull together some resources so she could open her flower shop.

There was always something going on in Echo Park.

There were good times like Ti Chi Classes on June's Japanese Deck and Coy Garden a few doors down (built without a permit, Echo Park Style, I'm sure.) or the long nights of African Drums at Lazaro, the Brazilian Impresarios Jungle-like garden next door, complete with fire hole, plenty of Cachaça, ganja, and on special occasions the beautiful "Las Mulitas Spectacular."

And there were quiet days, too, Lacy playing the funky old upright she dug up at a Piano Store on Washington Blvd.

Me, I was involved in my studies, looking for side work; Lacy was happy; I just went with the flow; I figured everything was hunky dory till one day, Lacy sat me down.

"I can't continue like this, Justin. It can't go on this way," she declared.

"What are you talking about, Lacy? What's wrong?"

"Don't you know? Isn't it obvious?"

She started tearing up, and I had no idea what was happening.

"Justin, either we get married, or I'm leaving," she firmly declared.

Blindsided. Stammering. Then, weakly,

"Jeez, Lacy, what are you talking about?"

"I am dead serious; either you marry me, or I am leaving."

"What are you talking about, leaving? What's wrong?"

"We've been in this house exactly two years, and you didn't even know that did you?

You don't care. You never intended to marry me. You don't love me, do you? If you loved me, you'd marry me. I might as well leave. This relationship is going nowhere," she declared.

She began to sob uncontrollably.

To say that I completely understood her would be untrue, but I couldn't stand to see her crying; besides, things were going fine. I didn't want anything to change. I couldn't bear to see her go. Grabbing her around the waist, I hugged her tightly and said,

"Okay," the words leaving my mouth before I even processed it.

"Let's go to the courthouse now. We can get married today, okay?"

I didn't know if I wanted this or not—maybe I did, maybe I didn't. I knew that saying no would change everything, and I couldn't quite fathom why the thought of change unnerved me, but it did.

"Do you mean it?" she asked.

"Yes. Will you marry me?" I said, believing I had to.

A shotgun wedding—just without the shotgun.

Happily, she grabbed me around the waist and covered me with kisses.

We were downtown in front of a judge in less than an hour.

Lacy and I giggled so much as he read the oath that he asked us to leave the courtroom and reconsider. Minutes later, we returned, composed, and the satisfied judge called in a young girl to witness our vows. She smiled at Lacy and me as the judge spoke his words.

That night, a couple of fellow USC students came over with champagne, half a bottle of Ancient Age, and a neatly wrapped bouquet, which Lacy immediately put in a watered vase.

We sat on the covered porch of the old red bungalow as the evening cooled and the LA lights flickered brightly below.

Together, we laughed until the morning light found its way over the bougainvillea and onto the porch, reminding us we were not alone.

Our friends bid us a fond adieu and the good life as they trod down the broken cement steps to the street below.

Lacy held me tightly and kissed my face.

"What a wonderful wedding," she said.

"Thank you so much."

The Church

On weekdays, I drove the old Nissan five miles south to USC, returning to Echo Park in the early evenings.

One fine day, the old girl broke down near Figueroa and Olympic, so I hoofed it back to Echo Park, thinking I would get "Guy," the Algerian Echo Park Avenue "credit mechanic," to fix her the next day.

Some people might be upset by a breakdown like this, but not me; I reasoned that nobody would steal the old Nissan because it was safely parked on a public street.

Besides, it would be a pleasant walk, and I'd be back in Echo Park in a couple of hours.

As it was a lovely afternoon, rather than a brisk walk, I meandered along, looking around.

After a few blocks, I found what appeared to be an old baroque-looking church in a little alley right off Figueroa.

What an odd place to put a church, I thought.

A hefty-sized older Black man with salt and pepper hair and a round, friendly face was sitting on the church steps. He smiled as I approached.

"Is this a church?" I asked.

"It was back in the old days, but now it's just a warehouse for Piedmont Textiles. No praying around here anymore, except maybe that Saturday will come sooner."

"I hear ya," I replied.

I stared at the church for a moment and wondered if the parishioners would ever have imagined that this was what would become of their sacred place—a storehouse for textiles.

I imagined the congregation all decked out in their turn-of-the-century garb, Model Ts parked out front, or perhaps even horse carts tied to a railing in front of the church.

"I'm Justin, Justin Larkin." I reached my hand out to his.

"JD," he said, extending his hand to shake.

"Well, JD, you might not believe this, but my father-in-law owns Piedmont, and I had no idea he had a place in Los Angeles. He never once mentioned it."

JD looked at me. I'm sure he didn't believe my words, but he continued,

"I met Mr. Wilkins once, and he seemed nice enough."

"He's okay," I said.

"Hey, listen, JD, do y'all ever need help around here? I could use a bit of extra cash. I'm studying at USC. Do you have any work in the afternoons?"

JD looked at me and smirked.

"Well, seeing that you're related to the owner, I gotta give you a chance. Sure, I'll give you a try. Come on down any afternoon around two, and you can hump some cotton onto Benny's trucks. We load for the next day's deliveries starting around 2 p.m. It pays seven dollars an hour, cash."

I was a naïve sort. I figured I had pulled some strings with old JD; only later did I find out Piedmont would have paid a corpse seven bucks' cash to load the trucks.

I think sometimes they did!

Doctor Wang

On special occasions, I'd declare myself a holiday and treat myself to breakfast at the International House of Pancakes on Figueroa near the campus.

I'd spend the first ten minutes struggling in a somewhat vain attempt to scrunch the Los Angeles Times in front of a vast plate overflowing with bacon, eggs, and hash browns.

They gave you a separate plate piled high with flapjacks and another with a cup of coffee on the side.

On one such occasion, an older Chinese gentleman occupied a stool to my right. He had placed the same order but somehow arranged the plates so that his newspaper was perfectly placed between the various plates and easy to read.

I studied the geometry and precision of his design and copied it. Then, I inserted the newspaper in the amalgam at the same angle, and it worked.

He noticed me looking at him as I worked with the newspaper.

Somehow intrigued, and without further notice, in a loud voice that I am sure everyone in the joint heard, he said,

"I've seen you on campus. What do you study?"

"Philosophy. Are you a professor?" I asked.

"Yes, I am Doctor Wang; pleased me you," he said in some Chinese English.

He reached out over the empty stool between us to shake my hand.

"Justin, Justin Larkin, pleased to meet you, sir."

He firmly shook my hand and buried his head in his Chinese newspaper.

'What a pleasant man,' I thought to myself, 'confident and to the point, unlike the other creeps that habituated this berg,

After a bit, I interrupted his breakfast.

"Excuse me for staring, but I could not help but admire your arrangement of the plates and how nicely your newspaper fit within them. Please forgive me for copying."

The professor looked me over a bit more and then declared,

"Not at all; on the contrary, it demonstrates a practical and rational character. Well done. What do you study again?"

"Philosophy, I'm in the Graduate School. I transferred from Tulane."

This time, the professor gave me a gaze – one that made me a bit uncomfortable, I might add – then returned to his paper and, speaking as if to it, not me, grumbled in what was clearly disgust:

"Humf!"

After a few minutes, the professor looked up and asked,

"Tell me, why do you study this philosophy?"

I pondered a bit.

After all, as a graduate philosophy student, one is expected to ponder before one speaks, and I wanted to exhibit a thoughtful, if not profound, response, so I gave one I sensed would impress.

"I am deeply interested in investigating fundamental questions about life, knowledge, meaning, and truth."

The professor replied,

"So, you say you will investigate issues, discuss points, and argue ideas. And you do this while pain, suffering, and lamentation thrive worldwide. And all you do about any of it is think?"

His response took me aback.

Although this guy was not complimenting me or my chosen field, his words rang true to a large extent.

"I never really looked at it like that, Doctor," I replied.

"Philosophy is stupid and useless. My advice to you is to make yourself useful and study computers."

Somehow, as simple as this statement was, it made perfect sense.

I recalled my own critique of Annie and her Marxist philosophy, which I had argued was nonfunctional and could only result in personal unhappiness.

In contrast, the Existential philosophers I championed were less concerned with changing this crazy world and more focused on surviving within it.

On reflection, though, at least Annie's guys were trying to fix things—even if their solutions were absurd—whereas mine just searched for meaning in the wreckage.

I was perplexed.

Dr. Wang was right; it was the improvement of the human condition that should be our endeavor, and this is done through the determination of test solutions that can solve real problems.

What better tool was there than the computer combined with pure logic?

I have always felt one must be open to new paths. Perhaps this meeting with Dr. Wang was more than mere chance.

Could it be that it was somehow predestined? In either case, I knew I needed to pursue this.

I followed Dr. Wang to his office after the meal, and we continued our discussion into the dark of night.

His office was chaotic, with books in total disarray, stacks of papers on the floor, and empty bookcases.

He was a fascinating character: oddly, when someone knocked on the door, he would waddle through the disarray of books and papers and open a crack in the door,

"Go away, I'm busy now," he would tell whoever was knocking.

Then, he would return without an explanation, and we would continue our discussion.

Finally, he said, "Okay, you want to study computers?"

Without thinking, I replied, "Yes."

"Okay, then, we will do it."

At that point, he led me out of his office, and we walked across the street to the IHOP, where our cars had remained all day long.

That evening, I broached the subject with Lacy.

"I met a fascinating gentleman today at breakfast. It turns out he's the Chairman of the Computer Science Department at USC, and we had an intriguing discussion about solving human problems using computers.

It got me thinking… that philosophy minimally impacts the human condition, and I want to do more.

Lacy, I am convinced that this is the way to go. Dr. Wang is willing to take me on as a student. He feels the logic I learned in philosophy will be useful, and, at most, I will need two extra years of study.

What do you think?"

Lacy thought a bit and replied,

"That sounds like a wonderful thing. If you feel that you can do more for others, as you say, this is wonderful. I don't know anything about computers, but you know I'll always support you in what you do. So if you believe in it, go for it."

You'd think changing majors at a prestigious university would be difficult, but it was straightforward.

Wang and I wrote some crap about computers and logic being the same fuckin' thing, and both departments signed off on it.

I think the Philosophy department was glad to see me go; they were pompous dicks anyway, and leaving that department was something I never regretted.

Even Doctor Wang thought it was funny how facile it was.

"Stupid people," he said,

"Stupid People, it was good that you come here, much more useful."

As simple as this change of a graduate major was, my relationship with Doctor Wang was not what I expected.

I figured we were buddies and would work one-on-one; perhaps I could be his assistant and earn extra money, but that would not be the case.

I rarely saw him, and when I did, we barely spoke.

He never helped me solve a programming issue or gave me any advice about anything. When I would stop by his office, he'd give me the same brush-off that he gave others when they came to his door; through the crack, he'd say,

"Don't mess around, Justin; why are you here? Go do work!"

I figured it was sage advice and followed it. I came to believe that our first meeting was our interview, that he sized me up and threw me in the water.

When it was time for my dissertation, he was my Chairman. His only advice was,

"Justin, I am going on vacation, so do you work carefully and make no mistakes. If you see the smallest error, you must correct it, as dozens are hidden, and you cannot see them. I will read your work once, and if it is not perfect, you cannot see me for six months."

During my time at USC, Lacy opened a little flower shop on Glendale Blvd. in Echo Park.

The shop was like a tropical oasis in the city. Walking in there was like stepping into another world, a rainforest with Lacy in the center – a flower among the flowers.

It was an amazing and beautiful place; many more should have seen it, but that was not to be.

Lacy would sit in a perpetually dying tropical jungle that needed to be entirely replaced every three or four days, a sad and costly endeavor.

The word spread, as she demonstrated a true knack for creating tropical arrangements with an elegant simplicity. Her arrangements were in great demand in the finer homes in nearby Los Feliz and Laughlin Park.

Lacy and her designs fit well with the ladies of these estates, and why not?

Both were beautiful and refined.

However, this feeling was not mutual, as Lacy detested their arrogance. Declaring that they reminded her of everything and for every reason, she left Charleston.

Instead, she preferred to spend her time at the household, commiserating with the kitchen help or perhaps the gardener or handyman. If they were single or without family, she would invite them to Christmas dinner.

By Lacy's admission, these years were her happiest.

At the time, I had no idea, as she worked so hard and long, worrying and struggling over placing a twig in a vase..

At last, in a final fling, every stem and twig found its correct, special place where it was born to sit.

Standing back, Lacy would look at her creation with complete satisfaction, as if the inspiration came from above and somehow that twig brought order to the universe.

"Oh, that's so beautiful. Look at that beauty," she would say.

I laughed to myself, agreeing that it was beautiful, undoubtedly, a work of art, but also that it was merely temporal.

Each morning at 4 AM, Lacy would go to the Flower Mart, with a point, a nod, and a few words to her comrades of the dawn, she would then, in an instant, wrap the flowers in yesterday's Los Angeles Times to be carted away for display and death, their funeral, a departure full of glory and splendor.

This was a part of her story, her happy life, her newfound life, but what about the past?

It had not disappeared.

The ghosts remained: her past in Charleston and her mother and father. That life remained strained.

Mr. and Mrs. Wilkins rarely phoned Lacy and never visited, and as for me, her husband.

I don't even think Mr. Wilkins knew that I was working at his fuckin' warehouse.

The Phone Call

Time passed quickly, and to be honest, things were going pretty well at the university.

I enjoy studying and learning, and even then, I was sure learning was much more fun than work.

Of course, I know some people don't feel that way; I just do.

I was making good progress, and of course, Wang wouldn't talk to me. I often stopped by his office when I was near his building and even looked for him at IHOP, but we never crossed paths.

I knocked at his door sometimes.

No answer. But I knew damn well he was in there.

It was like he could recognize my knock but refused to open the door.

Look, he wasn't giving me trouble, and the dissertation was coming along fine. I just wanted to tell him about an article I submitted for a computer science review. It had been accepted, and I thought he'd be impressed.

His ignoring me made me slightly paranoid that I was on his bad side, but I let it pass.

I had to.

Maybe he already knew about the article; he reads a lot, or perhaps somebody told him. The academic world isn't as big as you think. The professors have their conferences, they mingle, they keep up with each other.

I say this because a few days later, I got a call—from Professor Kapel at, of all places, Ole Miss.

He introduced himself and said,

"Justin, I read your paper, and I was impressed. That was fine work. Tell me a little about yourself—your hopes, your dreams."

That was all I needed. I rambled on for about twenty minutes. I can't even recall a word of what I said. Now and then, he'd engage me, and finally, he got to the point.

"We have an opening for an adjunct professor in the fall semester, and we'd like to offer it to you."

To say I was surprised—well, yeah, I was surprised. But mostly, all I could think was: This is what I wanted. This is what I worked for.

I could already see it—swimming in the faculty pool, a real professor, tweed jackets in the fall. Sure, it wasn't philosophy, and maybe it didn't make complete sense, but what does?

"I haven't finished my dissertation, Dr. Kapel," I said. "I guess they call it ABD—all but dissertation."

But I knew he already knew that.

Kapel didn't seem concerned.

"Justin, it pays $20,000 a year, but there are consulting opportunities, and it's much cheaper here than in Los Angeles. You'll be fine."

Truth is, I'd have done it for half that. I know it wasn't a lot, but it wasn't about the money but the opportunity. This was my dream, to be a college professor, and here it was happening in real time.

I would make it work for Lacy; we would be happy and content. We could make a life for ourselves, have kids, be happy.

But I knew I had to get past Lacy; it would not be simple, and I knew that in my gut.

She loved L.A., and Ole Miss was in the South; I had more than a hunch this would be a hard sell with her.

"Dr. Kapel, thank you very much. This sounds great. Can I tell my wife and call you back tomorrow?"

"Sure, Justin, that's not a problem. Of course, tell your wife; it's a good move to keep them current. I am sure she will be delighted."

"We look forward to having you here. Talk to you tomorrow, and congratulations. "

I hung up, stunned. This was surreal in a good way.

I imagined the reaction at Tulane. The turds who kicked me out would hear about it, and I knew exactly what they'd say.

I imagined myself at a football game and the Rebels kicking the Green Wave's ass, like they usually did.

I'd run into Dr. Bougiere with his PhD in Physical Education. Excuse me, Kinesiology.

What a fucking joke!

"Justin, Justin Larkin, is that you? It's been a long time," he'd say.

"Yeah, some years, Bob. I finished my doctorate at USC in Computer Science. I'm teaching at Ole Miss now."

Bob would look at Lacy, his expression caught between recognition and confusion, the dummy trying to process it.

"Hello, Dr. Bougiere, how have you been?" she'd say, smooth and composed.

"Lacy Wilkins of the Charleston Wilkins—you stayed with Professor Rankin and worked in the library. Is that you?"

She smiled, effortlessly. "It's *Larkin* now. Justin and I are married."

Bougiere would be slammed, not knowing what to say.

"Well, you look wonderful. How have you been?"

"Just fine, thank you." Lacy would say with a curtsy.

Then I'd slap him on the shoulder, just like the dummy did me when I left his office.

"Well, Bob, we gotta go—our Rebels have a thirteen-year winning streak to keep alive."

That would wipe the shit-eating grin off his face. The same grin he had when he got me kicked out.

How this SOB ended up as a dean is a mystery to me.

This was more than perfect.

So maybe this wasn't Harvard, but it was a start—Ole Miss, the history, this would be more than cool.

But something nagged at me.

Lacy.

I wasn't sure how she'd take it. And she had to come.

I wasn't stupid. Her love of L.A. and, more than that, her history in the South, I already knew what was coming.

I wasn't looking forward to this conversation.

When she gets home from the flower shop, she is always tired; naturally, she is up at 4 AM and usually doesn't eat much, if anything, until she gets home.

As she entered, I greeted her with,

"Lacy, I've got some fantastic news. I got a call today. Guess what?"

She walked past me into the kitchen, took off her jacket, and tossed it through the open door onto the sofa.

"Justin, I have to get dinner ready. I'm starving."

She pulled pots from the cupboards, filled one with water, and put it on the stove.

"Just a minute, just give me a minute. Let me get this going so we can make some rice."

I followed her like a puppy.

"Lacy, stop. We need to talk. I got a job offer today."

She sighed, seeming slightly perturbed, and sat at the little kitchen table.

"Okay, Justin. What kind of job?"

I sat across from her.

"Lacy, I got a university job offer."

She looked at me with delight and confusion for a second. Then, something shifted. I could feel it.

"Justin, you haven't even finished your dissertation. How can you get a job? Are you dropping out?"

"Lacy, it's normal. They'll let me finish it while I teach."

She smiled, genuinely proud of me, but I could still see that concern; it was a mixture of something I couldn't explain.

"That's great, Justin. I knew you could do it," she said, but there was something uncertain in her voice. She smiled, but beneath it, I could sense hesitation, part pride, part unease.

She gave me a big hug, then pulled back and stood close.

"So, where is it? I hope we don't have to move."

I exhaled. "Lacy, it's at Ole Miss."

Her face changed instantly. The warmth was gone.

She looked amused, but not in a good way.

"Justin, you know I'm not going back to the South. What do they pay anyway?"

Lacy said, as if looking for another reason to refuse.

"20K, but there will be consulting work, and it's cheaper there. We will be fine," I replied confidently.

"Justin, I make more than 25K at the Flower Shop, and business is growing constantly.

Besides, I love it, and like I said, I am not moving back to the South."

I walked out of the kitchen. I didn't bring it up again during dinner but had a plan. If I could match the 25K, I had a chance.

The next day, I called Kapel.

"Dr. Kapel, see, the thing is... I'm making about $24K here. If you could go to $25K, I could get my wife to go."

The line went silent for a few seconds.

Then, his tone changed. Flat. Cold.

"Justin, I didn't know you were in it for the big bucks."

And then, just like that, he hung up.

<h1 style="text-align:center;font-family:cursive;">La Luz de Jesus</h1>

The Piedmont warehouse on Figueroa was a wooden structure about half the size of a football field.

Large, cantilevered beams and skylights covered the wood-framed edifice. Elaborate stained-glass windows faced Figueroa, shedding an eerie blue light into the open space.

It was in great disrepair: The floorboards creaked from the excessive weight of the heavy fabric bolts, not to mention the balcony, which was so laden with bolts of every color and design that only through the grace of God did it not tumble to the floor.

It was bad enough going up there in the first place, but worse was that sometimes we had to grab a bolt right up near the top of the balcony, up near the stained-glass image of Jesus.

Just being up there gave me the creeps.

Near the warehouse's entrance was a little office with a tattered and filthy carpet. Wood-paneled walls sported pin-up calendars dating back decades, which were of no use, date or year-wise.

Remnants of scotch tape from long ago removed notes left a scum on what must have once been the pastor's pristine office. A beat-up desk and credenza were littered with old phone books, bills of lading, and algae-covered coffee cups.

On JD's desk sat a black rotary phone, a large computer monitor, and a fax machine covered with thick black grime.

This was Piedmont Textiles' operational center in Los Angeles, the locus of all distribution of their fabrics to the Southern California market and beyond.

Orders flew off the fax machine with details of size, quantity, and lot number to be loaded onto the back of one of Bennie Goldman's trucks parked in front of the church.

Each bolt had to be carried down the ten front steps that fronted the church, the same ones that parishioners used in days bygone.

As the orders came in, JD would announce them in his particular way:

"Two bolts 4635 unprinted, two bolts 4635 unprinted, outside."

Bennie Goldman would be out there yelling and screaming, cigar hanging from his mouth,

"Put 'em in Sonny (the name of a truck; all his trucks had names).

Stack 'em high, boys. Lots more coming!"

When the truck was completely loaded, he walked into JD's office and drank stale coffee from a big old industrial coffee maker until more orders came in and the next truck was loaded.

By the time I got there, the orders would be coming in fast, and by five in the evening, we'd have at least three or four trucks filled to the brim.

Finished, the lumpers would head into JD's office one by one and face Bennie, sitting on an old oak swivel chair, the wet cigar still hanging from his lips, eyes glued to the Daily Racing Form.

The men handed Bennie sweat-soaked, crumbling slips with folded bills inside.

He'd unwrap them, glance at the paper, look up at the guy, then fold it back and slip it into his coat pocket.

I have no idea how this worked, but there was never any trouble, so I guess they trusted one another.

It was a beautiful thing.

The office belonged to JD, the head warehouseman. Bennie used it as his own and declared,

"I wouldn't waste no goddamn money on an office," and he meant it.

JD was an older fellow, around fifty; Bennie was probably at least eighty. Brooklyn-born Bennie died a few years ago, and his last words were,

"I'm Bennie Goldman, and I'm from Sheep's Head Bay."

I went to Bennie's funeral, where the rabbi and others gave speeches about Bennie, saying all sorts of fancy things. I figured they were talking about a different guy.

JD was originally from Texas.

He had more wives than you could shake a stick at, and sometimes his "wives" would come in early Friday and wait hours for JD to get his paycheck—getting their cut, I reckon.

JD died, too, a few years back; he was still relatively young – I think his wives might have gotten to him. I went to his funeral. It was in a storefront church in Watts. Five people attended, including the reverend and me.

How those women could show up every Friday for a paycheck and not make his funeral was a shame.

A loudspeaker suddenly blasted one day in the warehouse, echoing throughout the church.

"Larkin, get your ass to the office now!"

I dropped the end of the bolt that Blunt and I were carrying down the creaking balcony to one of Bennie's trucks waiting out front.

"What the fuck are you doing?" Blunt screamed as I dropped the bolt on the floor. The whole balcony shook with a loud thump.

"Fuck, Larry, didn't you hear? I have to go to the fuckin' office."

"Next time you do that, tell me. You almost cut my nuts off when you dropped this fuckin' thing," Larry said obviously pissed.

"Okay, okay, sorry, man," I said.

I headed down to the end of the balcony and descended the creaking staircase – at risk of life and limb, even without the bolt.

Larry's eyes were on me. He sat beside the bolt, leaning against the soft fabric.

The sun's rays shone through the stained-glass figure of Jesus and lit him up in a yellowish hue, blessing him.

I'm sure.

JD was gone, and Bennie was nowhere to be found, but the aroma of his fifty-cent El Producto remained.

Mashed Styrofoam cups half-filled with bad coffee covered the beat-up walnut morass JD called "my desk."

I guess that when Harry appeared, they found places to hide; neither liked to be around when the brass was near.

The brass was there all right: a tall, well-dressed Chinese gentleman stood alone and as far away from anything that could pass germs as possible.

"Hello Justin, I'm Harry Wa, Director of West Coast Operations for Piedmont Textiles."

Harry spoke in a stout and confident British accent, demonstrating wealth, education, and stature.

"Yes? I'm Justin Justin Larkin. Pleased to meet you," I declared while holding my hand out for him to shake.

In kind, Harry reached over and grabbed my hand, firmly shaking it long and hard, and then continued,

"As director of Piedmont on the West Coast, we were looking for a computer engineer to assist in automating our company. I reached out to my Uncle, a professor at U.S.C., for a candidate, and he highly recommended you.

Last night, I spoke to your father-in-law, Mr. Watson Wilkins, from Charleston, South Carolina.

When I mentioned your name, he indicated that you were his son-in-law. He informed me that you were working in our Los Angeles warehouse. Frankly, I couldn't believe it. I was shocked."

"Shocked?" I asked.

"Yes, Justin, may I refer to you by your given name?

"Sure, yes, certainly. Justin, thank you," I said.

"Yes, shocked, an educated man, especially in computers, and related to the founder, working in the warehouse – it doesn't make sense.

Who'd you kill?"

"Nobody," I replied.

"Justin, would you be available for a dinner meeting this evening? I have something I would like to discuss with you."

"Sure, but I'm really not dressed for dinner, Mr. Wa. My Levi's are covered with holy dust from the balcony; I'm sad to report," I said.

"Quite a witty retort, this being a sanctuary in its former life.

But do not worry; the restaurateur knows me well. It will be just fine.

Furthermore, it's a fine Cantonese Restaurant in San Moreno, one of my favorites, and there, a man of such knowledge as yours is accorded great respect regardless of your attire. It would be my pleasure, I insist," Harry replied.

"That's great, but I'll need to inform my wife and J.D.; I have two more hours of work here in the warehouse," I said.

"I took the liberty of letting J.D. know you'll be working with me this evening. Of course, you'll be compensated. As for calling Mrs. Larkin, you can do that from my car phone," Harry said.

"In that case, I'm ready whenever you want," I replied.

"We'll go now. After you, Dr. Larkin," said Harry, and we exited the church.

"It's not Doctor yet," I replied.

"Don't worry, Uncle has great confidence in you; he speaks very highly; you will be Doctor Larkin, but don't tell him I said this," he declared.

"I won't, but thanks for the vote of confidence; I still have considerable work."

Parked next to Bennie's truck was a bright red Maserati, and off to the side stood JD and Old Bennie, cigar seemingly glued to his lips, both of their mouths wide open as this lumper entered the Maserati with the West Coast Director of Piedmont Textiles.

"Wow, Harry, nice ride!" I said as I sat in open admiration of such opulence.

"It's a company car. We should get you one, too. Let's figure out a way," he said.

The Deal

Harry tore out of the parking lot like a bat out of hell and whipped onto the 9th Street on-ramp, cutting a sharp right like he was cornering at Le Mans.

As he drove, he said,

"Do you like Chinese food? The place I spoke of in San Moreno will knock your socks off. It has excellent service and the best Cantonese cuisine this side of Hong Kong."

"Fantastic, but can I call Lacy now, so she won't worry?"

Harry handed me the phone. I dialed, and Lacy answered.

"Hey Lacy, I'm in the car with Harry Wa, the West Coast Director of Piedmont. He's a great guy."

I nodded Harry's way, and he smiled.

Then I continued, "He's taking me to dinner. I'll be home a bit late," I said.

I noted some hesitation in her voice as she replied,

"When will you be home?"

"Probably a couple of hours," I said, looking at Harry for confirmation.

"I don't feel good about this. Be careful," Lacy advised.

"No worries. I'll be home soon. Love you," I replied and hung up the phone.

It was clear that Lacy was not happy about this meeting. I was confused again, but this could be an excellent opportunity I would not bypass.

Her mood put a damper on things, but I tried to put it out of my mind.

"Ya know, I'll never be able to figure out women. They have some odd moods," I confided to Harry.

"I am sure she is a fine woman. She comes from a very distinguished family and has a brilliant husband. Like my father always said,

'In quality, there is complexity.' So if Lacy is complex, which I take she is, she is of more value, but my father also advised that one should beware of spending too much time in a vain attempt to fathom a woman's mind, as those waters run far too deep."

"You have a wise father, Mr. Wa. I'll remember those words. Thanks."

Harry made me feel a bit better, but I know Lacy, and though her words were short, she was not happy I was going to dinner with an executive of her dad's company.

She did not like it at all. I anticipated a shit storm when I got home, and I was right.

The restaurant was a small upscale place, full of well-tailored Chinese business types and beautiful, immaculately attired Chinese women.

Brushing the warehouse dust off my jeans as best I could, I took a seat, and without hesitation, Harry started talking to me and a waiter who stood patiently at the tableside.

Now and then, Harry would bark Chinese to the waiter, who would dutifully scribble down a character or two until dismissed by Harry, who then focused on me.

"Listen, Piedmont is having huge financial problems. My firm, HTS Holdings in Hong Kong, took a 45% stake in Piedmont to help it through its financial difficulties. One condition was that an executive from HTS take over the West Coast office, and I was that person.

In any event, we needed some computer work, so I figured I'd call USC and get a student at a better rate. I called Dr. Wang – he's my uncle, not my real uncle, but a close friend of the family back home, so we call him Uncle.

We needed someone to assist us in automating our systems, and Uncle mentioned your name.

He said that you were about to finish and that you were also his most inventive student. So, I called Mr. Wilkins in Charleston and told him we could either automate in LA and lay off staff or move production to Asia and close the Charleston Plant.

He grudgingly agreed to the LA cuts and automation. I mentioned that we had a USC wiz to do the work, but he was aghast when I told him your name.

He asked how a philosophy student could run computers. He didn't even know what you were studying!

Justin, I was shocked that he would have his son-in-law work in the warehouse, especially an educated and talented son-in-law.

We would never do that in China except as a punishment.

Let me be honest with you. The numbers are bad, but Piedmont is a great brand. We can turn this company around by moving production from Georgia to Asia."

Food started arriving, and we both dug in. Between mouthfuls, Harry continued.

"Justin, I need you to automate the file room. That's the first task. We have over twenty people there, and the system is antiquated. Someone must pull a paper file whenever they need even the simplest piece of paper. The whole process needs to be automated. Any ideas?"

"Gimme a minute. Some of my best ideas come when I eat," I said.

The food was excellent, and it did get me thinking.

As I was concentrating on some delicious brown gravy and tofu concoction, it came to me, so I blurted out:

"We can implement an automated document management system and back file scan. While there are upfront costs, the labor savings over time are incredible."

"Brilliant, absolutely brilliant. Uncle was right; you're a genius," he remarked.

Upon reflection, I must admit that the solution was not brilliant, and Harry probably knew it too.

Any competent engineer would have made the same remark, but arguing with such a compliment is hard.

"Justin, call me when you are done at USC tomorrow. I'll pick you up in the Maserati; you can drive it if you want."

The Word

I figured Lacy would be happy about me getting a "real job" at Piedmont, but what do I know? She was not supportive at all.

"I don't like it. I don't feel good about this. I don't," Lacy said.

I replied, "What could go wrong?

It's a great opportunity for us. Not only will we have more money, but what excites me even more than money is that I'll finally have a chance to apply what I've learned about computers to a real-world situation and a real business. I'd be making myself useful to your dad.

He'll see and appreciate what I've done for him, you, and us."

"I don't know, Justin, I just don't know. I have a bad feeling in my gut about this. It's not good. Please don't do it. Working with the family doesn't feel right to me. I would really like to keep things separate."

"Come on. What does your gut have to do with this? In any event, I hear you; I will be careful. If nothing else, we'll have more money. Don't worry," I said.

"We don't need any more money; we're doing just fine," she insisted.

The way I saw it, money was money, and we could use it; unlike Lacy, when an opportunity comes my way, I take it, so I took the job and made a mental note of her reservations.

On occasion, Lacy would speak to her father on the telephone, and after a bit, she would hand me the phone. I guess she wanted me to have some positive bond with him. It would have made her life easier if I had his respect.

However, the way I looked at it, he had me pegged as someone odd or perhaps offensive. He called me "college boy," not to my face, but he said it to Lacy. It was not meant as a compliment, that's for damn sure.

I suspect he saw me as a poor fuck with a bunch of talk that produced nothing.

He seemed to share Lacy's disdain for white-collar guys like Harry; he seemed to respect guys like "JD" and that worker he invited for dinner back in Charleston.

Or at least that is the impression I got.

He seemed to respect success and not talk; he knew his daughter was living a life of relative poverty, and I suppose he didn't think much of me.

I figured the only reason he put up with his doctor sons-in-law was that they had money, status, and position, and as far as he was concerned, I had none of those things.

In his world, those things count.

Lacy loved her dad and respected that he got his hands dirty in the Mill.

Sometimes, I felt she felt the same way as her dad.

What I did have was his daughter, and I guess that pissed him off.

Knowing that, I had to be careful about what I said about him.

Lacy loved her Dad and had a great deal of respect for him.

She told me repeatedly,

"We lived a good life, servants, and a beautiful home in Charleston. People were always stopping by; the house was always full of people. We'd also have big, extraordinary events at Christmastime, Easter, and the Fourth of July. We were never alone, and Daddy was always happy and fun. He was so funny. The only real sadness I recall was Velma and her illness. I guess God put Velma there to teach me that the world wasn't always rosy, and he taught me that he sure did.

Though he never complained or cried, things weren't easy for Daddy.

His daddy, our Grandpa Hiram, left him with a real mess when Daddy returned from fighting in Europe.

Seems the business was on the brink of bankruptcy due to the troubles of the Depression.

It wasn't just Piedmont that was in trouble. All the mills were in the same situation, yet when we entered the war, government orders flooded all the mills except ours.

We never received even one government contract during the entire war.

Grandpa blamed Roosevelt for making things worse during the Depression by dickering with the economy; naturally, he made his feelings known to whomever he met all over the Tidewater.

When dishing out contracts, the administration remembered him as a rabble-rouser, and Piedmont was left out of the mix.

That made Grandpa even angrier, and he talked even more.

Daddy said if he'd just shut up, they'd have given us business, but he was a man of his convictions, and it cost us plenty.

We almost lost Piedmont.

By the time Daddy returned, conditions had gotten so bad that Grandpa Hiram was fixing to sell the mill. Daddy was dead against it, opening a massive rift between them.

That's when Grandpa moved out of the house to a little place near Hilton Head, and I hardly ever saw him. I knew there was bad blood and felt terrible for both of them.

Daddy could have walked away from all the people we owed money to, but he didn't.

Grandpa thought it stupid to pay everyone off and blamed the government for his downfall. Daddy paid back every red cent and got the mills going again all on his own, with Grandpa up in Hilton Head.

Daddy respects hard work; he's not afraid to get his hands dirty in the mills or elsewhere. All the workers, black or white, love him.

Grandpa Hiram, in many ways, wasn't fit for the mills. He was a scholar in his own right, and he was very well-read.

He could have been a senator or congressman, anything like that. He was a Yale Man, just brilliant. 'More interested in his books than the mill' is what Daddy always said.

Most of the books in the library are his. Whenever he returned home, he would spend most of his time there.

It seemed like he was visiting long-lost friends.

Auntie Shirley said Daddy was a real hellraiser as a kid and played hooky most of the time. He spent days running around Charleston Bay with whomever he found on the streets.

She said he could handle himself well and was good with his fists.

Naturally, this drove Grandpa crazy, but what could he do?

Grandpa always wanted Daddy to attend university, but that was not the case.

He never liked books, schools, or being in one place too long; he was a regular Huckleberry Finn. Somehow, Grandpa got him enrolled in Duke, but he was back home within a month. Then Grandpa sent him off to Tulane. He attended a few classes there, then enlisted in the Army, and ended up in the 82nd Airborne. He was a paratrooper and jumped all over Europe. He even fought with the Golden Gloves and was a champ.

He keeps the newspaper clippings; he's proud of that title, like the college degree he never got.

Daddy is a rough, wily fellow. He had to be.

He didn't have it easy, what with the Depression and the war and the condition of the mills on his return. It took a rough man to pull it together and turn things around, and he was up to the task, but to me and my sisters, all he showed was kindness and love."

I knew Wilkins and I were coming from different places. I truly wanted his respect, but I never got very far. When he'd call, Lacy would say,

"Justin, say hello to Daddy."

I'd grab the phone and say,

"Mr. Wilkins, how are you? And Ms. Wilkins, how is she?"

"Fine, Justin, we're doing fine. And you, Son, how are you?"

That would be all I needed to start; it doesn't take much to get me yakking. I'd go on about the latest book I read, how I was progressing in college, who knows what I'd say, but I'd say it all, and it would all be about me, and if I had to exaggerate a bit to make it sound better, I would.

Now and then, I'd hear a "yes," so I'd keep going, but the truth is he probably wasn't listening or didn't care, and finally, he'd just say,

"Can I speak with Lacy?"

Dejected, I'd hand over the phone.

This is how it always was, but after my move into the office from the warehouse, I noticed an even harsher, more sardonic edge to his voice.

I sensed that he genuinely resented my working for Piedmont.

When I worked in the warehouse for cash, he was okay with it; at least, I was doing something worthwhile. But I guess office work, punching things into a computer, did not seem worth the pay I was getting.

I asked Lacy if her father was mad at me, and she responded:

"I told you, please quit as soon as you can. It's not good for you to work there."

"Lacy, you were right. I gotta admit it; that old gut of yours was right again. But the checks are great.

When I graduate, I'll quit for sure. In the meantime, I'll be careful; I'll leave if it gets too bad. I'm with you on this 100%," I replied.

Lacy seemed relieved and said,

"That makes me feel much better. Quit as soon as you can."

The next day, I approached Harry with my feelings that Wilkins wanted me gone, but he ignored them.

"Wilkins has no idea what you're doing. If it were up to him, we wouldn't even have computers. Don't sweat it; you're doing great. Keep up the good work. We see eye to eye. You and I can take this company far!"

About six months later, with my dissertation done and approved by Wang, I was no longer under pressure.

Lacy was making enough, so in the worst case, we could get along if I quit.

In addition, the document management project was complete; that was for sure.

Harry fired twenty-five office staff, saving hundreds of thousands a year and achieving a return on investment on the automation costs in less than three months.

He was elated, but I was persona non grata among the employees. They called me "The Terminator," among other things.

"Harry, please get me back to the warehouse. The office folks hate me, and my father-in-law thinks I'm a deadbeat and that I'm ripping off the company with the salary you're paying me; it might be better for all concerned if I went back with JD.

Lacy is beaking me like crazy; I guess her Daddy is putting some pressure on her. I'm unsure, but she keeps telling me it's not good to work at the office. And Wilkins was far less upset when I was working in the warehouse; it's OK if you send me there, and now that the migration is completed, there's less need for me up here.

Harry leaned in, his voice low but firm.

"Are you out of your mind?

We need you here. Justin, you just saved us a fortune—you're too valuable to be wasted in a warehouse.

Leave Wilkins to me; I'll handle him. Be patient.

Hong Kong is on my side, and they have a lot riding on this, just like you do. And let's be honest, a man like you should be thinking bigger. Lacy's a woman of style—she deserves more, and so do you. Wilkins will come around eventually, trust me, whether he sees it yet or not."

Harry wouldn't let up: instead of reducing my hours and involvement, he increased both, dragging me to every meeting, lunch, and seminar that involved company management or operation.

One day, he pulled me aside and said,

"Listen, Justin, your work on the migration project was brilliant. Sure, Wilkins hasn't gotten it yet. All he sees is revenue; he doesn't seem to understand that a penny saved is a penny earned. Frankly, it's idiotic to me.

We'll be up tens of thousands of dollars in six months, but he wanted to know about the twenty-five people I fired instead of lauding us. He was even talking about hiring them back!

Can you believe that?

We need to work together. I am very frustrated. I'm going to move you to sales.

That's all he understands."

As it turned out, selling involved talking to people, something I like to do, and I immediately succeeded. The odd thing was that I knew very little about textiles; besides that, they were heavy, so I talked to the clients about anything: travel, history, art, politics, personal affairs, baseball scores, anything that came to mind.

Oddly enough, this method worked.

I booked so many orders that the Charleston plant was doing triple shifts.

It was amazing, and all I had to do was talk.

Suddenly, Wilkins was calling me day after day for status reports.

He was delighted, as his beloved Charleston Plant cronies were working their asses off, and the Chinese had to completely halt their idea of moving the operation to Asia.

The company was in the black because of little old me.

I figured Harry would be happy. He wanted me in the old man's good graces, and now I was, but he instead seemed more frantic than elated.

He asked me out to dinner, which usually meant he had something to tell me.

There were no wasted efforts with this guy. Everything had a purpose; that was becoming clear.

"Justin, what can I say? What you've done in sales is impressive. Now, imagine what we could do if we ran this place.

Wilkins is exultant and slightly confused, but the numbers don't lie. They're far beyond what I expected.

We need to take advantage of this opportunity.

Ask Wilkins for ten percent of the company; you deserve it.

He's your father-in-law, the father of his daughter, and you have proven your worth, even in his eyes.

Go for it."

"Yes, but an interest in the company? Why would he do that?" I asked.

"Listen, in his mind, sales drive a business. As good as your document management savings were for the company, they didn't make one loom run.

What you are doing now is powerful stuff.

Trust me: he'll give you the ten percent. And Justin, not only do I need you here, but think of the good we could do if we grow this company.

We'll employ many people: technical, production, clerical, warehouse guys like J.D., vendors like Bennie, and lots and lots of Bennies.

Of course, you, your family, and the Wilkins will make a lot of money, but you'll also be helping many other people. You'll feel good, and Wilkins will be proud."

Harry had a great point. I'd never really thought about it that way.

By selling, I created opportunities for people, doing real good and helping people, rather than just talking about it.

This was indeed a way to "make myself useful."

It was clear now Dr. Wang was only half right. The first part of the statement – "make yourself useful" – was brilliant.

The simplicity and elegance of that statement felled me and caught me off guard, leading me down the path of studying computers. But now it's clear that one does not become useful by studying computers alone but by selling; selling creates opportunities, and a computer capitalizes on them—and sometimes destroys them.

My first act with computers destroyed twenty-five lives, yet in selling, I brought happiness and wealth and started a chain of events, all with positive results.

Sales would undoubtedly make me useful; the facts were in front of my face. Scores of people and their families all work, eat, and live because of my sales. I discovered a new and valuable path, and I would take it."

Harry continued,

"Call him in the morning. We can make this company grow. We can make good things happen. He will understand now, I am sure."

The following day, I called Wilkins from the house without thinking.

"Hello, Mr. Wilkins. It's Justin."

"Oh, yes, Justin. Isn't it a bit early for you to be at work?"

"Yes, Mr. Wilkins, but I wanted to speak with you about Piedmont."

"Sure, Justin, but you're doing an excellent job. Let me tell you something, honestly.

Initially, I was convinced you would fail in sales because you lacked knowledge about textiles. I told Harry this clearly, and we had quite a disagreement.

However, I realized I was mistaken and that numbers don't lie.

What you're doing is fantastic, and you will be rewarded.

Keep up the great work!"

"Mr. Wilkins," I replied,

"In a roundabout manner, it's about the sales that I am calling you. Let me preface this by saying I am not interested in more money. That is to say, I am satisfied with what I am getting, and I indicated to Harry that same mindset.

However, he feels that, given my success, perhaps we would all benefit from my being incentivized with a ten percent stake in the company.

Let me be clear: I am not asking for this, but Harry seems to think you would support the idea, and he feels that I can contribute."

There was a bit of silence on the line.

Then Mr. Wilkins replied,

"That might work out; it might be of benefit. So let me be clear about what Harry is suggesting: he is saying that the HTS Group is willing to give you ten percent of their interest in Piedmont as part of a package to incentivize your continued employment at Piedmont?"

"Well, not exactly," I replied.

"Well, what do you mean exactly, then?" Wilkins snapped back.

"Mr. Wilkins, that's why I'm calling you. They want you to give me ten percent of your interest."

"I see," said Wilkins, and he hung up the phone.

Wilkins

Unbeknownst to me then, if Wilkins had given me ten percent interest, HTS would have a majority in Piedmont; I guess they figured I would be more compliant than Wilkins.

I guess that when Wilkins hung up, he immediately called Harry; nothing else could explain Harry's sudden change, which I would soon find out. I am sure he told them in no uncertain terms that he was not releasing any of his stock to me.

I made my way into the office, sat behind my desk, kicked my feet up, and called a client.

Soon enough, I was completely engaged in discussing politics or art when Harry barged in, flinging my office door wide open.

He was raging mad, overcome with anger.

"Get off the goddamn phone! You're wasting time!" he screamed.

The client could hear it, and likely the entire office; he even left the door wide open.

I really hate being "loud-capped" and embarrassed in public. Embarrassing me in public pushes all my buttons. I wouldn't even take this from Lacy.

Instinct took over. Taking the receiver by one end, I chucked it at Harry, barely missing his head. Reaching the end of the twisted line, it boomeranged back and missed me.

"Listen, Asshole," I said, "I could give a fuck if you fire me; this place is a fuckin' madhouse! Go fuck yourself."

At this point, I was fed up with Piedmont and couldn't comprehend the politics.

Besides, I'd promised Lacy I would leave if things got too crazy, and they just did.

Harry called Wilkins right away; I knew that because Wilkins gave me a call and told me so.

"Justin, forget about Harry. I run this goddamn company, not Harry. He wanted you fired, but that's not going to happen. You take the day off and meet me at the Yorkshire Grill on 6th and Grand tomorrow at 8 a.m."

Then he hung up.

Wilkins must have taken the next flight from Charleston to Los Angeles.

He slept at Checkers on Grand between Fifth and Sixth and met me at Yorkshire Grill just down the block at 8 a.m. sharp. I spoke first.

"Mr. Wilkins, there's no problem here. I plan to leave next week. I don't want to create any friction between you and Harry."

Wilkins heard me but just nodded and said nothing.

We finished breakfast and walked up the hill to the Wells Fargo Towers, a few blocks away.

Wilkins was silent but fuming.

When we passed Willard, I saw him pick up the phone.

I was sure he informed Harry that Wilkins and I were on the way (heads-up!)

We exited the elevator on the 21st floor and entered the offices.

Harry was waiting there to greet us. He opened his office door, and Wilkins walked in first, with Harry following closely behind.

Harry slammed the door as he entered.

I stood outside in his secretary's office and listened through the door. You could hear them yelling and screaming.

I had visions of Cats and Dogs running up and down the office walls in chaos.

I couldn't take it. I didn't want to be the cause of this confusion, and I was apprehensive about the outcome and what part I might play in it.

I wanted out.

This was way more than I bargained for, Maserati or not. I had to break in.

I knocked on the door, opened it, and said,

"Mr. Wilkins, can I speak with you briefly?" He stepped out and closed the door.

"Mr. Wilkins, listen, I heard you in there; there's no need for HTS and Wilkins to split up, no reason for this dissension. Buying them out is costly; don't worry about me; please don't do anything to hurt your company. I'm glad to leave—I don't want to cause any problems. "

Wilkins looked through me and replied,

"I know what I'm doing." Then he turned and walked back in.

Harry and Wilkins stayed in the office for a few more minutes.

Then Harry came out, gave me a dirty look, and walked down the hall.

Wilkins exited after Harry cleared the office and was out of earshot.

Curiosity and concern overwhelmed me. Looking at Wilkins, I asked,

"What happened?"

He replied nonchalantly,

"I bought them out. I'm paying cash. I need to come up with the money in three months, and I will. Harry is out, and he's not coming back. I need you to watch the place. You went to college, and you'll figure it out.

Take Harry's Office. You're in charge of Los Angeles now."

"What…" I stammered, "What about the car? The Maserati."

"He's leaving it. His wife is picking him up."

It was odd that the Maserati was the first thing that came to my mind.

Some might think this was a great day, a fine accomplishment, but it was the worst day of my life.

I walked into Harry's Office, and it was now mine.

To be safe, I sat down behind the conference table and stared out the huge windows overlooking Los Angeles far below.

The Boss

Word spread fast. I took the elevator to the ground floor and walked past Willard at the concierge desk.

"Congratulations, Mr. Larkin!" he said. "I hear you're in charge of Piedmont in LA now."

Ignoring Willard, I thought to myself,

"In charge of what? Is this what I want to do for the rest of my life? Surely this ain't what I planned! What I wanted…"

But what could I do?

It seemed the train had left the station, and I was on it. I had no other choice. Wilkins had nobody else; he needed me.

Regardless of what Lacy thought, we could use the money—she was pregnant, and I had that to think about, too.

How could I raise a kid at that little house in Echo Park?

I needed to give her the life she deserved, the life she had known as a child. This was a gift horse. What would I do? Check its mouth?

Then, right then, I stopped thinking.

I figured I'd go along with it. Time passed fast; the first two years at Piedmont weren't that bad.

The money was fine, and I got a Jag – the Maserati went to Lacy's bitch sister Ashley.

It was like I was in a mist, losing track of things and hurling down a path not of my choosing, to which I saw no end or chance of retracing.

We hired a housekeeper for Lacy, and she started looking for a bigger house. She found one she liked behind Laughlin Gate, a ritzy section of Los Angeles near Griffith Park.

Wilkins insisted it was better if the company bought the house and held it in trust; then, we wouldn't have to pay any taxes on the extra salary needed to pay the mortgage.

I went for it, but Lacy didn't like the idea of the company owning our home.

However, she wanted the house, and Wilkins would only front the money under those conditions, so reluctantly, she agreed.

Things were careening out of control.

Only a few years before, I was to become a professor in Tweed, take long, restful lunches on a beautiful campus, and swim in the pool at the faculty club in the late afternoon.

Now, I had fancy cars and suits, and I spent my days on the telephone, eating lunch at my desk or entertaining a client at some fancy downtown haunt, attempting to be whatever they wanted me to be to get the sale.

It was hard work, requiring extreme concentration and effort.

I was losing track of myself.

Upon return from inane lunches in lieu of scholarly discussions with colleagues, I screamed at warehousemen, listened to secretaries' bitch and moan, attended workman's compensation hearings, or stood in dirty sweatshops, arguing over nickels and dimes.

Lacy complained. "You've changed, and I don't like the change."

The way I look at it now, she may have been right.

Success

It's not that I'm so fuckin' smart, but facts were facts, and after I took over the West Coast Operation, my efforts drove the company.

As a matter of fact, we carried all the other regions.

The Chinese would have taken over the company if it weren't for me.

Even Wilkins had to have known that, right?

Jade and Ashley would always get their cut; I could deal with that; the business was huge, making bank, so what if Lacy's sisters didn't do shit?

There was plenty of money to go around. I had a cool car, and so did Lacy. We had a house to kill for, plenty of stuff, our wonderful son David, and our health.

As far as I was concerned, that's enough.

What could Wilkins say? Is it an accident that Piedmont was making money? Be real: all they had to do was look at the books; it was all there and all me.

I worked my ass off, it's no damn accident!

Wilkins never said much; sure, he let me run things and gave me my way, but my last meal with him was breakfast at the Yorkshire Grill the day I got the job.

Eventually, he stopped calling me, and when I called him with a question or when I wanted his advice, he avoided the call or told me to try again later.

I worked hard for success; it was not without effort. I don't care what anyone thinks; I know it's true—that's all that matters, right?

One day, he called me entirely out of the blue. I figured it was to discuss sales or some of my management questions; I respected his experience and wanted to probe him for answers to some questions. But as it turned out, it had nothing to do with business.

"Justin, I found this stunning villa in Jamaica, an outstanding value. You like the Islands, don't you?"

"Yeah, sure, Mr. Wilkins, you know I do. Is it wise to purchase a vacation property? Is there not a better use of company funds?"

"I bought it, and the deed is done. I had to, Son; it was too great an opportunity to pass up; you'll love it. Take the family; call Grace when you want to use the place, as she'll keep track of who's there.

Let me tell you, David's gonna love it. Okay, gotta go. I just wanted to tell you that Piedmont now owns a Villa. Congratulations. Oh yeah, one more thing, are we making any money out there?"

"Mr. Wilkins, you see the books, we're doing great! You've gotta know that."

"Yes, that's right. Keep it up; things are going well."

I'm no fool. I knew what he was doing. He was adding to his Legacy. For a fraction of the purchase cost, we could just as well have written off stays at the best resorts on the island.

But what could I say? After all, it was his company; ultimately, he was in control, not me.

He was the least of my worries: as long as I kicked ass, he stayed off my back.

Lacy was giving me the headaches, while Pop was giving as little credit as possible and living off the fruit of my efforts (and we were indeed living in high style); Lacy was unhappy with my business preoccupation.

"Justin, what happened to the philosophy, the religious discussions, and the tears you shed over ideas? All you talk about now is Piedmont, JD, and some guy named Benny.

What do I care what some textiles cost?

When we go driving, you point out this truck or that truck and give me a dissertation on what kind of diesel it is and how you have one of those or these.

I am getting sick of this; it's boring. When was the last time you even read a book?"

"Well, excuse me, how do you think you got that house? Or how did you get David into that fancy private school on the Westside instead of some shitty public school?

And that fancy car you drive, and the help at home?

Do you think it grows on that silver dollar tree in Echo Park? No fuckin' way. I have to work my ass off! What are you whining about here?"

"Justin, there is no doubt you are an excellent provider, but what good does it do? You're never here; you're always angry, pissed off about something, and when you are here, you're distracted; you don't even listen to me.

Do you think I like to listen to you ranting in the morning on the phone, screaming and cussing at some employee? What's wrong with you? We're getting older; you're not twenty-one anymore."

"Well, what do you want me to do, quit?"

"That's fine with me; I could move back to Echo Park anytime; I don't need all this. Do you think it's good for David to hear you ranting? It's gotta stop!"

What could I do? What could I say? It was true – all of it. I'd changed.

I was focused on the road ahead. Like it or not, that's what a man has to do. I was on a highway, I could see no way off, I couldn't let Wilkins down, he depended on me, and I didn't believe I could let Lacy and David move back to Echo Park.

I had to provide, and doing what I was doing was the way to do it.

There was no way out, so I let it all pass and made the best of it, fumbling through life. I would try to be a better husband.

"Lacy, I love you and David very much; I will try to improve and do what I can. I love you both."

"Okay, Justin, Okay."

She clearly had doubts, but she put up with me.

Sometimes, in chaos and frustration, I heard Kaya's voice resonate from somewhere, echoing in a strong tenor through the darker caverns of my thinking.

In my mind's eye, she would come over to my house, lie on the floor, and want me to sex her up, no bones about it. I would rub her tits, and she would grind her body against mine.

Her quirky nature, exotic looks, and wonderful voice – I longed for those times when each moment seemed so special when each moment was.

The more distance and time put between us, the more entranced and obsessed with her I became.

Lacy and I would go to the Jamaican villa about once a year. I honestly looked forward to those times. Lacy would come, but without enthusiasm; it wasn't her thing. She'd prefer Paris or Rome – somewhere with "culture." She was bored with the beach but tolerated it for us.

David would roam the shores, wild and free, running from the forested cliffs to the sea and back.

I would sip dark rum, read Henry Miller, and wander in and out of the warm water, speaking to anyone who would listen.

Tosh, a local Rasta fisherman who parked his boat on our beach, was especially fond of David, and David was fond of him.

He would rise early each morning and go with Tosh to the sea.

The village where the house was located was called "Revival," that's what it did for me; it revived me spiritually and mentally.

Wilkins named the Piedmont estate "Calm."

Calm was a colossal affair – in many ways very similar to their home in Charleston – with an extended front porch and tall columns, plantation style, a throwback to the days when slaves wandered the island at the service of their white masters.

A small cottage overlooked the sea, a miniature of the big house.

Lacy and I preferred the cottage, which was on a cliff overlooking the Caribbean Sea, which stretched beyond the horizon.

We never stayed in the big house.

Living like that against the backdrop of the island's poverty seemed somehow offensive.

Besides, the cottage was all we needed or wanted.

Jade and the rest of the family never even visited the cottage, so it was like our very own place, and we were happy with that arrangement.

Like Echo Park, warmth permeated the cottage.

Like his father before him, Tosh had fished the waters for as far back as anyone could remember.

Each day, he would pull his little skiff onto the sands just below the cottage, where it could sit perfectly safely.

Tosh was forty, but his skin was wrinkled and lined from the countless days spent at sea in his uncovered skiff.

An old, raggedy, red, black, and green Rasta hat covered his long dreadlocks, which reached down to the top of his bell-bottom pants. He also wore trunks of many colors, hand-me-downs from long-departed tourists.

Tosh rarely spoke, but when he did, nobility and wisdom were inherent in each uttered word.

Wilson, the house administrator at Villa Calm, was in his fifties, with graying hair. He carried himself with the dignity and demeanor of an English butler.

"I learned my trade in London, where I attended the university," he told me the first time we met as if to separate himself from the others.

While I was not sure if what he said was true, there was no doubt that he ran the house with the efficiency and detail of a trained hotelier of the highest order.

The staff consisted of Rasta girls from Revival Village.

I have no idea how the Rastafarians came to this area or why Wilson hired them, but they did an excellent job keeping the place shipshape.

The Rastafarians were always there, and the Wilkins' extended clan was not; this was really their home—that was how it felt to me.

Sometimes, they let us come and pretend it was ours.

There was a little nightstand by our bedside at Laughlin Gate. Turning over, even my still-groggy eyes could decipher the digital clock on the nightstand on Wednesday, February 12th.

It was 72 degrees, 09:52 A.M.

Lacy'd long ago departed for the flower mart, as enamored with the mornings as I was with the night; it's as if we functioned in different time zones, crossing paths only at the setting of the sun.

The bedroom was quiet and still, and I was alone in a lovely world (essentially of her making). The California sun shone through the French doors, distant views of the mountains and the immense lawn unfolded below, and the shimmering blue waters of the pool created a mirage floating above its surface.

At these moments, I felt that all the hard work was worthwhile. Then, a sordid and terrifying realization arose as if out of nowhere.

In a matter of mere hours, I would again be immersed in a mundane mix of commerce and sweat and somehow so engaged in them that any recollection of this elegance, tranquility, and refinement would fade, only to be replaced by the bellicosity and the disdain of the commerce that created them.

An even more disconcerting thought I knew all too well was that I would enjoy the folly and be enraptured, thrilled, challenged, and even invigorated.

This world of beauty and calm would fade into a distant memory as if I had never tasted it.

"Today is a special day," I recalled. "It's Eric Day. Shit, I have to be downtown by noon. But it's only fuckin' 09:52; I'm good."

Relieved, I decided I had time for coffee and perhaps a swim before rushing downtown, time to appreciate the fullness and brilliance of a fine morning.

I wrapped myself in a robe of fine Egyptian cotton. Light streamed through wide-open doors, revealing a scene of beauty and calm all but lifted from a storybook.

Millions must imagine they will find this world if they make it to Hollywood, yet this is a life few who live in this town will even see, and far fewer will live.

Yet, as I stood there, the soft, rich carpet of emerald grass beneath my feet, I took in the scene before me—a near-Olympic-sized pool, it's still waters reflecting the deep green of the hills framing it.

Beyond, Griffith Park stretched into the horizon, the planetarium gleaming in its pristine whiteness above.

In that moment, I was acutely aware of my blessings.

How I came upon such opulence is still beyond my comprehension; while it was surely not by mere luck or happenstance, not unearned, at the same time, it was clear to me that it made no sense.

But I jettisoned such thoughts.

Drawn toward the small pergola off to the side of the pool, I made for the fine espresso machine twinkling, reflecting in the sun; hot and thick liquid dripped from its slender silver spout into a small tasse placed there for my use.

Mine alone.

Savoring the warmth and invigorated by the potent elixir, I moved closer to the pool, setting my cup on a glass tabletop of fine Deco design, and plunged into warm, clear waters.

Submerged, submarining for a few yards, not enough to exert myself but enough to wash the morning from my skin, I arose to a surface surrounded by evergreen, deciduous, verdant hills.

Again and again, I have been amazed at my good fortune.

I could happily have spent the day at home… but no, I could not tarry; it was a special day for young Eric, and one must be a man of one's word. One like me must be an example for one like him.

I promised Eric this meeting but would not keep him waiting. After all, effort and focus brought me luxury, and I owed those who made it possible maximum diligence and attention to detail.

Fortunes can always fade if you don't keep them burnished, and that wouldn't have been fair to either Lacy or David or Wilkins, for that matter.

Duty and responsibility were burdens an honorable man would and could not sidestep.

Of late, Eric had been a driving force of Piedmont's success.

His contribution and sales were real; as I became more involved in operational details, I counted on others to assist in the sales. Eric had been my star. I ignored him at my peril; I was well aware of that.

I promised Eric we would spend the day celebrating his accomplishments and sales.

My mission for the day was to make him feel appreciated. I figured this would motivate sales, a useful expenditure of my time.

Eric was far more traditional than I, and that is a simple summary of our differences.

Refined and orthodox in his approach, his manner was as different from mine as night from goddamn day. I sold by building relationships with passion and gut.

On the contrary, Eric was focused and directed, neat and punctual, detailed and comprehensive – he sold by logic, information, and competence.

Born and bred in South Pasadena from as blueblood a clan as one might find in Southern California, Eric was handsome and blonde, a scion of wealth, taste, and refinement. He was a sales leader at Piedmont, his totals fast approaching mine, and since I was now otherwise occupied with good old Harry's duties, I was convinced that the day would soon come when his numbers would exceed mine.

I was never completely sure why he applied for a sales position at Piedmont, but the brand fit well with his impression of himself.

It was also well known that Wilkins richly rewarded success in selling; my saga clearly demonstrated that, if nothing else.

There is no formula for a salesman's success; judgment is based on results. I took a chance on Eric, and it paid off in spades. The more he sold, the more our numbers rose, and that was what it was all about.

Increasing sales and revenue is a measurable goal, not some abstract philosophical principle that puts nothing in a wife's or boy's mouth and employs no one.

Not some act of intellectual masturbation which sucks resources from the public trough and gives nothing back.

Outside the office, Eric and I had nothing in common. While he loved playing golf and attending polo matches, I had never been on a golf course or watched a polo match on television.

I considered such things to be frivolous and a waste of time. I would instead read a book, though I no longer made time for that.

Friendly and well-mannered, Eric never spoke of politics, philosophy, or anything other than business, yet he never failed to ask about my wife or son.

He was barely twenty-five when he married a lovely woman, Janice. Though she had borne him two children, she looked as if she had just stepped off the runway with one more on the way. She had delicate features, beautiful blonde hair, and a pleasant manner; she was a woman of class and sophistication like Lacy.

Yet, whereas Lacy seemed uncomfortable in her world, Janice appeared at peace with things as they were. But who can know the details of a man and woman's affairs?

Eric did not speak of these things, but I was under the impression that their marriage was without strife, unlike mine.

I took a short swim, ending up at the bathhouse near the east end of the pool to shower, shave, and prepare for the coming trials; I knew a lunch with Eric would take all my effort.

He bored me to tears.

Hesitating for a few more moments of bliss, I stared up at the blue dome of the sky and felt the warmth that surrounded me. I counted the passing wisps of whiteness above, noting the green of the trees gently moving back and forth in the breeze and birds passing in the azure skies.

Far too soon, I will be downtown. .

The bathhouse sported a sizeable walk-in closet where Lacy had neatly arranged the Brooks Brothers suits her daddy preferred me to wear.

I figured a tan suit, brown dime loafers, and a blue long-sleeve Ralph Lauren would be appropriate for an afternoon of drinking and dining with Eric.

Dressed and coiffed, I glanced at the mirror.

"Lacy would be proud," I declared.

As I walked back toward the house and out the side gate to the driveway, I found the Jag sitting pretty, still fresh from yesterday's detail. Pulling out of the driveway under Laughlin Gate, I quickly glanced at the clock.

"Oh fuck, 12:45? Where did the time go?"

Passing Mulholland Fountain, I took a right on Fletcher and pulled up the on-ramp to 101. The freeway winds around the mountainside on its three-mile climb towards downtown Los Angeles.

As the Freeway climbs higher and higher, the cliffs of Elysian Park straddle it like the walls of some ancient city, and in the distance, the towers of Los Angeles glimmer in the sun.

Exiting the freeway at Flower, the Jag drifted down the incline. I took my foot off the accelerator, and the cat stopped gently at the red light. Bums passed my window as I waited, their faces sad and forlorn. I was impatient, waiting to turn right, and I gave them the pass.

Knowing Lacy, they may be Christmas guests someday.

Traffic gathered as I crossed Broadway, where throngs of Mexicans walk streets crowded with old and detailed edifices, once the home of barons of industry, now housing seedy clothing stores and electronics shops.

I continued to Alameda, home to warehouses and industry, factories, railroad yards, and produce markets with vendors ending their day at high noon after cleaning their booths and stalls, sweeping and washing, ammonia and soap cleansing the bacteria, sending it to the Los Angeles River and the Pacific beyond.

Little Tokyo

The main gate to Little Tokyo is diminutive, like all the things in this place, its name being an apt description.

The gate abuts Second Street, fronting a Zen-like plaza a few blocks from the expansive city courthouse, police station, and jail.

The Government Center, full of bloat, waste, and corruption, sporting massive front lawns and poorly arranged faux grandiose landscapes, juxtaposes interestingly to this Japanese village built on a human scale.

Pulling into Joe's Parking Lot right behind the Brewery off Second, I slide into the first available spot as an attendant meanders over and hands me a ticket. It's a short walk down Second, past a little Shiatsu shop at the entrance to the Japanese Village.

Yesterday after work, I barked to Eric,

"Meet me tomorrow at noon at the first restaurant in Little Tokyo Village. The place stinks of fish; you can't miss it."

Late as I was, I was sure he would be waiting; Eric would not desert his post. And there he was, a lonely lost soul, a very white guy surrounded by Asian businessmen chattering away in a foreign tongue.

Noticing me enter, Eric leaned back on his stool, balanced on his rear legs, and looked happy and relieved.

He said,

"Justin, I was about to leave. You're almost two hours late! What happened? I was calling and calling, and your voicemail picked up. The office said you weren't there either; they sounded happy."

"Fuck those guys. Sorry, my cell must have been on mute," I said.

When I pulled my flip phone out of my pocket, I noticed it was, so I fixed it and stuffed it back in.

"Shit, sorry about that, "I echoed.

"No worries," Eric said.

"It's okay. Your instructions were perfect. This place does stink to high heavens, but sitting here, I got used to it."

Laughing as I sat down next to Eric, I said,

"What, no women? You're sitting here for two hours, and no chicks attacked you? You're losing your touch, old man."

Eric laughed, adding more Coke to the half-filled glass he'd been nursing. I motioned with my right hand to the bartender/sushi chef, who was wearing a bandana on his head.

He acknowledged me and shouted,

"High!"

at the top of his voice, slamming a carafe of hot sake in front of our faces.

Then, the chef lifted the carafe and poured the warm, transparent liquid into tiny blue thimbles, one for me and one for Eric.

I raised my glass, saying, "Salut!"

I reached over, our glasses touched, and I continued.

"Eric, what can I say? You are doing a wonderful job. Congratulations, and thank you very much."

Then I looked at Eric, his fine suit and professional composure, and said,

"You represent our brand well, clearly better than I. We are all happy for you."

Looking up at the sushi chef, I asked,

"Please, just bring us an assortment of everything, the best you have. Spare no expense."

The chef watched me as I continued,

"My friend here is a great salesman. Treat him right. He is number one."

The chef looked at Eric and said, bowing,

"Oh, number one? Thank you, thank you."

Each plate the chef placed before us looked superior to the previous one.

"Justin, there's more to come, more sales. I want to make enough money to pay for the notes at a house in Pasadena near my parents. My drive now is a bit long, and houses are high near Las Lunas, but you have been great, and if I can keep going, I can afford it.

Our parents will kick in the down; we're looking at about two million. With Piedmont's name, I don't see any problem. I can do it."

"You'll do it," I affirmed.

"I have no choice. I have to! We have another kid on the way," Eric replied, smiling.

While I wanted to change the subject away from money, Eric persisted.

"Justin, I have ideas. We're all going to make money. This is serious. It's about responsibilities to the company and our families."

"Chill out, Eric," I waved him off.

"Relax, fuck business shit," I insisted and continued.

" Do you know why I love this place? Oh, not this bar in particular, but Little Tokyo in general. I like the smallness and scale and have some excellent memories."

Eric seemed interested; he leaned forward.

"Memories from here? What kind? What memories in particular?"

"Years ago, when I was in college, I came down here to meet a girlfriend, someone I knew in high school," I said.

"A high school sweetheart. I had one of those, too; I married her!" Eric said.

"Yes, a high school sweetheart. There was this sushi cart right outside this place, and one day years ago—it could have been twenty years ago or maybe more.....," I said, fading in and out.

"They sold sushi from a cart?" Eric asked.

"Yeah, right out there, just outside the window, in front of the restaurant, right on Second Street. It was twenty-five years ago, but in my head, I keep seeing myself buying sushi repeatedly from that cart."

"God, twenty-five years ago. So, is that why we're here today?" Eric enquired.

"It's like I can still feel Kaya's vibes down here.

Now and then, I come just to get that feeling," I said more to myself than to Eric.

"Kaya. What kind of name is that anyway?" Eric asked.

"I have no fuckin' idea. She's Japanese, so maybe it's a Japanese name. Not sure." I explained.

"Nice name, but Lacy sounds better to me," Eric said confidently.

Forget Kaya! Man, that was just a high school sweetheart. You're married, and your wife is terrific. Janice loves her."

I sat staring out the window. It was like whenever I went around there—dreamy, foggy, hazy, an indescribable feeling.

Eric seemed lost in his world, too, as he poured sake from the carafe into his thimble and then, demonstrating superb manners, filled mine.

We sat drinking and not talking, and Eric gazed out the window.

As for me, I saw the sushi cart and stood beside it again, hand in pocket, pulling out bills with gusto, drifting through the window... An undersized Japanese man, scarf wrapped across his forehead, serves up the sushi.

Kaya is delighted, pointing at various concoctions and using the proper Japanese names to describe them.

Glancing at Kaya, I am engrossed in her smile. The sushi touches her brown lips, and then she fades and disappears.

It's the end of the reel—a short one, yes, but the film loops forever and ever.

Eric emerged from his reverie and said,

"Justin, are you alright?"

"Yeah, sure. You wanna go somewhere else?" I asked.

"Sure. You're the boss. Any other ideas?"

"Yeah, I'll meet you at the Athletic Club. They have a beautiful bar there. Let's get outta here," I said.

I paid the tab, and we left, walking past 'the spot.'

Eric kept going.

I lingered there a second to take one last look.

I swear that cart is still there!

Fifteen-Year-Old Dickel

"The Duke," as they call the Los Angeles Athletic Club bar, is a bitter disappointment.

The stained light oak bar has an air of newness, like a basement bar on some upscale suburban ready-built.

Immaculately clean, it lacks any soul.

Spirits of boredom pour out of the walls of the joint. To add insult to injury, the bar was empty, except for Tom, the bartender.

"Hey, Justin, what can I get you boys?" asked Tom.

"How about a couple of Duke's martinis? That's your specialty, right?"

"The best martini in LA, and coming right up," he replies with barely a twinge of excitement.

As Tom shook the martinis, Eric and I sat staring at the length of the bar. Not one fuckin' person there. What the fuck, I thought to myself. I was never good at planned affairs; I just wanted this day to end.

Eric probably hated it as much as I did; I bet he thought he was doing me a favor.

Most likely, he was thinking about his long drive home. The way I figured it, if we could down this shit in half an hour or so, he could be on his way. It was nearly 5 p.m.

"Enjoy, men," Tom said.

He set the drinks down and walked off, not even attempting to cheer us up.

Eric looked at the walls, and I stared into space, now and then faking a lame toast.

Both of us were pretty much talked out.

In fact, we had little to discuss. Besides work discussions, Eric was a straight-on guy with little interest in art, literature, politics, or science.

It was all about the job and the family. He was nothing like me, come to think about it; he's really more like Wilkins.

On top of that, he was half my age.

Tom pushed another of his "famous" Duke's Martini's on us. He must have had some quota, and looking at the empty bar, I figured he wouldn't make it.

"To Duke's Bar, the most boring bar in LA," I declared.

Tom looked over, smirking, and said,

"Now, Justin, cut it out. We were loaded about an hour ago. We had five librarians in here."

"Librarians. That sounds about right," I retorted.

Eric took his drink and slowly sipped the remaining brine from the glass, looking towards the walls, windows, and beyond.

My mind traveled to a million different places, above the high ceilings and staid walls amidst the silence and peace.

I find some solace, but today was about a good time for Eric, not my contemplating things.

"Eric, this place is depressing. Let's take a little walk up to the Seven Grand. I can't take this anymore."

Eric nodded in agreement; I guess he felt sorry for me for putting on this lame shebang.

I wish Lacy was as concerned for my feelings as Eric seemed, but he wasn't married to me.

When I think of it, I admire Eric the most. He always seems to think about the other guy. I suppose that's why he's such a good salesperson; people must sense it.

We hoofed it over to the Seven Grand, just half a city block up Sixth.

It was twilight, and the streets were filled with buses and cars full of commuters ending their day. We turned into the small entrance to the Seven Grand but found it blocked by a gargantuan bouncer guarding the entrance like an NFL lineman guarding his quarterback.

Eric was in the lead, and the lineman declared, "You're ID?"

Eric handed his license to the bouncer, who carefully inspected it and looked Eric up and down. Anticipating similar treatment, I attempted to pass my license to the bouncer, but he waved me onto the vestibule.

Off to the left was a dimly lit hallway with an ancient wooden stairway heading up at a steep forty-five degrees.

Dark walls enclosed both sides of the stairway, which was crowded with people heading up and down—so much so that we were jostled up, emerging in an ample, open space.

A huge, worn oak bar extended the entire length of the room, which had dark paneled walls covered with Western memorabilia and other ancient funk. This eclectic mix, without any fundamental or underlying theme, was cool, oddly, like some Disney amusement.

It was nearly 6 p.m., and the bar was already packed. We moved with the masses, circumnavigating an antique pool table as if it were the Kaaba itself.

Approaching the bar, we were greeted by a young bartender with Brycleemed hair, definitely a good omen.

"What can I get you guys?" he asked.

The back of the bar was crammed from end to end with every whiskey one might dream of.

I spied a cool-looking bottle of George Dickel bourbon crowded amongst the panoply.

"What about that Dickel? Is it any good?" I questioned.

Pulling the bottle from the wall, the bartender put it before us and said,

"Excellent choice. Fifteen-Year-Old George Dickel, excellent choice."

With a smile, first looking at Eric and then the bartender, I said,

"That's all I drank in New Orleans. People appreciate Dickel down there and barely know about Dickel in L.A.

Just regular old Dickel: that's what I drank in New Orleans. I never knew about fifteen-year-old Dickel, and if they had it, I'm sure I couldn't afford it, but ordinary Dickel worked just fine, if you catch my drift."

The bartender nodded in agreement, and Eric looked my way.

The bartender asked,

"So, do you want the Dickel?"

"How much is the bottle?"

"You want the bottle?" he asked.

"Yes, how much?" I repeated.

"One-seventy-five."

"Leave it. We're celebrating."

"You sure are!"

He left the bottle and a couple of shot glasses.

I felt better for Eric. He had a good bottle and lovely scenery, which was the treat I wanted to give him for his successful sales.

Concentrating on the long bar, a relic of some old Western Movie Set, I suspect, we grabbed our shots, swung around, and hung our arms on the rail like gunslingers looking for a fight.

As luck would have it, two handsome women—a blonde and a redhead—pushed their way up through the growing crowd, seeming to head right for us, the redhead in the lead. We made room at the bar, and they looked expectantly at the barkeep for some refreshment, the redhead oddly gazing at me.

This was more like it!

Eric looked them over and then, holding up the bottle as a visual aid, said,

"We have this fine fifteen-year-old Dickel. Want some?"

The girls looked at each other, a bit surprised. Then the blonde smiled, looked at Eric, and said,

"Sure, why not?"

Eric raises his hand high and beckons the bartender, who rushes over.

"Can we get two more shot glasses?"

"Of course," said the bartender.

He quickly produced the glasses and laid them on the bar. Eric poured two drinks and handed one to each girl.

I decided to chime in.

"Let's drink to Eric; it's his frickin' birthday.

The girls smiled, and Eric looked at me like I was crazy.

But before he could say anything, the redhead raised her glass and started singing.

We all joined in.

"Happy birthday to you, happy birthday to you, happy birthday to you, dear Eric!"

We downed our shots, and Eric said,

"Well, thanks a lot, but it's not my birthday; regardless, that was exceedingly kind. Justin is a joker, but a nice one."

"Welcome," I replied with a smile.

"Do you guys work downtown?" Eric asked them.

The redhead replied,

"No, we're from Seattle. My name is Haley, and this is Rebecca."

Haley motioned to her blonde friend, standing at her side.

"I'm Eric, and this is Justin!" Eric said.

"Pleased to meet you," I said.

"What brings you all to L.A., business or pleasure?"

Rebecca answered,

"We're attending a nursing convention at the Wilshire Grand. We heard the Seven Grand is the place to be, so we're here!"

The girls smiled, but Haley's flaming red hair falling gently on her soft white shoulders grabbed my attention.

I couldn't keep my eyes off the well-proportioned undulating mounds surrounded by soft, blue-hued seersucker fabric exuding an innocent but evident sensuality.

What a goddamn beauty, I thought to myself.

To my surprise, I must admit, I noted that her red lips and bright blue eyes were focused on me like a laser light.

Fragrances of soft lotions demanded my attention. The whiskey was warm within. I reached out to touch her face, and my hands moved down over the dress and the mounds. I couldn't believe I was doing this, but I was.

Surprisingly, she stood there looking at me, expressionless but permitting. I awoke from this semi-trance long enough to look askance and find Eric staring at us, mouth open wide, but I was not disturbed.

Haley and I were tête-à-tête.

"Do you think it is an accident that I came over to you?"

Aghast and utterly confused, I say, "What do you mean?"

"Something is wrong. That I could see. You were pulling me here, and I wanted to come," she replied.

"What do you mean? I didn't even know that you were here. I don't know you!" I protested.

"It's written all over you. Something is very wrong. I could feel it, even from a distance. Let me touch you."

Haley reached out her hand, and I touched her soft white skin. The palm of her hand was damp. I took it and held it tight as we moved closer, pushing against the bar and each other, touching our sides to feel each other's bodies.

If time was passing, I was unaware.

Her smells wafted against mine, and we comforted each other, now and then sipping the fifteen-year-old Dickel, which cast its haze. The noise of the crowded bar was muffled, fading, all but nonexistent.

I was awakened by Eric, who pushed against my shoulder, his cell to his ear.

"Hey, Justin, it's my wife. I need to leave now. It's okay. I can return to my car if you want to stay here."

Slung back to reality and aware that Eric might not understand, I turned to Haley and said,

"Will you excuse me?"

I asked as I reluctantly separated myself from her.

Haley looked at me and said,

"Yeah, sure, go ahead."

Nudging Eric, I said,

"Let me speak to her."

Eric handed me the phone, and, composing myself, I said,

"Hello, Janice. It's Justin. We're at Seven Grand, down the street from the Athletic Club. I'm sure you'd like it—it's hopping."

"Yes, Eric told me," she replied. "Sounds great! We should go there sometime, with you and Lacy."

"Good idea."

"Justin?" she asked with some concern.

"Eric, is he okay with driving home?"

"I'm not sure, but no worries. He can stay at the Athletic Club down the street; I think it might be safer. What do you think?" I suggested.

"Good idea," Janice agreed and then said,

"Now, you two guys don't pick up any girls now. Be good."

"Of course not. You know better than that," I replied.

"I was just joking. Sure, tell Eric to stay at the club."

"Here, I'll hand him the phone," I said.

"Not necessary. I need to tend to the kids. Tell him what I said, and you all have a good time. You deserve it."

"Okay, goodbye."

I hung up the phone and glanced at Eric, who was looking at me the entire time.

"It's cool, Eric. You stay at the Athletic Club tonight. Janice wants you to have an enjoyable time. Are you having a fun time?"

"Yeah, sure, but I am exhausted. It's past 11 o'clock. If I stay downtown, I think I'll check in now. I have to make some calls in the morning anyway, and I have some emails to get out tonight. You stay and have fun."

"Shit, 11 o'clock. Where did the time go? Where's Rebecca, the other nurse?" I asked.

"I have no idea. Somewhere around here. We spoke for a few minutes, and then I ran into Randy Moss from Haute Designs.

We have a chance with them. It was opportune that I came here after all. I got a meeting next Thursday at the showroom."

"Haute Designs. I can't fuckin' believe it. That could be a million a year, at least. You're fuckin' amazing! You don't fuckin' stop! Go get some sleep; we'll talk in the morning," I say.

"Justin, are you sure you don't want to come back now?" Eric said, looking at me seriously.

"Naw, I'm fine. You go ahead."

"Okay, Justin. Head back soon, and don't get in any trouble?"

As Eric left, he looked back at me and shook his head in obvious disapproval; I could tell, but what the fuck?

I returned to Haley at the bar and told her,

"Eric is leaving. That dude doesn't stop. He was selling while we were talking. He is truly an amazing talent. And a good guy with a great wife and kids. He's as loyal as the day is long."

"That's important to you, loyalty, isn't it?" asked Haley.

"Yes, sure is. What else is there?"

"I suppose you're right, but loyalty needs to be reserved for the deserving, don't you think?" replied Haley.

"I have no fuckin' idea! Were you always a nurse?" I asked.

"Yes, but I did do a bit of modeling."

"I'm not surprised," I said.

She smiled and continued,

"When I finished junior college, I went straight into a nursing program."

"Have you ever been married?" I inquired.

"No, but I lived with a doctor for a few years. I'm a surgical nurse by trade. My ex-boyfriend said I was the best nurse he ever had."

We both laughed at once.

"I bet!"

She smelled wonderful and was soft as hell. The haze of the Dickel, the sweet perfume, and the tenderness of Haley overcame me. It was as if I were naked in that place.

"Haley, you're a beautiful woman. You must pine over some man day and night?"

"Justin, that is a better question for you than I, don't you think?"

"Is it that obvious?"

"It's written all over you. What is her name?"

"Kaya," I answered.

"Such a nice name," Haley said.

Haley moved closer as if imploring me.

Her perfume, mixed with a fine body powder, engaged my senses. Soft breasts pressed hard against my chest, her lips against mine. Oblivious to our surroundings, we held each other tighter and tighter with an ever-increasing passionate embrace. Instinct drove my hands lower, under her dress, between the soft petals, warm and wet with excitement.

Then, in unison, suddenly aware of our surroundings, we released and grabbed our Dickel shots as if they were doses of some medicine capable of bringing us back to consciousness.

Our composure re-established, Haley looked at me straight on and said,

"Justin, let me explain now. I want to tell you what you need to know. You're a fascinating guy. I'm glad we met. It's rare for a man to be so honest. You are in love with two women, it seems—"

However, before she could finish, my cell phone rang.

It was Lacy.

Chasing Shadows

I squeezed my way down the stairs, past the bouncer, and into the night.

The crowded street presented a stark contrast to the din above. It was loud, sure, but the sounds echoed away rather than folded in.

People of every sort gathered around the taco wagons that lined Seventh Street.

The smell of burritos and salsa wafted in the air as yellow wax paper blew in all directions, upset by the passing cars. My cell phone had long since stopped ringing. I knew I had better call Lacy fast, so I hit Redial.

Lacy picked up.

"Hi, Lacy."

She hurried a response. "How's it going? Is Eric, okay?"

"Yes, he's fine. We're having a fun time. All's well. I bought him a bottle of old Dickel."

"Justin, how many drinks have you had? You're safe to drive home?"

"Yes, yes, but Eric is staying at the Club. Janice doesn't want him to drive back home. And it might be safer if I stayed down here, too."

There was a pause as if Lacy was unsure of her response. Then she spoke.

"David has been asking for you all night. Speak to him!"

"He's still up? It's almost midnight."

"He won't sleep until you come home; you know that. He dozed off a few times, but he kept waking up. Speak with him!"

Lacy handed David the phone.

"Hello, Daddy, when are you coming home?"

As much as I wanted to speak to David, I had to make it quick.

Somehow, I didn't feel comfortable talking to my son in that condition, whatever that condition might have been, but I did it anyway.

"Hello, David. Daddy has to work late tonight. I may have to stay downtown, but in the worst case, I'll see you in the morning, so be a good boy and sleep now. Daddy loves you very much."

"Okay, Daddy, I love you very much, too!"

"Can I speak to Mommy?"

David handed Lacy the phone.

"Good. I'm glad you spoke to him. He was waiting for you; he wouldn't sleep until he talked to you. Go ahead and stay downtown tonight. No sense in risking a DUI. I'll see you tomorrow. Call me when you're at the Club and ready for bed. I want to make sure you're safe."

"I will, thanks. I'll call you soon. I better get back to Eric now."

"Bye," Lacy said and hung up.

I headed back up the stairs as quickly as possible. I wanted to find that woman and get her thoughts on Kaya.

She seemed to know what was happening, but I didn't know how or why. But I thought she might be able to help me—she seemed insightful and sensitive.

Besides, she made me feel good.

This time, the stairs were more challenging to climb.

Missing a step, I fell against the banister and recovered quickly through the crowd of people lining the stairs and back to my bottle.

But much to my chagrin, Haley was no longer there, just the bottle.

I craned my neck in all directions but couldn't see her.

Leaning forward to the passing bartender, I asked,

"Hey, did you see that woman I was speaking with?"

Rushing by, he called back,

"Sorry, sir. As you can see, this place is packed. Honestly, I have no idea where she is."

I handed him a $100 tip for the Dickel and my business card.

"Thanks a lot."

He smiled, looking at the card and the money.

"If she comes back, tell her to call me."

"Sure, Mr. Larkin, and no worries, I'll keep this excellent bottle of Dickel under the bar. It'll be here next time you return; you can count on it."

Making my way around the bar, I looked at each face for Haley, the same way I always searched for Kaya, hoping by chance we would somehow, somewhere, meet, though it never happens.

The way I figured it, the girls returned to the Wilshire Grand, and if I hurried, I could find them.

It was just five blocks, so I jetted down the stairs, hopscotching around the crowds that filled the stairway, and headed down Seventh Street.

I knew damn well I looked outlandish, running down the street like a lunatic in a business suit, slick with the sheen of whiskey sweat, ignoring streetlights and anything else along the way.

Arriving disheveled and with hair in all directions and reeking of bourbon at the front desk of the Wilshire Grand, I made a cursory check of the bar and the lobby before heading to the front desk.

"Sir,"

I began to say to the concierge.

"I know this will sound odd, but you have a group of nurses here for a convention. One of the ladies left her cell phone at the Seven Grand, and I need to return it to her.

She's a nurse with red hair and has a friend, a good-looking blonde. Haley and Rebecca are their first names. They were together. Have you seen them pass by?"

The concierge looked me up and down.

He had some qualms about releasing any information, so I reached into my wallet and pulled out a business card.

I put it on his desk and said,

"I'm Justin Larkin with Piedmont Textiles."

He looked at the card and then up and down at me for a bit.

"Mr. Larkin," he replied,

"I really can't be sure, but I think some ladies with a similar description came by about ten minutes ago. Unless you know their full names, though, I cannot connect you to our house phones."

"Sir!"

Pulling my cell phone out of my pocket and holding it up to his face,

"I have her cell. Can you tell her the gentleman from the Seven Grand is here with her cell phone?"

"If you would like, I can take the phone and give you a receipt. If she doesn't claim it within thirty days, you can come and pick it up."

It was apparent I was getting nowhere, and I was not going to give him my phone, so I hesitated.

"Oh, well, thanks. I'll see her at the seminar tomorrow and give it to her."

The concierge smiled thinly.

"That's a fine plan. Is there anything else I can assist you with?"

"No, thanks!"

Leaving the hotel, I turned and headed back up Seventh to the Seven Grand for one more look, hoping the girls were parked in some cubby or outside on the smoking patio.

Pushing through the crowds and the din, looking in and out but to no avail, I headed back toward the Athletic Club to get a room for the night.

Taking the elevator up to the room, I pulled my phone from my pocket and opened the door.

It was past midnight, and it was too late to call Lacy.

I felt like shit, like a cold was coming on, as I set the cell on the nightstand to the right of the bed.

When I did, the house phone fell to the floor.

I left it there, its blaring dial tone finally fading into silence.

A chill overcame me and sweat poured from my face.

I buried myself under the covers and fell asleep, wrapped tight in damp cotton and thick loathing.

Morning Next

My frickin' phone was blaring in my ear. Half asleep, I grabbed it, and it fell to the floor.

I reached under the bed on my hands and knees, grabbed it, and jammed it to my ear.

"Hello," I say.

"Hey, Justin. You, okay?" says Eric with evident concern in his voice.

"Sure, I'm fine. Where are you?" I replied, but I didn't mean it.

"Downstairs in the café," he said.

"Great, not a problem. Wait there. Give me thirty minutes. I'll meet you there."

"Okay." He said. Then I hung up.

I quickly showered, picked my suit off the floor from where I left it, and quickly dressed.

When the damn elevator stopped, it was so full of people I just motioned them to pass. I ran down the stairwell to the lobby and entered the café facing Hope Street.

Eric sat quietly at a corner table, as calm and composed as ever.

Unlike my disheveled appearance and unshaven face, Eric was clean-shaven and well-groomed.

Reeking of a combination of stale bourbon and Haley's dusting powder, I approached the young man.

He seemed not to notice me coming towards him as he continued reading the Times with a half-filled glass of fresh-squeezed at his side, only turning his head up when I pulled out a chair and sat down.

"Hey, man, ya know that redhead I was talking to last night. She's like psychic or something. She had some great insight into things. Imagine meeting someone like that at a bar?"

"Justin, insights my eye, anyway, it's none of my goddamn business, but I bet you were talking to her about something real soft.

It just wasn't right for you to hang out with her all night like that. Watch it. That's all I can say!"

"Listen, I got back here a few minutes after you did last night. I wasn't with her all night. I have no fuckin' idea what you're talking about," I declared with halfhearted enthusiasm.

"Just be careful. I know you're my senior and my boss and all, but this talk about Kaya and now about some redhead… in a bar. Don't do anything stupid. That's all I'm saying, man.

Things are going too damn well to mess things up. Lacy is a great woman, wife, and mother. Don't mess up your life. That's all I can say."

Picking up a section of the Times, concentrating on it a bit, I thought to myself,

"Where in the fuck does this little asshole come off talking to me like this?"

Staring out the window, I saw the city in full motion:

FedEx and UPS on every corner, Angelinos ambling from place to place, streets crowded with the 'day people,' all prim and fresh ready for another day of the bullshit the working world provides. Then I let him have it.

"Listen, I don't know what you're thinking or why you're all pissed, but I was just having a bit of fun. You know, this job isn't easy, there's a lot of stress. All your ass does is sell; selling is fun. You try sitting in the office listening to some sniffling secretary complaining about how she can't get along with her co-worker or some asshole from the warehouse filing a bogus workman's comp complaint, or some city dick talking about a 'code violation,' or worst of all, talking to some attorney trying to rack up more billable time at three hundred dollars an hour, those bastards are the worst.

Compared to that, selling is a breeze; I know everyone can't sell, and you're a master; I'm just saying I have to deal with a lot of shit you don't, so don't be such a fuckin' prude."

Eric looked at me hard and replied,

"I know you have a lot on your plate, and you do a stellar job; I'm just saying you can do whatever you want with your life, but I have a family and responsibilities. Frankly, as a friend, I was surprised at how you acted.

Listen, you can count on me; there's no way I will reveal your secrets. This is between us, and I appreciate you being honest with me, but that's not how I am.

In the end, we just work together; that's it."

With that, Eric put down his paper and left the café.

As he did, he said,

"I'll see you at the office."

My mind wandered as I watched him amble out and walk down Seventh.

Look, I did nothing wrong. Perhaps I have some issues, but it was nothing serious.

I'm just more curious than Eric. Maybe he can live some life in Pasadena and die, but I need to learn more. I need to do more. His quiet life is exemplary, but he's not me.

I figured I'd return to Wilshire Grand and find the redhead; she knew something.

I knew this obsession with Kaya was crazy, but I felt I could work it out, and Haley could help if I could find her.

As I walked past the Athletic Club's front counter, the concierge spotted me and asked,

"Mr. Larkin, will you be coming back tonight?"

"No, thanks, just check me out; I had two rooms last night."

The concierge replied,

"Yes, Mr. Larkin, and breakfast; it'll be on your statement. Have a wonderful day."

"Yeah, sure," I said under my breath.

To get to my car, I had to exit Olive Street and walk down the stairs to the underground lot.

I found the Jag just where I left it.

Driving up the ramp, I made a left on Olive and a right on Seventh Street and pulled to a stop at the Wilshire Grand valet, directly in front of the hotel's entrance on the right of the building.

"I'll be back in twenty minutes."

I told the valet, handing him my keys and taking a paper ticket from his hands.

The concierge at the front desk had this shit-eating grin on his face; I must have looked like shit: stumbling, wrinkled suit, pale skin… I looked like I'd been in a bar fight or come off a junk binge.

I imagined working at a hotel desk; he'd seen it all, but maybe I was imagining things.

"Is the nursing convention still here?" I asked hurriedly.

The clerk replied,

"Yes, sir, the last session ends at noon today."

"Okay, thanks."

I mumbled, heading back toward Starbucks on the Seventh Street side of the hotel, figuring I'd get a latte and wait.

But dammit, the line was too fuckin' long, and I looked and felt like shit, so I decided to head home, clean up, and come back later to find her.

It Can Get Worse

By the time I got home, Lacy was gone.

I cleaned up and took a nap so I could head out around four; Lacy usually brought David home at five, so if I left at four, I would surely miss her, which was my intention.

At about 3:15, I put on another suit, grabbed my laptop, and drove back to the hotel.

Lacy hadn't arrived, so all was good.

The hotel had a Starbucks overlooking the lobby; I parked there and watched for the girls while simultaneously creating a mobile office: the laptop and papers in front of me, the cell phone at my side.

I noticed that half the other patrons in Starbucks were doing the same thing.

Looking at them, I chuckled to myself. What could be their purpose? Was the whole world on a chase?

The night duty concierge (the guy from last night) arrived at five, and as soon as I made eye contact with him, he waved me over.

"Sir, I saw you there and took the liberty to check the register. All the nurses from the convention have checked out. Would you like to leave the phone now?"

"Shit, I was hoping she'd still be here, I know she needs her phone. Thanks a lot; I'll take it to the lost and found. What a bummer!"

Holding the phone high to make clear my intentions, I meandered into a small room near the back of the hotel. There was a row of chairs at the back of the room.

I stood there for a few minutes, looking lost. Then, pulling a bit of courage from within, I departed, heading towards the concierge and making sure to give him a big wave as I passed, saying,

"It's done!"

Exiting the hotel, I sported a smirk. I'd kept the cell phone tucked in my pocket, treasuring its weight and feeling like I had just pulled off a major caper.

The Jag was still quietly parked near the valet station, right where I had left her, out of the sun's harsh rays and the noise of passing traffic.

After getting out of the garage and on the road, I called Eric to check the status back at the office.

"Hey, Eric, how did it go today? Is everything okay?"

"All operations are running normally; there is one thing, though," he said.

"Oh no! What one thing? What happened?" I asked.

"Nothing bad; I just wanted to tell you that Mr. Wilkins called to compliment me on my sales. He is delighted with our numbers; he says he will give me a raise."

"Great! Excellent work! I'm heading home now. Thanks for keeping a lid on things, and congratulations on the raise. You deserve it."

"Not a problem. Have an enjoyable evening and give my best regards to your family." Eric replied.

I hung up with a sigh of relief.

This whole episode had been exhausting from the start in Little Tokyo until that moment.

Oddly, I was never more than fifteen minutes from home, yet it felt like I'd been out of town for a week.

Dusk hovered over Laughlin Park as I passed under the Laughlin Gate and parked the Jag in the drive.

Entering the house, I could hear Lacy moving around in the kitchen.

"Lacy!" I hollered.

Walking the short distance from the front door to the kitchen, I knew she was there, but she did not reply. Upon entering the kitchen, it became clear that there was a reason for her silence; she was clearly upset and had "that look" on her face.

As I approached, I attempted to throw my arms around her. Rejecting my advances, she pushed me away and moved down the kitchen counter, putting more distance between us.

"Lacy?" I said. She didn't reply.

"Lacy, why aren't you talking?"

Finally, she fixed me with a dour look and said,

"What do you expect me to say? This is a goddamn mess! You stay out all night! I know you returned because you left tracks all over the house, clothes around the bedroom, breadcrumbs all over the kitchen floor, and dirty dishes in the sink. Am I supposed to be happy?"

"What the fuck are you talking about? What mess? You know that I was with Eric. I called you from the bar where we were celebrating his sales. I told you all about this. You told me not to come home. What the fuck is up with this?"

Her face tightened with anger, and she said slowly, firmly,

"You called me a bitch!"

I had no idea what she was talking about, but it was as if a switch had turned; she had a look on her face I'd never seen before – a scary look, an out-of-this-world look.

Did I drunk dial her? Could she know about Kaya? Had she finally had it with Piedmont? Could it be something else? I needed to calm her down, and I knew that.

"Lacy, I didn't call you a bitch, I swear."

"Justin, you screamed that I was a fucking bitch, and the whole neighborhood heard it. You're a goddamn liar. Do you hear yourself? You called me a fuckin' bitch."

What was she talking about? I didn't call her that, or I can't recall doing so.

Maybe I did?

I was confused and frozen, but it didn't matter. She'd made up her mind and was quickly heading in my direction. I hightailed it out of the kitchen and proceeded toward the front door as fast as my feet could carry me.

She must have grabbed a lamp on the go; I know that because the fucking thing shattered across the floor, pieces flying in front of me.

Front door open… I jetted out of the house toward the driveway and my car.

I made it to the Jaguar with Lacy a few feet behind.

I could feel her right on my tail.

Flooring the Jag, tires screeching, something bounces off the rear bumper, shattering in the street.

"Fuckin' bitch, goddamn fuckin' bitch, fucking lying bitch, she's one crazy-ass motherfucker. I didn't say shit, but I'm saying it now! She's fuckin' crazy!"

Blasting down the road, in thirty seconds, I was at Los Feliz Boulevard and made a quick left at Riverside Drive. I headed east to Glendale Blvd right past Rick's Diner and into the shopping center near Rowena.

I pulled into a spot in front of Winchell's Donut House.

The public phone there was a scummy mess, marked with the leftover tracks of the bums who habituate the place.

A cruel, grimy, sticky combination of donut glaze and dirty black coffee coats the receiver and the keys; it was the perfect appliance for an anonymous call.

Pulling my little black phone book from my vest pocket, I flipped through the pages (with now sticky fingers), finally finding the word

"Gamer" scrawled in a semi-legible slant across the 'T' page—a code for Kaya.

I dropped a quarter in the slot on top of the phone; I could hardly wait as the money fell to the bottom of the unit with a hard clink and dial tone.

Carefully, I dialed the ten digits, and after two rings, Kaya answered, her voice resonating within me the way it always had.

In my mind's eye, I could see her on the other end.

"Hello?" she says.

"Kaya. It's Justin, Justin Larkin."

"Oh, Justin. Hello, Justin. How are you?"

She seemed excited when I called. I searched for words, the way I always did when I spoke with her—never mind the interceding decades—but nothing profound came to my lips; rather, the most ridiculous and benign comments slipped past them. There was never a plan, rhyme, or reason; it was all in the moment.

"Kaya, I just called to see how you are, how you're doing."

"I am doing simply fine, just fine. My son is just returning from Japan, and I'm on my way to the airport to pick him up," she declares.

"I didn't know you have a son. You have a son?" I asked rather stupidly.

"Yes, one son," Kaya replied.

"Wow, that's great, great,"

"I have to go now; we're on our way to the airport. Can we speak later?"

"Sure, when should I call you?" I asked.

"Call me tomorrow, okay?"

"Sure, I'll call you tomorrow."

I replied, hanging up the phone.

Early Morning

The office sofa was surprisingly soft, much softer than the bed might have been at home, with me facing in one direction, Lacy in the other, tension in the air, and a shotgun under the bed.

The first morning light streamed through the large plate glass windows overlooking the city, lighting them with a red-blue tint.

Moving quickly, I went into the streets, where homeless people were covered in ancient and filthy rags and old newspapers curled in building entries.

A brisk morning dew and slight mist shrouded the otherwise deserted streets on the uneventful five-block walk to the Athletic Club.

Re-entering the locker room, warm shower under my belt, I donned my blue gym trunks, exquisitely decorated with "LAAC" in cursive script on the side, and a blue tee shirt bearing the same logo.

While jogging the indoor track, my sadness and anger were overcome with pleasant thoughts.

At least something good had come from the morning hours: the dawn of a new day. The early rise and brisk walk in the crisp morning air with Brahms's strings ringing in my ears made me realize that beauty and peace abound if one opens one's eyes!

I jogged down the six flights to the small cleaners adjacent to the club and entered, removing my headphones to speak to the small, nervous Hispanic woman who greeted me.

"Hello, my suit was dropped off an hour ago. Larkin is the name," I said.

"Yes," she replied.

"Um… I'm here to get it?"

She looked at me with a corkscrewed mouth.

"Sorry, sir, the suit is not ready. Did you specify *Rapido* when you brought it in?"

"I didn't bring it down. I had Greg from the club bring it down; I am sure he did; he speaks perfect English," I declared.

"Sir, he didn't say *Rapido*. Can you come back in an hour?"

I gave her a look that could've killed and was about to unload on her, but I thought better of it – no need to spoil the excellent mood.

But my emotions overtook me. Hating myself for it, I heard my voice growl,

"Give me my goddamn suit."

She handed me the crumpled ball of slacks and jacket, and I stepped into the two-by-two-foot dressing room.

Nothing but a short curtain separated us, a curtain that terminated three feet from the floor, leaving a gap designed by some miscreant to humiliate me.

I am sure.

I put the squashed mess on as best I could, rubbing the legs and jacket with my hands to smooth the wrinkles, knowing all along that the attendant was probably laughing her ass off as I continued my struggle.

My hands were in plain view, and I rubbed my legs, which were fully exposed in the gap between the floor and the curtain.

The beautiful morning was over for me!

Cursing to the four winds, a lunatic in a wrinkled suit, I slinked down the street, passing a bum in similar attire.

A Splinter in the Heart

Back in the office again, safely at my desk, I gazed down at the city below and the people waking up for another day of whatever they do to earn their keep.

Behind the conference table, I logged into the personnel department's pre-employment screening portal.

I organized it personally a few years back to allow human resources access to public records databases, including credit and criminal checks, property ownership, pending and completed lawsuits, marriages, births, divorces, prior employment history, and other useful criteria.

Company Policy, which I also wrote for this portal, strictly prohibited its use by anyone except for the initial screening of new hires, but I couldn't help myself.

I typed in her married name, Kaya Gustafsson, and the results trickled onto the screen.

I sat perfectly still save for my eyes, which carefully rolled across every tidbit of information.

Sure, I'd known her phone number and address for years, and naturally, her married name, but a lot of the recent information was listed under her maiden name, a clear sign of leftist feminism.

The results painted a clear picture; I could connect the dots. Her employment and connections reminded me of the Echo Park Lefties, a type I knew well.

Her records demonstrated a strong association with left-leaning production companies, few religious connections, and sporadic employment.

Her husband turned out to be an itinerant jazz artist, born in Sweden (a Socialist), without a doubt.

They'd lived on the West Side of Los Angeles all these years; it was as clear as an open book: a West Side Liberal, you can take that to the Bank.

No doubt Kaya laughed at the Lord!

Indeed, Kaya and I had grown apart on politics and theology, but perhaps that was simply a consequence of our separation.

That said, the best thing for now was to ignore those things. We can undoubtedly reconcile such things once we are together.

In any event, emotional concerns are always of higher order, clearly trumping mere temporal matters such as these.

As Eric strolled into my office, I noted a new air of confidence in his walk, a swagger that I found a tad bit disturbing.

Then again, why shouldn't he swagger? He was the man like I was once – sales are king.

Eric walked toward the window to view the city far below. I followed but felt a twinge of vertigo, so I backed off behind the conference table again.

Feeling better, I said,

"I was reviewing some data online about Kaya."

"Justin, don't tell me you used the personnel portal; I thought that was prohibited for personal use," Eric replied incredulously.

"Who's in charge here? It's not going to hurt anybody, and besides, I found out some interesting things: she's a producer of a bunch of left-wing garbage, and her husband? He's a two-bit horn player; she could have done so much better; it's a fuckin' shame she's wasting her life like that!"

"Justin, you're crazy."

"Dude, there's more. I checked out her financial condition. It looks like there have been some hard times.

From what I can tell, she supports the horn player, and it looks like, at one point, they were so low on cash that they had their car repossessed.

What a waste!

She was such a great girl! How she could attach herself to a loser like that is a mystery to me. I bet that socialist Swede got her involved in these leftie productions to boot. What a waste."

Eric just looked at me, his jaw dropped open.

"Larkin, what's come over you? You're obsessed! You need to see someone; you need a rest. Why don't you take Lacy on a vacation or something?"

"What the fuck do you know? Look, I'm a curious fellow, and there's no harm. It's simple research; I'm just looking up an old friend. What's wrong with that?"

Eric looked at me hard, right in the eye. Then he grabbed me by the shoulders and pushed me down hard onto a rolling Steelcase swivel chair, which shot across the room, finally coming to a hard stop against the picture window.

A plate of glass was the only thing separating me from a twenty-three-story fall to my death.

His face against mine, he screamed,

"Justin, have you forgotten who you're married to? Have you forgotten for whom you work? Have you forgotten that your father-in-law is the chairman of this company? Think, man, think!"

"Eric, listen, quick, pull me away from this window; this is fuckin' dangerous!"

Eric pushed the chair away from the windows toward the conference table, and I recomposed.

"Listen, Eric, please relax. Sit down on the other side of the table, the window side, please."

Eric sat down where I pointed, and I took my position safely on the opposite side and I continued.

"First of all, I've done nothing wrong, and second of all, there's nothing to worry about, so chill. It's nothing, just curiosity."

"Well, I hope so, but you gotta cool it. I mean it. This is getting really serious. I'm concerned," Eric said somberly and intensely, as if he meant it.

"I'm fine, but hold on a minute. I'll show you it's nothing. I'm going to call her right now."

"What!" Eric screamed.

Pushing the Steelcase chair even closer to the conference table, I hit 32# on the black desktop phone.

The speaker kicked on, and the number rang. I looked up at Eric.

His mouth was wide open, but nothing was coming out.

"I preprogrammed the number, smart huh?"

A female voice answered the phone.

"Hello?"

Eric was silent, watching, terrified. Then I spoke:

"Hello, Kaya. This is Justin, Justin Larkin."

"Oh, hello, Justin," Kaya said.

"Kaya, listen. I've come across this source that wants to fund a project, and they need some help, so I thought of you. It would also be an opportunity to get together after all these years, killing two birds with one stone."

"What kind of… what are you talking about? Kaya responded in a voice of surprise and confusion.

"I don't want to tell you about this over the phone. Can we meet somewhere?"

"I don't know. I don't know," replied Kaya.

This was my opening, and I took it.

"I haven't seen you for years; naturally, I would love to see you. That is obvious. You're an old friend.

However, in this case, it's about a project I came across that may interest you and pays very well. Sure, there are a few bucks in it for me, but that's not what's important here. I want you and my other friend to do well. You'd be perfect for this project; my buddy's company would have the needed person.

It's a win-win all over the place.

Can you meet me at the Tropical Café on Sunset today? I'll tell you all about it."

"Justin, I don't know; let me check my agenda."

Kaya paused and then said,

"No… wait…"

We can hear her thumbing through some pages, and then she speaks.

"I do have to be at Public Television Studios on Sunset at 2 o'clock, so that's right down the Street from the Tropical; I'm finishing a project there, and I haven't been to the Tropical in years. So, okay, Justin, great timing. How about 1:15?

Kaya paused a bit, and I couldn't believe my plan was working, so I held off. Then she continued.

Now, Justin, are you absolutely sure there is funding? I really could use another project. I don't have time to mess around but will make time if you have a project."

She said, with a trace of hope and warning in her voice.

I heard it and replied to assure her. There was no way I wanted to mess this up; this was clearly a time when the economy of language was of benefit.

"Yes, yes, funding, there is funding, no problem – I'll see you then," I said.

"Okay, goodbye, Justin. 1:15 at the Tropical, then.

As she hung up, Eric backed his chair away from the table and looked at me in disbelief.

"What's this about a job in a film? Is this bullshit?"

"Yeah, and so what?

Listen, Eric, there's something I have to find out. Something is missing in my life; somehow, this person is the key. Dude, I am totally frozen. I can't do anything until I resolve this."

"What are you talking about? You built a business. You have a beautiful wife and house and a fine son. What is the problem here? Do you want to ruin all this? Eric said.

"I don't know. I know something is missing. It's like when you have a splinter in your foot. It won't kill you, but it's a gnawing pain, and you can't ignore it. I went to a shrink, a good one, and he couldn't tell me anything. I even saw a gypsy fortune teller,"

"What did she say?" asked Eric in amazement.

"She uh… she knew about Kaya. She said there was another woman in my life and told me Kaya cared about me."

"Justin, what are you going to do?"

"I'm going to meet Kaya and see what happens."

"Man, this is a bad idea. Think about your family—the business. You could lose everything. I'm serious—don't do it."

As Eric left the office, leaving me to my devices, I sat and pondered. I'd barely heard a word he said. Or rather, I didn't consider his words at all. I was doing this thing.

The elevator descended to the lobby like a whirlwind; I sleepwalked past Willard at the front desk, handed my ticket to the parking attendant, and rolled out of the lot onto Grand Avenue, heading toward Third and Sunset.

After making a hard left on Sunset and a quick right on Parkman, I passed the Tropical and parked in the alley behind the old Chinese pharmacy.

The Tropical always had a funky feel, but lately, it seemed scummier than before. It seemed like they didn't clean it, and if they did, it was just a surface clean, as Lacy liked to say.

I'm not entirely sure why I invited Kaya to meet me there, but the place was peaceful, making it a good spot for a conversation.

If Kaya was telling the truth, she had an appointment nearby, so perhaps it was a fortunate choice, or maybe she genuinely wanted to see me.

It's also possible she was intrigued by the prospect of a job, and I happened to be the one who could offer it to her. I'm uncertain which of these possibilities is true, but I decided to cover my bases like any good salesperson or gambler.

Carmen was behind the bar. There were only a few patrons in the café.

Most of the morning crowd had already made it off to wherever the deadbeat lefties and wannabe artists go during the day, only to return at night to hang out.

"Hey, Carmen, you see a beautiful girl waiting for me?"

"You crazy, Justin. No beautiful girl is waiting for you!" She smiled and laughed.

"Just wait," I say.

"A beautiful girl is coming. Please, a café con leche."

Taking a second to look around the room, I noticed that it had changed a great deal from the days when "The Cuban" owned it. Back then, businessmen of all types would stop by for a good shot of espresso and a cigar.

One day, the Cuban died, and Jeff purchased the place.

The old Cuban would be turning in his grave if he saw what the place had become. Its walls, now covered with pictures of Fidel and Che, clearly in admiration, told it all.

Little do the Commie motherfuckers who come here realize that the legitimate Cubano who opened this place and ran it for years was a fervent anti-Communist whose family had suffered harshly under Castro.

If the Cuban visited it now, he'd burn the place down, I'm sure.

Carmen handed me the drink.

When the Cubans were here, they took their time and were proud. Now it's slam bam—thank you, ma'am—no wonder the country is going down the tubes.

As I sipped the lukewarm, tasteless brew, I meandered towards the back wall of the café, plastered with pictures of Che fishing off the

Cuban shores beside his hirsute buddy Fidel, just like a couple of happy tourists.

Finding a table near the Sunset entrance with an excellent view of the comings and goings, I sat and waited. A large picture window faced Sunset Boulevard; there was no way I could miss anyone who entered.

Cars and buses traveled by. I was almost hypnotized by the motions of people crossing back and forth and cars stopping and starting.

The café's aluminum door swung open and shut as customers came and went.

Suddenly, I heard the screech of a nearby chair against the concrete floor.

My eyes flitted upward.

Time stopped.

All motion ceased.

There was silence—a reverence where, seconds before, there had been noise and confusion.

Now, vehicles outside the plate glass window moved as if they were on air cushions, and all disorder and chaos disappeared.

Motionless, we stood face to face; then, without even a word, we grabbed each other and embraced, my arms around her yellow blouse and hers around my wrinkled and musty garb.

I buried my face in her shoulder with my eyes closed tight. She pushes her neck tightly under my chin.

We held each other for what may have been seconds or hours.

Loosening our grips, I was dazed and confused, tête à tête and overwhelmed, but I spoke.

"Kaya, I'm so glad you came."

Her perfunctory reply surprised me; it was as if I were a stranger.

"Of course. It's really nice to see you," she says.

She stood in silence, but I was not to be denied.

I took in her light brown skin, inhaled the scent that wafted off her amber hair, and concluded that she looked the same as the last time I saw her—nothing had changed.

"Kaya, just talk, just talk! I love your voice. Please talk."

Dismissing my words and speaking as if in a rush, she said,

"Justin, that's sweet, and it's great to see you, but I have to be at KCET in thirty minutes, so please tell me about this project. That's why I came here."

"You've only just now arrived!" I exclaimed with a bit of distress.

Looking at me in a way that revealed a note of sympathy, she said,

"You always do fascinating things. I always knew you would, but dear, I am short on time today. We can talk longer some other day. I need to sort of cut to it right now, OK?"

"It's been twenty years since we last saw each other, and every time we've spoken, the conversation always ends before it starts," I said.

"What do you want from me? Listen, I only came here because you said you had a project. I just wanted to see if I could help."

My disappointment was unmistakable. She threw me a charity smile

. "Look, sure, I wanted to see you, Justin; sure, it is nice to see you."

She reached over and touched my hand, then pulled away and continued,

"But I do need to mention one thing that is of some concern."

"Mention what?" I asked.

"Listen, it's not really a big deal, but now's as good a time as any, and this needs to be said."

"What, Kaya?"

"Balter, my husband, knows you've been calling our apartment, and he claims you're hanging up on him.

You need to stop!

He knows that it's you, and actually, it's really pissing him off; he told me he's going to call the police soon.

Balter bought this caller ID contraption; he's storing the call history and says he'll take it to the LAPD and file a complaint."

"Is it a fuckin' crime to call someone?" I said.

Again, Kaya grabbed my hand, this time keeping hold of it.

"I think it is a crime... so please stop."

I pulled my hand away and whimpered,

"What's wrong with me?

What have I done wrong?

You kept my letters! You told me that on the phone, remember?"

Kaya was silent, so I continued.

"I spoke to a shrink and then to a psychic. I told the shrink you kept my letters for over twenty years, and he was speechless. He didn't say anything."

"Do you want the letters back? If you want them back, you can have them," she retorted.

"No, I don't want them back, and I swear that shrink was confused. It was clear that your keeping the letters threw him for a loop. He couldn't say I was crazy. He couldn't say anything."

"Justin, you asked a shrink about us?"

"Yes, it's gotta be weird that I keep thinking about you. I know that."

Kaya just looked at me, clearly reconsidering. Then she said,

"Great. So, you talked to a shrink. Let me guess—he told you to stop this, right?"

"No, he said nothing like that! And there was this psychic. Truth be told, she was more impressive than the shrink. I said nothing, yet she immediately told me another woman besides Lacy was in my life. She knew everything.

Kaya, I told her you didn't care for me, but she insisted you did. When I told her about the letters, she swooned that you kept them for

20 years. I mean it. I never saw anybody swoon before, but she swooned… right in front of my face.”

Kaya didn't seem to hear what I was saying, or at least pretended not to, but I knew she was listening, even when she interjected,

“Justin, what is this project about?”

“What project?”

“Jesus… the project! The reason you asked me to come here in the first place. You told me there was a project.”

“Kaya, to be honest, there isn't one. I just wanted to see you.”

Kaya's frustration seemed mixed with delight.

“Okay, Justin, I see. Look, it was nice seeing you, okay?”

As she turned to exit, I grabbed her by the right arm and said,

“Kaya, we fucked up. We fucked up royally.”

She stopped and turned, looking pensive and sweet, and whispered,

“Oh, Justin!”

Leaning forward, she kissed me on the cheek and quickly turned away.

Before I could recover, she was out the door, disappearing as quickly as she came.

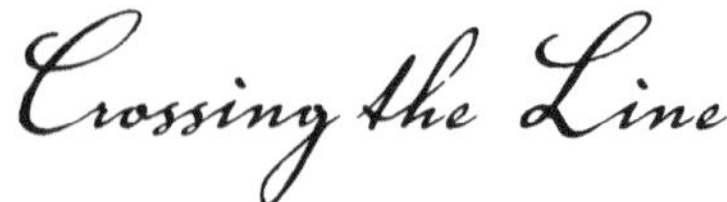

Numbness overcame me.

The stench of my wrinkled garments filled the room.

Kaya seemed just the opposite: clean, fragrant, and carefree.

Her exterior screamed abstract art, refined art, and a casual elegance with an elusive smile.

On the outside, she was the artist, and she was calm and mild; on the inside, she was a labyrinth, a rolling sea, an endless series of calculations of infinite complexity; one would be hard to know if there was order to the madness or merely absurd convolution.

Sitting down, I gazed out the window and attempted to create some order, some perspective.

All I could think of was Lacy, but a few miles from there.

What was she thinking? What was she doing?

Moreover, what am I doing?

Tired and perplexed, I reasoned it was no time to face my family.

The best course of action was to sneak into the house and gather some clothes.

I executed the plan with perfection.

I was careful to see that Lacy's car was not in the driveway; I rapidly pulled in and gathered what I needed for the next few days, quickly throwing it all into a suitcase.

Running out to the car, I set the suitcase in the backseat and jammed out of Laughlin Park, down the street, and past the gate without catching a glimpse of Lacy.

I headed toward the Athletic Club, which I figured was the best place to stay until I worked this stuff out.

I called the house solely to leave a voice message.

"Hello, Lacy. I'm deeply sorry about the other afternoon; my apologies, and believe me, I'm working on my temper and the 'working too much' issue, which I believe is the source of many of our problems. I am seeing Dr. Mankoff tomorrow. I'll stay at the LAAC for the next couple of days so we can both have more peace, and I'll do some serious thinking about fixing this. Believe me, I know I need to spend more and better time with you. I understand that now. Call me if you need me. I love you; things will be fine. Lacy, I love you; please forgive me while I figure this out."

That should hold Lacy while I worked through it all.

And it wasn't totally dishonest.

Maybe my words were entirely true; I was not sure anymore.

I did know that my experience thus far with Kaya indicated that she wasn't being honest with me, was conflicted, and worked both sides of the fence.

I had to take affirmative action and clarify matters.

Standing by and doing nothing would not help either Kaya or myself; I needed to act immediately.

Getting a room at the Los Angeles Athletic Club was never a problem.

Opening the door to my room, I placed my suitcase on the bed, opened it, and grabbed some trunks. I took the elevator down to the jogging track, and after working up a good sweat, I headed back to the room for a shower.

With my suit pants strewn over the bed, I changed into fresh blue jeans and a dress shirt.

I figured I'd head towards Kaya's Westside apartment.

After speaking to her and seeing her in person, it was obvious to me that it was in our mutual best interests to resolve this long-simmering issue—the sooner, the better.

We were both suffering, but to be sure, she was in more denial than I was.

Despite my predicament with Lacy, I was feeling good.

It's hard to describe now — I felt a distinct kind of excitement, an out-of-this-world feeling, and utter disconnectedness from my actual life.

I noticed a Bose Wave on the nightstand, worlds away from the drop-a-dime monstrosity Lacy and I adored at Jerry's.

But that day seemed like decades ago, and it was.

Grabbing my suitcase, I took the elevator to the ground floor. (I wasn't about to leave without a change of clothes again.)

Who knew what would happen?

I bypassed the front desk and walked down the fifteen steps to the parking garage below.

There she was — my Jaguar, clean as a whistle. That Fernando was great. He had the valet key and must have seen me come in.

If you're ever at the club and need a clean car, Fernando's your man!

I jumped in and made a left onto Seventh Street, drove past Grand, took the next left and a quick right onto Sixth Street, up the entrance ramp of the Harbor Freeway South, and then sped up to eighty, making my way toward Kaya's home on Veterans Avenue, opposite Westwood Park.

Her apartment complex was called "The Westwood Park Apartments."

Clever…

A few Sundays a year, mainly in the summer, I'd find myself parked at this curb, staring at Kaya's apartment on the off chance that she would appear, and I could catch a glimpse of her, but I never got so lucky.

Sometimes, I'd stop at the local Trader Joe's market or some Chinese fast-food joint, hoping she'd be there or perhaps touch something she once touched.

Sitting opposite her apartment and scanning her driveway, tension mixed with excitement and tinged with outright fear.

What if I was noticed?

In front of Kaya's house, I experienced the same anxiety that I did on each visit to Little Tokyo.

In Little Tokyo, however, there was no fear of discovery or of violating any law; here, there was.

My god, I was in front of her house!

Looking out on the park side of the street, I noticed boys tossing a hardball back and forth with ever-increasing speed.

The bright sun continued its march across the sky. An errant toss sent the ball directly in front of the Jaguar, where it abruptly stopped.

I dared not retrieve it, but no matter; a freckled-faced boy of about thirteen with a regular boy's haircut ran in front of the car, bent down, and grabbed the baseball.

Standing up in front of the car, he gave me a long look after tossing the baseball back to his friend, who was standing a good seventy-five feet away in the park.

His eyes lingered, piercing through my windshield as if he knew who I was and what I was doing, and then he ambled back into the grass and his game.

A few seconds later, I heard a rapidly approaching engine. Glancing at the rear-view mirror, I saw an LAPD cruiser pulling up behind me.

It stopped less than a car's length away.

A cop sprung from the black and white and walked to the driver's side of my car. I noticed a second person holding back in the car. Out of habit and theory, I opened the door to meet him on equal terms, mano-a-mano, but before I could get out, he barked,

"Sir, stay in your car."

I closed the door as the six-foot copper stopped by my window, staring down at me with a half-smile on his face.

Then he crouched down so his face was at the window level of the low-slung Jaguar.

"Sir, can I see your driver's license, registration, and insurance card?"

"Sure, Officer, but what is this about?"

His face tightened a bit, and he repeated,

"Sir, can I see your driver's license, registration, and insurance card?"

Reaching toward the right visor, I looked for my little document holder, but it wasn't there.

"Fuckin' shit!" I blurted out.

"What did you say?" asked the officer.

"Sorry, Officer. I can't find the document holder. It's gone, but this is my car."

Glancing toward the park, I saw the kids who'd been tossing baseballs approaching the car, apparently drawn by the scene.

"The fuckin' guy who cleaned my car must have misplaced it.."

"Sir, can you please watch the profanity? Not only does it disturb me, but there are kids around here."

"Oh, sure. Sorry, Officer, but can you please check your computer? My name is Justin Larkin, and this is my car. I am sure you can find the ownership details through the plate numbers."

The cop seems bothered and replies briskly,

"Sir, we don't have that information on the computer, and even if we did, the law requires that you carry your registration and insurance card at all times."

Laughing, I looked up and said,

"Come on, Officer. Are you telling me that simple information about this car is not in the database? That's impossible."

The kids watched with ever-increasing intensity and interest as the officer stared down at me.

"Your driver's license, now," he demanded.

I could feel eyes focused on me. I lifted myself up on the seat to pull the wallet from my rear trouser pocket, but it wasn't there.

I'd probably left it in my suit pocket on the bed at the Athletic Club.

"Sir, I must have left my wallet in my suit pants at the Athletic Club."

The officer did not seem impressed.

I was thinking, Come on now, Justin, use your skills; you can outsmart the son of a bitch.

"Officer, I'm sure you understand. You're married, aren't you?"

He only stared at me blankly, which I took to mean yes.

"Well, sir, I checked into the LA Athletic Club today," I whispered, leaning a bit closer to his ear and lowering my voice.

"My wife was a bit upset with me, so to keep the peace, I stayed at the Club, if you catch my drift. I'm sure you must have been in a similar situation. In any event, I am pretty sure my wallet is in my suit pants at the Club. So, there ya go, that explains it all; there is really no problem here."

Much to my chagrin, his face remained stern.

"Sir, can you please step out of the car and put your hands on the hood?"

I complied.

What choice did I have?

Now, one minute before, I was sitting in my car, minding my own business, now only a few minutes later, there I stood, opposite Kaya's fuckin' house, right near a public park, surrounded by a bunch of kids and with my hands on the frickin' hood, who would have imagined?

"Officer, please listen. I am Justin Larkin, and I own this car."

"Sir, just stay there and keep quiet, please. Keep those hands on the car."

Suddenly, I felt like shit; I actually started to feel sick.

The crowd grew bigger each second. It now seemed like half the park surrounded me and was watching the show. The officer returned to the squad car and said something to his partner, who appeared to be typing away on the cruiser computer.

Then he swaggered back to me and said,

"Listen, sir, please keep your hands on the car!"

My hands were on the fuckin' car; I didn't move them; what was his trip?

He looked at me as if he was going to reason with me, and in a calm voice said,

"Sir, let me explain: the initial reason for this stop was an investigation involving incidents with children near this exact spot over the past several months. Naturally, we placed cameras here, and they recorded a Jaguar matching yours at this spot on several occasions."

"I just got here."

"Sir, we know exactly how long you have been here. There is a camera right over there."

He points to a light pole, and I see a camera pointing at me.

"So, you have been recording me?"

"We sure have. Anyone under that camera has been recorded and archived for our investigation."

That set me off for some reason—or rather… enraged me.

They were recording citizens. Stealing their privacy?

Just then, all the lights went out in my head. Taking my hands off the Jaguar, I did a little jig: I was literally hopping mad.

Seeing red, I stalked toward the policemen.

"Hey, Mr. Cop: you can go fuck yourself. What is this, Nazi Germany? What or who gives you the right to go around poking into citizens' private lives, taking pictures of them when they don't even know it? What's this shit coming to?

Who the fuck are you anyway, the fucking Gestapo?"

The officer was foaming at the mouth – what else could I expect?

The cop grabbed me and threw me across the hood of the cruiser, pushing my cheek against the sun-warmed metal. He put his face close enough to whisper in my ear.

"Listen, citizen asshole, move your fuckin' ass again, and I'll going test my newly issued taser against your, sorry ass."

He straightened up and let go, stepping away to get something from inside the Crown Vic. As luck would have it, he had positioned my head and eyes with a perfect view of Kaya's house.

And what timing!

There she was, pulling out of her long apartment driveway in a beat-to-shit white Toyota Land Cruiser, which stopped halfway between the end of the driveway and the street.

The driveway had a strip of grass down the middle, and I could see oil dripping from the Land Cruiser, making spots on the lawn.

I wondered if Kaya knew about the leak.

Her husband Balter, a large white fellow, was carrying two huge suitcases, and trailing him was a nicely dressed little boy about seven years old.

Balter looked across the street and then continued to load the Land Cruiser. The cop returned – I guess he got something from the cruiser – and put his mouth close to my head so the crowd wouldn't hear.

"You called me a fuckin' Gestapo. I don't like that," he said, grabbing my neck.

I gasped and then said in a muffled voice,

"No, no, what I mean is that having cameras all over the place is right out of 1984."

The cop drew back a bit and looked at me.

"1984?" he asked blankly.

Before I could explain the allusion, a backup unit arrived.

At the wheel was a short, stocky Mexican American kid, probably an ex-Marine, who pulled his cruiser alongside the Jaguar, double-parking on Veterans.

Leaping from his cruiser, he asked,

"What do you need, Sarge?"

"Watch this guy!" came the reply from my "friend."

The Sarge walked away, leaving the other cop a few feet from me, with his hand on his pistol.

I made sure I kept my face pressed against the hood. His head was half-cocked, and his eyes were aimed at me like laser lights. His feet were planted firmly on the pavement, and he stood guard as a few minutes passed.

The Sarge returned with a small pad. Out of the corner of my eye, I see him scribbling something.

Finally, he stepped over to me and put his mouth next to my upturned ear; the other was still crushed against the hood.

"So, you think I'm a Nazi? That's what you said, right?"

I figured it best to shut up.

Moving away from me, the Sarge swaggered around a bit and then stopped in front of the Jag and announced for all to hear,

"Maybe you're the guy you claim to be, but you have provided no proof."

Pausing for a few seconds, he looked up at the crowd, and then he announced as if on a PA system,

"And let me be the first to inform you that even if this car is yours, you are violating several sections of the vehicle code, including failure to produce a valid driver's license, registration card, and proof of insurance on demand. Therefore, this vehicle is subject to impoundment. Please remain where you are."

Walking back to his cruiser with his deputy watching me like a hawk, he parlayed with his partner, who I assumed was communicating with HQ via the onboard computer.

I knew this was looking serious, but the facts were that I was innocent, at least of any crimes they had in mind.

So, I shouldn't have been worried.

Paperwork is paperwork; it's really not that bad. That said, the scene in front of all these kids and Kaya across the street had me sweating like a pig.

Why Kaya did nothing to help me was disconcerting, to say the least.

"Officer, please come here! I need to explain something!" I yelled out.

To my surprise, Sarge strolled back and stood five feet from me.

"Officer, please, can you come a bit closer? I don't want all these people to hear."

He stepped a few feet closer, and I pleaded,

"Listen, Officer, see that woman in the Land Cruiser across the street? She knows me. I'm not a pedophile, far from it. I was waiting for that woman in the Land Cruiser. Can you see the Land Cruiser over there?"

"Yes," he replied after a slight neck twist and a gander at Kaya's Car.

"Just ask her who I am. She's a friend of mine. I just saw her today. She'll confirm who I am."

"What's her name?" the officer demanded.

"Kaya Gustafsson," I said.

The Sarge looked down at the pavement and started to giggle.

"Then why didn't you just knock on her door? Why were you sitting here for an hour watching these kids?"

"Officer, it's a personal matter between Kaya and me. Just run across the street, and she'll tell you I'm Justin Larkin. Please."

The officer backed up and said to me sternly,

"Mister, if this is a waste of my time—"

"It isn't," I interrupt.

"Trust me. Just go ask her, and she'll tell you who I am. Please go quickly before she leaves."

As he walked across the street, Kaya was carefully backing out of the driveway, suitcases neatly stacked in the rear of the Land Cruiser.

That dick Balter sat upright in the passenger seat, like some pompous ass, while the kid was strapped tight in the backseat.

The Sarge marched across the middle of Veterans like some traffic cop on Broadway and Sixth.

Kaya stopped the vehicle and rolled down the window as the Sarge approached.

He leaned into Kaya as I craned my neck to see what was happening.

The gawking crowd remained entranced.

Sweating my ass off, I felt the same way I did on the operating table in New Orleans years earlier, with my fate in God's hands.

Sarge and Kaya were deeply discussing, with Balter animated and leaning towards Sarge.

Finally, Sarge moved aside, and Kaya gently pulled the Land Cruiser away and out of sight.

Sarge returned and said,

"The gentleman in the car confirmed that a car resembling yours was parked where it is now many times, and the lady in the car, Ms. Gustafsson, seemed to agree.

What could I say?

Things had gone from bad to worse any way you cut it: no driver's license, no insurance card, no registration, and the cops claiming they had video proof I was some pedophile.

Furthermore, Kaya's husband claimed he had seen my car in this exact spot many times, and he was right.

Only I knew for sure that it was my car and also that I was not a pedophile. I knew I could provide all the documentation needed, and Kaya knew that, too, so why didn't she say anything?

Sarge stood looking over me; the Mexican American Cop also covered me.

"Listen, Sarge, this is bullshit, and you know it. This is my car, and your computer has to know it, yet you refuse to check. You claim you have a video of me at this spot, but if you do, it will show I have never left my car.

So, it seems that Orwell only got it half right: Big Brother is here alright, but George neglected to tell us that Big Brother is an Idiot. What do you think, Sarge? Is that the deal?"

Sarge just looked at me and sneered, then directed his attention to the Mexican American cop.

"I've had about enough of this guy. Cuff him, read him his rights, and put him in my car; I want to bring this guy to jail personally."

"Lift your hands off the hood, step back three feet from the car, and keep your hands behind your back," the Mexican American Cop said.

I did as he said.

"Now spread your legs!" he shouted.

The officer put the cuffs on me, reached into my front pocket, and pulled out the Jag's keys.

How could this be happening?

He loaded me into Sarge's car, and Sarge took the driver's seat, started the car up, and asked:

"Have you ever been to Jail before, Mr. Larkin?"

"No."

"It's not that bad. You'll be able to make local phone calls. Do you take any medications?"

"No"

I sat stone silently in the back of the car ride to the jail, not knowing what to think.

I could hear the Sarge and his partner bantering, but it seemed like mumbles.

No words made any sense, just the coming night, the growing darkness, the hard seat, and the feeling that although it was almost dark, everyone we passed could somehow look in and know who I was.

Reason's Undoing

All I could think of were my dad's words: "Don't ever call me if you go to jail."

Not to worry, Dad, you're the last on my list!

I couldn't believe Kaya put me in that position. She was right there; she had to know it was me. One word and I could have been free, but it didn't come.

The Los Angeles Police Station is an unimpressive mid-century structure. Actually, like everything built, designed, or created by The City of Los Angeles in the last fifty years, it's a piece of shit.

One good thing about being a criminal is you entered the rear of the structure and weren't exposed to this abomination head-on. The cruiser rounded the block, turned, and entered a vast, mostly empty parking structure.

The rear entrance to the jail had a simple façade, resembling an old-school bungalow.

It was somewhat comforting and, to my mind, more tasteful than the grand entrance we bypassed.

Sarge handed me over to some fellow police officers (it seemed I was expected), who led me through the paces of fingerprints and mug shots.

Then, I was tossed into a 7x10 cell full of Mexicans with a telephone and a scummy toilet.

The Mexicans were crowded around the telephone hanging from a board attached to the cell wall. Opposite the phone was a worn and beaten wooden bench.

Just a few feet away, we could see, but not touch, a modern police station with happy cops chattering away.

And why shouldn't they be happy, with the generous pensions, guaranteed wages, and plenty of time to hob knob and eat donuts, not to mention those fancy uniforms and, yes, the gun – I'd be happy too!

Yet in my world, better said, our world, that of the hardened criminal, it was a different story: a toilet none of us would sit on, a bench as hard as a stone, and only one telephone for me, Jose, Jesus, and Pablo.

To top it off, we couldn't discuss our shared plight as we didn't share a language, which was a blatant attempt by "The Man" to break our spirits.

At last, an opening came, and I reached the phone. There was no way I was going to call Lacy. Based on our last discussion, she'd likely have let me sit in there forever.

Besides, there was no simple or even believable way to explain this. I've heard the whole story, and I'm not sure I believe it.

Eric was the logical choice, as he worked for me.

It always seemed that employees, while getting regular checks, would often go the extra mile if they knew what was good for them, and Eric, I was sure, was smart enough to know the drill.

He'll keep it quiet; I'll call him, I decided.

"Eric, listen, I'm in fuckin' jail, the jailhouse section of the Los Angeles Police Department."

"What?" he asked after a pause.

"Eric, listen and don't talk. I'm in a fuckin' jail cell in Parker Center or whatever they call it now. I was caught driving without my license."

"You're in jail?"

"Eric, just listen.

"I am at Parker Center, LA Jail. Go to the Athletic Club, get my wallet, and that asshole Deutsch, the fuckin' attorney. Get him down here."

"What's Deutsch's number?"

"Dude, I'm in fuckin' jail. I have no goddamn idea. Find it and tell him to come down here fast and to bring his frickin' checkbook or whatever habeas corpus shit he needs to get me the fuck out."

"Sure, Justin. Just one thing: does this have anything to do with that girl, Kaya? Just asking."

"No, not really. I was near her house when it happened, but this has nothing to do with her.

Get down here, fast!

Bring Deutsch!"

As I hung up the phone, I glanced at the Mexicans sitting on the crowded bench. I could sense a newfound respect in their eyes as they looked at me; my authority on the phone must have reminded them of their Patrón.

Who else but a boss would dare talk like that? They immediately slid over, making room for me on the bench.

We sat there for a few minutes, and then some cops came and chained us together like a Parchment Farm Chain Gang.

They led us up a long, industrial hallway, stopping in front of a metal door with a porthole window.

Behind the metal door is a bunkhouse lined with cheap metal frames and flimsy mattresses arranged in neat rows.

Each row has about twenty bunks stacked three high.

The room was near capacity. Guys were in the beds; some stood or talked while others slept.

A soft drone permeated the place.

Making my way to a free bunk on the third tier, I was afforded an unrestricted view of the comings and goings from a perch of relative safety.

Throwing the threadbare blanket over myself, I lay there and gazed at the clock. Each second seemed like an eternity. I guess I was there an hour or two when I heard this on the loudspeaker:

"Larkin, Justin Larkin! Proceed to the exit."

Hearing the good news, I jumped off the bunk and onto the hard floor, making it over to the porthole door.

The jailer glared at my face and said,

"Put your wrist up to the window."

I did, and he read my wrist tag through the window for a second. Then, with extreme caution, he slowly opened the door, ensuring no tailgaters, and led me down a long hall.

A solid metal door was at the end of the long hall. The jailer opened it and let me into a small room.

It was so small that it reminded me of a waiting room at a doctor's office; it was just the size of Doctor Markoff's office. The psychiatrist I mentioned to Kaya and Lacy.

In the back of the room was a small wooden bench of pine or maple—I'm not sure which—with a new stain job; it looked lovely and could fit about two people at most.

Two feet before me was a counter with bulletproof glass separating me from a large, busy office.

Before I could take a seat, a middle-aged woman in civilian clothes appeared behind the bulletproof glass window and said,

"Step up to the window, please."

I did, and she handed me an envelope through a slot in the glass window. The envelope contained my Jaguar keys, phone, and belt.

"Is it all there? Check it carefully," she said.

"Yes, it's all here," I replied.

"Then sign on this line," she directed as she turned over the envelope and showed me a line to sign.

"Ma'am, do you have any idea where my car is?"

"Yes, you're really lucky it wasn't impounded. There was a mix-up, and the officers never called it in. I checked the cams. It's right where you were arrested."

Look!" she said.

She turned her screen around so I could see. Sure enough, it was sitting right where I left it: my Jag was bathed by the streetlight that supported the camera.

"Just get it soon; you don't want to get a ticket for overnight parking," she said.

While it was comforting to know that my car was still there, my ire about the cameras and the city's continued extortion of its citizens set my blood to boil.

However, I reasoned it might not have been time to vent. I figured I'd better shut up and get out of the place.

"Stand back. The door on your left will open quickly, and you may leave when it does. Good evening, Mr. Larkin," the woman said.

The door swung open to a vast, empty lobby—an immense space with no apparent function, just dark marble walls. I assumed Eric and Deutsch would be waiting, but neither was there.

Kaya stood alone, as pretty as a picture, framed by one of the enormous walls, with my coat neatly over her arms.

$Free$

"Kaya, what the heck are you doing here?"

"Let's just go," she curtly replied.

"I have your wallet and your coat."

She handed them to me.

"Justin, your attorney took care of everything with the city; he said he posted bond, and there was this younger guy—Eric, I think—he said he worked for you. He wanted to drive you home. I told him and the attorney that your car was near my house, and I would drive you to get it."

"Let's go."

"Thanks," I replied with a smile.

What luck!

I thought to myself, almost laughing, I would have gotten arrested years ago if I had known that this was all it took to get a ride with Kaya.

It was beyond absurd, but I went with it—don't look a gift horse in the mouth.

Kaya was stone silent and walked fast out of the station, exiting on First Street past the Grand Façade. She walked so quickly that I had to push hard to keep up.

"Was my wife here?" I asked.

Kaya kept walking and picked up her pace; it was almost as if she were running.

"No, I thought I might meet her. I was going to apologize for any trouble or confusion that Balter or I may have created.

When I returned home from dropping off Balter and Jamie at the airport, I heard you were taken to jail."

"How did you find out?"

"A couple of kids at the park told me the police took you away. It was quite a spectacle. I called the West Los Angeles police station, and they said you were taken downtown for booking, something about the cameras in the park."

"What did Robert say? The attorney?"

"He said you don't have to appear for a month. He kept asking Eric if he should call your wife.

The attorney wanted to know who I was, but Eric shut that down— it felt like he was protecting you.

I told them we were friends and that I'd drive you home. I'm sorry if Balter and I caused trouble by not identifying you. Maybe we could've stopped this."

The walk from the police station to Little Tokyo, where Kaya had parked her car, took just a few minutes, but we had to cross Little Tokyo Village to get to the lot where she had left her Land Cruiser.

As chance would have it, we walked right past the sushi restaurant where Eric and I had eaten the day before and right over the exact spot where the sushi cart had sat the last time we were together, maybe twenty years ago.

Grabbing her arm, I held her fast so she slowed her pace.

"Remember that little sushi cart that was here twenty years ago?" I asked.

"Justin, come on," she said, reluctantly admitting it.

"Naturally… I remember it. I remember all the times we were together."

"Wow, I'm shocked. I always thought you viewed me as an appendage. I can't believe you remember."

"Of course I do, but I can't believe this is happening," she said.

"What do you mean?"

"That I'm dragging you out of jail! That all this happened. Your wife should be picking you up, not me. Why didn't you call her in the first place?"

"Come on now, Kaya, what could I tell her? That I was hanging out in front of your house and that the cops picked me up? Or perhaps because they thought I was a pedophile?"

"Okay, I get it, but Justin—"

She stopped cold, spun around, and faced me.

"What the hell were you doing outside my house? That was insane! I should've left you to rot. What's wrong with you?"

"You know why, goddamn it," I muttered.

She narrowed her eyes. "Tell me."

"Because I love you. Always will. And in the end, you'll be my final thought— my final word will be your name."

A smirk played across her face, gone as quickly as it came. Then she turned serious and said,

"Justin, shut up. You're crazy. I'm taking you home now."

It was as though we were back in high school.

I touched Kaya's arm as if by accident, and then with more intent, I grabbed it, held on, and we walked through the Japanese Village arm in arm.

The Land Cruiser was parked across the street in a multi-storied garage.

I opened the driver's side for her.

She got in and sat down, reaching over to open the passenger door, but I didn't wait; I climbed over, laughing and tumbling into the passenger seat.

"Justin, what's wrong with you? I have two doors," she gasped.

"Sorry."

As we pulled out of the garage, I asked,

"Where are your son and husband going anyway?"

"They're in Sweden—my husband's from there. He's filming a movie for the next month, and my son went with him."

"Hum, the database had him down as a musician; I need to look into that," I mumbled.

"What?"

Kaya asked, her voice laced with confusion and a hint of concern.

"Oh, nothing. Listen, Kaya. When I was in front of your house, why didn't you help me?"

"What was I supposed to do? Admit I knew you?

The cop asked if I recognized you—if I had said yes, it would've made things worse.

Balter was already furious that you called.

If he knew it was you, he'd have made sure you weren't just in for the night but the week.

And yes, he recognized the car—he always watches.

It drives me insane."

As we pulled out of the lot and headed up Second Street toward the freeway, I reached over and took her hand.

She didn't pull away, and we held tight.

Sooner than I wished, we arrived at her apartment.

Kaya pulled into a space in front of her garage, and for a moment, neither of us moved.

Finally, we let go, stepped out of the Land Cruiser, swallowed by the LA Night.

The Drive

The Jaguar was right where I had left her, curled like a comfy cat under a streetlight, bathing in a yellowish glow.

Kaya's gaze lingered on the Jag, her eyes softening in a way that pulled at me.

She'd always had a thing for beautiful cars—her lawyer dad once surprised her with a brand-new BMW, a gleaming anomaly in our modest neighborhood.

Now, the rusted junker we pulled up in was worlds away from that sleek Beamer, its muffler rattling with every move.

I saw the flicker of longing in her expression, a quiet ache for what she once had—or maybe for what she thought she'd lost.

"Can I come in for coffee?"

"That might not be a good idea," Kaya said softly.

"OK, I'll take you for a ride; how's that?"

"Justin, are you nuts?" she snapped.

The mess with the cops, the drive to LAX with Balter ranting about you the whole time, Jamie stuck in the back hearing it all—and then after all that, I pick you up from jail out of the goodness of my heart, I am not even sure why I did it, I think it was a mistake.

Wasn't that enough?

And now you have the gall—your ego—to think I'd ride around with you?

I can't even begin to fathom how your mind works.

You must be living in some bizarre fantasy world.

I don't love you, Justin. Don't you get it?"

But then her eyes drifted to the Jag, lingering just a second too long.

Something shifted—maybe it was the car, or perhaps it wasn't.

She sighed, her tone softening just a notch.

"Okay, but just a short drive. Ten minutes. No more. I really have to get back."

"Great, wait here, I'll bring the Jag around."

I ran across the street, figuring maybe the camera wouldn't pick Kaya up getting into the car if I pulled it across Veterans and picked her up in front of her apartment.

Those bastards couldn't be recording her building; I was sure that was coming, but I figured not yet, maybe in a few years, who knows how, but they'll figure that out – I'm sure there's a way, maybe satellites or something.

Besides, the night was dark, and a warm blanket of clouds covered the Westside, which should've obscured the camera a bit.

Reaching over, I opened the door, and she started to get in.

She lingered as if she was having second thoughts, then a quirky smile, an almost devilish one.

She hesitated, looked, and then slid in.

When she was in, she looked out the windshield, not at me.

"The seat belts are right by the door," I said.

"Do I need them? You're not going to crash, are you?"

"Are you crazy? No way." I said.

I have been trying to get her where she is now for twenty years; the last thing I would do is crash.

We took off, Kaya stealing a glance at me before leaning her head slightly out the Jag window, letting the night air catch her hair.

At that point, I didn't care if it was me or the Jag; she was in the same car as me, next to me, and that was all that mattered,

"Where are you going anyway? Do you even know Justin?" she said absentmindedly as her hair blew in the LA Night.

"I don't know for sure, but somewhere," I replied.

I didn't care where we went; I just wanted to be with Kaya, and I was. She didn't seem to hear me; then, like coming out of a dream, she turned and spoke directly to me.

"Listen, if this is a game, let me out right now. Do you know where you're going or not?"

"No game, Kaya. Just a drive."

I said with great sincerity, which seemed to satisfy her.

"Okay, just not too far. It's been a long day."

She said and then poked her head out the window, now and then gazing at the console; I am sure I saw a smile cross her face.

"Okay,"

I said, careful not to say anything that could alter her mood.

I figured I'd drive and see what popped up. She didn't ask for details. After a few minutes, she reached over and touched my hand.

"Cool car; I always did like Jaguars."

The streets were empty as if the West Side was making a path for us.

Kaya's slightest touch, whether accidental or not, sent sensations through my body, mind, and spirit. She leaned back and closed her eyes.

It was as if I were in a dream. Kaya was sitting next to me, quiet and relaxed.

I ate up every aspect of her, as I have been pining to do all these many years, but this was not a dream. It was real, and she was there. I shall not let her go! I thought to myself.

Her light brown visage, penciled and defined brows, and a slight slant to her eyes all returned as if they were never gone. The hair was coifed just so naturally, wild in a way yet confined, like her, organized chaos, like chaos on purpose.

Her smile told me everything and nothing simultaneously. The snug-fitting black sweater that highlights her figure, combined with her stare, is hidden but always there.

Her eyes, transfixed and transfixing, full of art and intrigue, my muse, was, on the one hand, ordered and defined and, simultaneously, full of chaos. I knew the chaos was the real part; it was just contained, barely, within.

The order was contrived.

Kaya fights the chaos, but I am drawn to it.

That chaos is there for us.

She opened her eyes, apparently after a long period of thought, and said,

"You have done well, I can tell. You have a beautiful car, a great job, and a family. You have become a very successful man; in some ways, I'm surprised, in some not."

"It's only money," I reply.

"Justin, that sounds a bit disingenuous. 'It's only money.'

You care about money, or you wouldn't have worked so hard for it; you wouldn't have so much of it.

On the other hand, Balter and I have had many opportunities, but if we didn't believe in a project, we passed on it. Now, it seems you will do anything to make a profit. It seems to me you always want something new.

And now, Justin, it's me. Am I right?"

"That's not completely true – I've always wanted you!"

I believe Kaya blushed, but it was dark, making it difficult to tell. Making a right turn on Wilshire Blvd, I headed toward downtown Los Angeles.

Kaya looked around, noticed our direction, and then said,

"I couldn't help but notice a 'Jah Love' bumper sticker on the back of the Jag.

"Are you a Rasta or something?" she said with more than a hint of humor.

"You noticed it?" I asked.

"Yes, it's perfect for you, Justin. It's out of context – the Brooks Brothers suits, the Jaguar, and the Rasta Sticker, still chasing two worlds at once, huh?"

I couldn't tell if that was a compliment or a jab, but that's how it always was; perhaps that is why I was so intrigued by her.

I loved it; she knew me, I guess, the real me, both sides like nobody else, not even Lacy.

However, now that I think of it, Kaya may have focused on the negative.

In contrast, Lacy may have focused on the positive; maybe, in retrospect, that's why Kaya did not want me, but I did not care.

I loved her and wanted her,

"Have you ever been to Jamaica?" I ask.

"I've never been." She said.

"We should go sometime; it's a fantastic place," I said.

Kaya laughed sarcastically and said,

"Oh yeah, sure, that would be a great idea!"

It was clear that she did not mean it, but then she pondered a minute, furrowed her brow, and asked,

"What do you do there, Justin?"

I looked at Kaya, and for a moment, it seemed like she actually wanted to know—about me.

I'd rambled on all the other times when we spoke, words tumbling out in a blur, and she'd cut me off, quick and clean, as if my story didn't matter.

But now, here she was, asking questions about me to me.

Or maybe I just wanted to believe she was.

"Nothing. I drink, eat, swim, look at the infinite, and do the important things. I stand in the ocean and look in all directions to see the wonders God has wrought."

"Yes, Justin, I can imagine you doing that, but what's the point of it?"

"That is the point: to do nothing, talk about nothing," I replied.

Kaya seemed a bit perplexed and said,

"Talk about nothing. What do you mean?"

"I mean, talk shit with people, people you might think are ignorant. Not Harvard grads, not hipsters – regular people, people at bars, people at the Waffle House, rednecks and Rastas, regular people. There's a lot to learn from these folks!"

She squeezed my hand, and we both looked forward.

"That's what I like about you, Justin, but you never could keep it together. There was always that temper, that anger behind it, that need to control everything. Have you gotten over that?"

"I'm trying."

"Well, you didn't do that good this afternoon," she noted.

"I guess not," I admitted.

I made a left turn at Vermont Avenue, heading towards Griffith Park, precariously close to Laughlin Park.

Instead of turning right at Los Feliz, I continued up Vermont, past the multi-million-dollar homes surrounding the gateway, past the Greek Theater, and into the wilds of Griffith Park.

The mountain's natural contours led us on a route winding around the illuminated Hollywood sign and into the mist.

Dark and threatening scattered clouds followed us from the Westside.

The silver moon shone, breaking through the clouds and casting streams of light to our left and right.

Veering right at the curve, we exited the tunnel below the planetarium, and the whole city lit up as if a spotlight had been cast upon its face.

Kaya leaned closer, now holding my hand more intensely. She pushed her shoulder beside mine, craning her neck to look below the cliff.

This is perfect!

That was all I could think.

Yet the naturalness of her moves was perplexing and difficult to fathom—things were happening so fast.

The contradiction between her voiced reserve from earlier and her physical ease now, as confusing and irrational as it seemed, made everything more perfect, more pleasing.

Her body spoke the truth.

We drove around the curves and said nothing; in a sense, it was like when I first met Lacy that night at the Camilla Grill, when we took that silent walk to Doc Rankin's house when there was no need to speak to understand.

However, this was different somehow. My passion, my stupid smile—everything was even more intense.

I had been looking forward to this since I last rode with Kaya more than twenty years ago.

As we came down to the other side of the park, the land became flat near Travel Town, and we crossed under a bridge towards the Equestrian section of Los Angeles that borders the river.

I made a hard left on a nondescript street.

The sky was darker now, and the clouds that had been menacing before made good on their threats and opened up, sending down torrents of rain that played a staccato drumroll on the roof.

I drove as if by intuition, by the gut, internal GPS leading the way.

Kaya held me closer, and the rain pounded harder on the slowly rolling Jaguar as I maneuvered it down the narrow street that soon became a gravel road.

A few hundred yards ahead was a small café, and as we drove toward it, the rain obscured the little building.

The place was hidden, as if in another world, accessible only to horse riders or plucky cars via this tiny, hidden gravel road.

A hitching rail perched in front of the café, the kind you see by saloons in old Westerns.

Fifty feet to the left of the rail was a small gravel parking lot with a huge, spreading oak tree.

Tagged to it with one hanging, rusty nail was a hand-painted sign reading

"Parking Lot."

I parked under the oak.

I shut down the car.

We sat there entirely alone save for the rain on the roof, speaking softly to us.

The Café

From the parking lot, the café came into clearer view.

Dark green wood siding framed a long picture window, revealing an old lunch counter and a few booths lined against the wall.

"How quaint!"

Kaya exclaimed and continued.

"Hard to believe we're just a few miles from downtown."

Through the rain-speckled glass, the place looked empty. A lone waitress stood behind the counter, her uniform straight out of the fifties.

"Come on, let's go in," I said.

Kaya hesitated, her expression flickering with doubt, as if weighing whether this was a step too far. Then, finally—

"Okay… yeah, but Odd, I've never seen this place before."

"It's like I've always said: when we're together, we make magic. Just start driving, and places like this appear outta nowhere."

"Don't push it," Kaya retorted.

We both turned our eyes toward the café. The entrance was a good hundred feet away, and the rain had thickened, coming down in torrents.

"I think I have an umbrella in the trunk. Want me to get it? I said.

"No, let's just go for it," Kaya said.

We wrapped our arms around each other's waists, raising our free hands in a useless attempt to shield ourselves from the downpour.

Running together, laughing, we reached the door, drenched but exhilarated—only to stop at the threshold.

She wavered as if running it through her mind for an imperceptible second.

Then, together, we pushed open the metal and glass doors.

Go Now

The café was deserted, and the waitress we spied through the window was nowhere to be found. The air conditioning ran at full tilt and chilled us to the bone, and the wet rain permeated our clothes to our skin.

"Let's go to the booth in the corner near the window," suggested Kaya.

We slid into the booth on the same bench, shaking and shivering.

Moving closer and closer to each other, we brought warmth to our bodies and huddled in the corner as one.

Looking around the place, I had the oddest, somewhat eerie feeling—not scary, just weird.

"Hey, Kaya, being here seems like an episode of *The Twilight Zone*. Do you get that feeling?"

"Yes," she said, looking at me before scanning the restaurant. Then she continued,

"I still can't believe I haven't run into it over the years. I've been to so many locations, but I must have missed this one."

Suddenly, the waitress, dressed in her café au lait-colored uniform and wearing a little square hat perched atop her head, appeared as if right out of Central Casting.

She was a girl of natural beauty in her early twenties.

Astonished, we began to laugh.

"What's so funny? Is it the uniform?" she asked.

"Yes, but it's cute on you," Kaya said.

"It's stupid, I know, but the owner insists. He says it's part of the 'ambiance.' What can I get you guys?"

Looking over at Kaya, I asked, "What would you like?"

Kaya smiled and looked up at the waitress.

"Well, what's good?"

The waitress replied,

"The hamburger platter is great. We grind our own meat and make our own fries."

"That's perfect. And Miss, can I have a strawberry shake with it?"

"Yes, absolutely."

The waitress turned to me.

"And you, Sir?"

"I'll have the same, but can I have a chocolate malted milk instead? My dad always had malted milk. I love the way the words sound. 'Malted milk.'"

Kaya gave me an odd look when I recalled the story, but from her expression, she seemed to get a kick out of it.

The waitress finished scribbling the order, turned, and left.

"How is your father, anyway? Is he alive?" asked Kaya.

"Sure is. He's alive and kicking—he's fine."

"I recall that you struggled with him and didn't get along. Are things better now?"

"How did you know we had issues?"

"Justin, it was so obvious. It seemed like he detested you. I felt sorry for you. I feared he might destroy you. You did an admirable job of ignoring it, but he treated you like shit; he did. I'm surprised you amounted to anything with a father like that; I sensed you were in great pain."

"Not that I'm aware of," I said quietly.

"Justin, you fixed it, didn't you? You guys worked it out, right?"

"Listen, can we talk about something else?"

"Sure, I didn't mean to bring up uncomfortable things, but I thought you'd have resolved this by now. I had difficulties with my mom—you knew that—but I worked them out before she passed away. I guess you haven't. I'm so sorry I ever brought it up. Forgive me."

"No problem, but I know how we can solve this mystery."

I said, trying to get Kaya to stop talking about my dad.

"What mystery?" she inquired.

"Remember the *Twilight Zone* episode about the café?

As I recall, it turns out there was no cook. That's how they discovered it wasn't real, that the café was just an illusion, a set created by some unknown force for some unknown purpose.

Kaya, all we have to do is ask the waitress to produce the cook, and if there's a cook and a real kitchen, we'll know for sure the place is real."

Kaya laughed. "You haven't changed a bit.

Still lost in your little fantasy world. There's really no need. We'll know it's real when they bring the food."

"Not necessarily. It could be prepared outside in a truck or something. Just ask to see the cook," I argued.

"Okay, okay, I will."

Kaya said with a grin, as if she were humoring me, but I didn't care.

The waitress returned with our platters and placed them in front of us.

Kaya glanced at me, then at the waitress, a flicker of amusement in her eyes.

'This looks great," Kaya said and continued.

"My friend here would like to thank the chef for the food on this rainy night. If he's around, can he step out?'

The waitress nodded and returned to the kitchen. As she turned, Kaya smirked at me.

"Justin, it looks like you're gonna get your wish."

I smiled at Kaya, a telling and knowing smile; she looked at me, half-cocked, and said,

"No! Justin, not that wish!"

As we began eating, the double porthole doors to the kitchen swung open, and a tall Black man with long dreads and a Rasta-colored skullcap on his head stepped out.

He looked at me for a long moment, his gaze unwavering, before speaking:

"Dawg nyam yu suppa."

Then, without another word, he retreated into the back.

Kaya set down her burger and turned to me, her curiosity plain.

"What was that about? You've been to Jamaica—what does it mean?"

I shrugged, forcing a grin.

"Something about a dog eating supper. Probably one of those cryptic island sayings—they're always throwing those around."

Kaya smiled faintly, but her eyes lingered on me as if waiting for more.

I looked out at the rain, trying to brush it off, but the phrase stuck with me. His tone, his stare—something in it I couldn't quite place.

Absolute quiet settled over the café.

The only sounds were those of Kaya nibbling on her burger and fries.

I pondered my good fortune, trying to ignore the faint unease his words left behind.

"Kaya, listen up,"

I finally said, breaking the silence.

She looked at me attentively.

"It's so odd that the cook is Jamaican; perhaps it's an omen.

I have a place, a villa, in Jamaica; my company owns it. I want you to come there with me."

She went back to her burger for a moment and then looked up.

"Maybe one day we can all go together—Balter, my son, and your wife and son. That would be nice."

"Kaya, you know damn well what I mean. I mean us."

"I'm not stupid," Kaya replied.

"I know what you mean, but that's crazy, impossible. What are you talking about? You're married; I'm married. It's crazy. Forget it."

Kaya started to eat again, then dropped the burger onto her plate and stared into space.

Finally, she looked up.

"Ya know, Justin, I didn't tell you the whole truth.

Balter knew it was you at the park. The police told him you were going to jail unless he admitted that they knew you, but he didn't care. He figured you deserved it. Balter sent you to jail. I begged him not to let you go, and he told me to shut up.

Justin, my marriage is not perfect."

"Whose is ?" I echoed,

But Kaya probably already knew something was wrong with mine; how could she not know?

"Balter is a bit of a player—handsome, with plenty of admirers. This film is in Sweden, and he gave me almost no notice. One day, he just dropped it on me. I don't believe it."

She looked out the window for a while and then turned into my eyes.

"Remember that fog after I left your car all those years ago?

The fog, the mist?

When I walked that half-block back home?

I promised to stay with you but then walked into the fog.

Do you remember that?"

"Yes, I remember, of course,"

I murmured, barely above a whisper, more to myself than anyone else—for I had lived it a thousand times, a million times.

"I entered the fog," Kaya continued.

"I had no idea it was that thick, or I would not have gotten out. I was lost; I couldn't find my door. I knocked on three doors before I found mine.

Justin, I lost you in that fog. You let me loose. You misled me.

Why did you turn me loose like that?

What man would turn a woman loose in the fog? I was frantic when I got home. You would mislead me forever."

"Kaya, I would never mislead you. You jumped out of the car. You wanted to go! I couldn't stop you. I would have driven you home."

"That's not what I meant. It was more than that. Why did you let me go?" she asks.

"How could I stop you? You wanted to go."

It was as if she were daydreaming, hypnotized, staring at the cool tropical rain, which was slackening, transforming itself into a mist, a fog, covering the café windows with haze growing thicker and thicker with each passing moment.

The oak tree departed, and then the parking lot sign was gone.

My Jag vanished; all was wiped out.

A strange and unusual look came over Kaya's face.

"Justin, we gotta go. We gotta go now."

Her voice was tight, low but insistent, and her eyes darted toward the windows, searching for something just beyond.

She rose quickly as if pulled by an unseen weight, her movements heavy with dread.

I threw a few bills on the table, and we were out the door.

I figured I could easily find the car.

Though I could hardly see it, I recall exactly where we ran and from what direction.

Kaya suddenly became panicked and frozen, and she held my waist tightly, which didn't make things any easier.

I felt my way as I feigned ease.

"Just hold on. It's not a problem. I know exactly where the car is. I'll find the way. Just hang on."

We inched our way through the mist.

Kaya hung on to me like a frightened child.

"Hold on to me tight. I have you; hang on now. I can feel my way around, so we don't hit the trees. I know the way; I will get us there. Don't worry."

"Justin. Be careful. Hold on so I don't lose you in this mist. Please, please hold on."

Her voice was filled with abject dread and horror.

Her body quivered as we maneuvered around trees toward where I recalled parking the car.

Eventually, I caught the front bumper, moved around, found the door handle, guided Kaya in, and closed it.

I worked my way around the car to the driver's side and got in.

Before I could say anything, Kaya, her breath coming in gasps, whispered,

"Justin, drive! Just drive! Get us out of here."

Like years ago, again, this primal fear was gripping her. She was petrified.

Strangely, I found the fog comforting, a soft, protective womb, yet Kaya was terrified.

This time, though, I was determined not to let her loose in it. I would make her safe.

We drove up the gravel road, back towards the highway, and then onto the freeway.

As the fog lifted, Kaya lay across my lap, huddled in fear.

"Hey," I said,

"As much as I love you being where you are, the fog is gone. That restaurant must have been in some gully. As soon as we got back up the highway, it lifted. It's fine now."

But she would not raise her head.

A few minutes passed before she looked up and said,

"Thank you. Thanks for getting me out of there. Can we go to Jamaica now?"

"Surprised" would not be the right word. Perhaps "aghast," "perplexed," "confused," or "befuddled"?

What had I done to make her agree?

My answer was sprite and matter of fact.

"Yeah, sure."

"Take me there now."

she moaned, putting her head back down in my lap.

Exodus

Scattered raindrops slammed against the roof and windshield with loud, disturbing pops, and renegade clouds wandered aimlessly.

Kaya raised her head, a bit calmer but still moved.

I could scarcely believe she'd decided to come, and on such a lark, who would have imagined?

Sure, it was too good to be true, but I would not look a gift horse in the mouth.

Maybe I just got lucky with the fog: the fact that it freaked her out and that Balter was a cad; why shouldn't I take my breaks when I get them?

I figured as much – a low-life trombonist, or whatever he was, who gets his wife's car hooked, fuck him.

Taking the kid to Sweden to 'make a movie,' let's get real, he probably had some woman there, and Kaya knew it.

There is enough bad luck in the world, and we all get our share; I say, take your breaks and run with them. That's how I have always lived, so why stop now?

Lacy was the opposite; did she even know that everything we had was because I went with the breaks?

Who are we to understand the universe and how it operates?

This was probably meant to be, and I had to work it right not to dissuade her. That meant working fast and not giving her too much time to think.

As she lay curled up on the seat, her head in my lap, in a fetal-like repose, I said,

"I have a few things left in my suitcase that I used at the Los Angeles Athletic Club."

Kaya registered a somewhat surprised look.

"You've been staying at the Athletic Club?

I thought you live in Laughlin Park."

"Yaa, I do, but I told you I spent the last few days there. Don't you remember?"

"I don't recall," she said.

Slowly, Kaya raised her head and looked out the window as if she were drugged.

Her movements were sluggish.

"We're about to pass the 110-South cut-off.

Should I take it?

Do you want to pass by your house and pick up anything?" I asked.

Without hesitation, as if suddenly awakened, she said with clarity and precision,

"Don't stop at my house; let's go straight to the airport."

Pedal to the metal, we continued south to the 105 freeway, which leads right to LAX.

"Hey, Kaya, we're passing our old stomping grounds. We just crossed El Segundo."

Now more awake, she replied,

"Who could imagine exactly twenty-five years ago that we would do this?"

I nodded in agreement as we passed the racetrack, exited the freeway, and parked in a pricy short-term parking at Los Angeles International.

This is no time to worry about a few bucks.

There was an odd silence as we walked toward the United Airlines terminal.

Kaya was at my side with nothing other than the little satchel she took with her when she left her house for an evening, and I grabbed the small suitcase I took to the Athletic Club when I escaped Lacy.

While our clothes had dried out a bit, Kaya's still showed the effects of the drenching at the café, and I was still in the same slacks and shirt I wore in jail.

We rushed through the parking lot to the United Airlines Terminal.

"How can I assist you?"

asked the United attendant, barely noticing our disarray.

"Two first-class tickets to Montego Bay, please," I replied.

The attendant looked down at the monitor, busily pumped away at the keyboard, and said,

"Fine, yes, we have space. How will you be paying?"

"With Visa," I replied, handing her my company credit card.

"May I have your passports, please?" she asks.

Quickly, I pulled my passport from the suitcase – I always leave it in my bag so it won't be lost – and handed it to the attendant. Then she turned to Kaya and said,

"Miss, may I have yours, please?"

I knew this was too good to be true.

There was no way that Kaya had her passport with her! We should have stopped by her house.

But Kaya calmly reached into her satchel, pulled out a passport, and handed it to the attendant.

The attendant looked at the passports. Noticing our names, she asked,

"Will y'all be traveling together?"

"Yes," we reply in unison.

"Fine. Can you please put your luggage on the scale?"

"Oh, no need for that. We have carry-ons today," I replied.

The attendant looked at us both with a half-cocked grimace.

Finally noticing our general disarray and lack of luggage, combined with the fact that I was purchasing first-class seats without notice, I could see her mind working.

I knew it did not make sense, and she had to be imagining stories. I start creating a thousand in my mind.

My best guess is that she imagined we were caught in bed and had to jet out the back door in the rain and get out of town fast, as her husband was gunning for us.

Luckily, she wouldn't have much time to ponder, as a line was building fast.

We would soon become just an ancient memory, or so I hoped.

"Y'all have a great trip to Jamaica," she said, handing us our tickets.

As we walked towards our gate, Kaya seemed almost detached, as if she was not even here with me, like she was traveling alone.

"Wasn't it lucky that you had your passport with you?" I asked.

Looking askew at me, Kaya said,

"Justin, do you think I would come to the airport without a passport? Come on… if I didn't have a passport, we would have had to stop by my house."

"I guess you're right," I sheepishly replied.

Los Angeles to Montego Bay

It is awkward now sitting next to Kaya as I am.

This has all happened so fast. I've had little time to think, and now that I am, I begin to reconsider. If I were able to get off the plane now, I would.

But we're miles high, so logic deems this is out of the question.

I am sure myriad thoughts and emotions are running through Kaya's mind, but there's no way to know, and I dare not ask prying questions.

I have enough to consider about my fate.

In truth, her concerns are the least of my worries.

I know now the consequences will be dire – how could they not be? – but perhaps there's a way out.

I can come up with something.

Looking over at Kaya, it is as if I never knew what she was thinking; then again, maybe I did.

Perhaps she has thought this through better than I: her family is in Sweden, and they may not even know she's gone, but my absence will definitely be noted.

Kaya grabs my hand tightly and reclines in her first-class seat; closing her eyes, she dozes off, seemingly satisfied and at peace.

I, on the other hand, am overcome with a sudden anxiety as I gaze at her face.

I'm delighted that she's by my side, but I wonder what the hell to tell the staff in Jamaica about her?

How do I explain my absence to Lacy and Wilkins?

What about David? What if he finds out?

Regardless, the die is cast.

It comes to me that I might well end up regretting what I've most wished for, but there's no turning back now; perhaps this is fate.

Kaya opened her eyes again, a startled look on her face. This little one that I had longed to touch, has she been thinking the same things as I?

"Shit, Justin, I have no clothes. I didn't bring anything—just what I have in my purse!"

What can I say?

It was not even a slight inconvenience; it was nothing like my concerns.

"Don't worry. We have everything you need at the villa and lots of help. The girls will take you to buy whatever you need; it's not a problem."

"Okay," she says, closing her eyes again.

I never believed I would be with Kaya. She would not speak to me for more than thirty seconds, and her letters were one or two words, cryptic.

Yet here she rests, seemingly without concern or care, and here I sit with all I've longed for yet unable to relax, in full contemplation of every possible pain and pitfall.

And now, as to money matters, how would I account for the expenditures?

Nowadays, it is impossible to hide the automatic dissemination of information on credit card use, including where it is used and for what purpose.

The world is already aware that I purchased Kaya's ticket and that I am going to use the villa to entertain her!

Further, I will do this in a house owned by my wife's father, in said villa where his company employs the servants, pays the bills, and stocks the kitchen!

The entire staff will witness this debacle, and electronic trails will be all over the island—cell phone records, ATM records, and even video recordings.

Privacy no longer exists in the goddamn world, even in Paradise.

Twenty years ago, dropping out of sight might have been possible.

Still, in a world of universal information exchange, it's no longer possible to escape, except perhaps through extraordinary means.

And here we were, not acting stealthily in any way, but rather as if we don't give a rat's ass who knows.

Still sleeping, Kaya reaches over and touches my hand.

Turning to my left, I gaze at her face, which reflects satisfaction and calm.

Should I not feel the same, as for the first time in twenty years, I am doing something only for me?

Montego Bay

Arriving at Montego Airport is always comfortable, even if the airport is a bit of a mess; at least I know I am here.

The place is a frenzied mix of cheap rum, knickknacks and gifts, hustle and bustle, kindness, harshness, poverty, and wealth.

Exiting the plane, I led Kaya quickly past gruff customs officials stuffed into their cramped cubicles.

The chaos, heat, crowds, and confusion define this place, unlike the nature that awaits us outside these doors.

Led along by the hand, Kaya gazes with amazement at the sights.

She wants to tarry, stop at a Knick Nack Shop, or wander into a record store, but I force a quick exit, almost falling outside into the front of the airport's circular drive.

Isaac is directly in the center of the drive.

I'll never know how he always snags that spot, but it is undoubtedly the best parking spot at Montego Bay Airport.

Leave it to Isaac; he always comes through.

I spy him standing before his '59 Caddy – long, pink, and glistening in the heat as he gently rubs a rag across its exterior.

The hills of Montego Bay are his backdrop, and Jimmy Cliff is blasting our fanfare from the limo's speakers.

Isaac's long and well-groomed dreadlocks give an entirely new meaning to Rasta; this is Rasta-Suave, if it is anything.

His dreads are the antithesis of the natural image but coiffed and cared for as if prepared for the Academy Awards.

At six feet tall, his lanky frame, tight white T-shirt, black bellbottoms, and brown-yellow skin impart a striking image that women adore.

Isaac moves forward, but not too far from his prized Cadillac.

"Justin, I am rejoiced to see yuh return. Neva thought I'd sight yuh 'til next year, so di pleasure even greater. Give thanks to Jah; yuh deh yah now."

Noticing Kaya and rarely failing to notice a woman, especially a good-looking one, Isaac looks her over critically.

"Justin, who is dis fine empress? So beautiful she is!"

He bows to her.

"Kaya works with me. She'll be visiting a bit; she's a photographer and is coming to take pictures of the island for a Piedmont advertisement."

Isaac is puzzled by my words; I can see it on his face. He glares at Kaya and then concentrates on her small satchel.

"Her camera is in my suitcase," I declare.

Isaac's eyes glow, and he turns away. Then, suddenly, he whips his head in our direction, with the dreadlocks following close behind.

If you know Isaac (and I do), this was a completely contrived action, ego, like a lion displaying his coiffed mane to impress a lioness.

His eyes light up, and an understanding smile spreads, but an understanding that I did not intend to communicate.

"Oh yes, she gon' be real help. Mi can see dat," he says, his tone dripping with sarcasm.

With all his confusion is erased, Isaac goes into full-tour mode, and any notion of his passing judgment fades.

Taking Kaya by the tip of her hand with the exaggerated motions of an English nobleman leading his lady into his carriage, Isaac directs Kaya into the rear of the Caddie.

"Miss, watch yuh step yah, but no need fi fear; dis yah di finest and most beautiful car pon di island, and it will provide yuh wid maximum comfort," he says.

"I'm sure it will; you're very kind," Kaya replied.

She settles in the rear seat of the Cadillac and then whispers to me as Isaac walks around the car to take the wheel.

"He has such fine manners. What a gentleman!"

I don't want to spoil Kaya's fun, but how easily women can be deceived amazes me. I know Isaac well, and with him, this is all a game, yet Kaya, like scores of other women, is hoodwinked by his pretty face and pleasing manners.

What's the use?

I play along, nodding in agreement as I snuggle next to Kaya, who does not refuse my advances.

Isaac gently pulls out of Montego Airport into traffic and heads toward Revival and the Wilkins compound.

Kaya gazes out her side window as warm, humid air pours in.

The hum of the rushing breeze blows past us and joins with the ever-present reggae that echoes from what seems like a hundred and one speakers planted in every conceivable nook and cranny of the careening pink Caddie.

Kaya stares at the distant mountains, the closer rolling hills, shacks, and occasional glimpses of the sea.

I hold her tight in fear, as every curve seems a death-defying ordeal.

Yet Kaya relishes each back-and-forth as Isaac speeds around cars, trucks, and inanimate objects littering the road, mere inches separating us from all these things.

Kaya is fearless, while I envision myself sprawled out on the rocks near the sea, dead, waiting to be swept away by the tide.

She is captivated, absorbed, and fully engaged in every move.

Amidst this fear, rising above it, I see calm and beauty becoming disorder and woe; even in the most tranquil places, menace and evil lurk.

Yet now, the blue sky and clean sea breeze drown out the shrill cry of disorder, and there is peace amongst the contradiction.

Unaware of our potential peril, Kaya remains relaxed and oblivious to our fate.

I know it is there, but even amidst the danger, I now choose to deny it.

The midday Caribbean sun bakes the car even as we careen over hills and dales, surrounded by humid and stifling heat.

Glancing briefly at the front seat and Isaac, Kaya removes her blouse, exposing her white ruffled bra, enclosing firm mounds tightly planted in each cup, as I recalled years ago.

She places her blouse on my lap, and goose pimples rise on her arms, the air blowing over her warm brown skin.

Then Kaya thrusts aside her ruffled brassiere.

Her nipples are hard, transforming a perilous auto ride in the country into a moment of warmth and sensuality.

"Ya man, it's a wonderful warm day. Look deh so. Mi have some refreshments fi yuh pon dis hot aftahnoon. Help yuhself." Issac says.

A simple Styrofoam box beneath our feet contains a bottle of Meyers dark rum and two whole iced coconuts sealed in plastic.

We help ourselves and fall into a trance-like state.

Her still-firm breasts rub against my body.

Bouncing along the highway, surrounded by tropical greens and the azure sea, contained within the intimate womblike warmth of the Caddie, and serenaded with rhythmic reggae beats, I grasp her by the waist, losing myself in the elements, mesmerized, silent, dozing, and rolling without consciousness as if on a somnambulist holiday.

Villa Calm

When we awake, we are pulling into the driveway of Villa Calm, a massive white plantation home similar to the Wilkins' residence in Charleston.

It is situated on a few majestic acres overlooking the Caribbean Sea, and I know that, in the end, I am the reason this place now belongs to Piedmont.

There is no chance it would have existed without my efforts.

The fact that I, one of the masters of the villa, arrive with a beautiful Asian woman and not with my wife and son as expected puts the staff in, let us say, a difficult position.

Yet, somehow, I don't much care.

Excited at what I consider my good fortune, I jettison shame.

A large lawn faces the sea, and the villa's entrance is a semi-circular pathway leading directly from the house.

Off to the right and near the cliffs is a small cottage open to the sky, with giant palms framing the view of the villa.

The little cottage is, in effect, a miniature Villa Calm.

It has two floors; the second-floor bedrooms boast exquisite French doors leading to a balcony, which juts precariously off the cliff, giving a view of the waves below.

Pulling up the drive, we see Wilson, the villa manager, an employee of Piedmont, a graying Black man with a regal stance and dignified air.

Seven Rasta girls surround Wilson, regaled in colorful island garb.

All stand perfectly framed by the Villa as if posing for a photograph.

Isaac pulls the Caddie in front of the group and runs around to open the door for Kaya, who is frantically buttoning her blouse.

Dressed, she exits confidently, as if she has been here before. She immediately wanders off towards the cliff as Wilson approaches me.

"Welcome, Justin,"

but his eyes are transfixed on Kaya as she wanders to the cliff as if somehow drawn to the sea by unseen forces.

I am the master of this Villa, but Wilson scarcely notices my presence. Finally, his gaze turns to me, yet he continues in a sardonic tone,

"It is nice to see you here. How long will we have the pleasure of your company? When might we expect Lacy and David?"

I can see the wheels turning in his head, and it ain't good thoughts he's having; I reply nonchalantly:

"Sadly, they aren't coming. I have this damn promotion project for Piedmont, and Kaya, the woman I brought, is assisting me. She is a film producer from Hollywood, and when I told her about this place, she said it would be perfect for a shoot."

Wilson looks down as I continue,

"Perhaps Kaya can stay in the cottage, and I will stay in the villa?"

"I will so arrange," says Wilson.

"Excellent," I reply. "There's one more thing. The airline has misplaced Kaya's luggage. Can you get her what she needs?"

"Naturally, we will take care of that. The girls will assist," replies Wilson.

He motions to the Rasta girls, who form a semicircle around him as he gives them directions.

Finished, the girls hurriedly head towards Kaya at the cliff's edge, where she stands between palms that extend to the heavens.

The Rasta reaches her, and she waves as they wander the path beyond the cottage, disappearing from view.

Wilson picks up my suitcase, and we slowly walk down the narrow path toward the Main Villa.

The infinite and the unknown surround me on both sides.

Covered in Salt

Settled into a room in the villa, I wait until I'm sure Wilson is gone and then take the long path to the cliff cottage by the sea.

Darkness surrounds me; the path lights barely illuminate my way. I walk carefully, not knowing exactly what to expect.

Entering the cottage, I call out to Kaya, but there is no reply. Slowly, I ascend to the second floor and the bedrooms overlooking the cliff and sea,

"Kaya, are you here?"

Standing on the balcony overlooking the sea, partially draped in a colorful sarong, Kaya turns to me.

The air smells of coconut and garden flowers.

I see that her firm breasts are uncovered.

The scent of ganja permeates the room, and I see spiffs in the ashtray. Taking hold of one, I inhale an ample amount.

Kaya walks toward me, and I to her. But she stops abruptly, turns, wanders to the balcony's edge, and stares over the sea.

I linger behind.

Her silhouette reflects in the bright blue, shimmering glow of the night.

The moon shines dimly against a backdrop of stars, so plentiful that scarcely space is left between them.

The night is so luminous that night and day are shades of one another.

Indeed, the creator has wrought something pleasant and fertile in this place to provide an easy and abundant life.

Kaya stands barely covered in her vibrant sarong, framed by this universe, her nakedness so irresistible.

She turns again, beckoning; there can be no doubt.

This time, I see clearly.

Then I am pushing her against the railing, and she relents as if she is expecting, nay, demanding my advance.

She eases into position and holds me in a passionate grip.

If the railing were to give way, we would surely tumble to our deaths, but considering this as a potential last moment, these the last breaths, I wouldn't mind at all.

I have no fear.

Up against the railing, she lifts her sarong, exposing her fragile and perfectly coifed petals.

Her right leg rises high as she leans hard against the ancient timbers.

She is open and ready for me, and I enter.

Consciousness departed, entwined. I pushed deeper, pushing her against the balcony railing, unmindful of danger and indifferent to the consequences.

Entering the flower again and again, the sweet nectar gently flows as I lunge endlessly into her, the sky, the sea, and the quiet night our backdrop.

At times, it seems the railing will fail, as the creaking timbers sway with our passion, but we ignore these dangers.

She pulls me closer, pressing harder.

We ignore the danger and all else but that which we share—here, there, within and without, above, below, and all around.

Our sweat mixes as we move rhythmically, mindlessly, harmoniously, irrationally, without thought or contemplation.

We are bathed in the spray carried aloft by the wind.

Damp, warm, and covered in salt.

Morning

When I awake, I can't find Kaya.

She is gone, as are the moon and stars that shone last night.

The day has come.

In the brilliant morning, a warm sun and sea breeze drift through the open French doors, the curtains flapping like winged birds.

The sweet scents of the Jamaican morning waft through the space.

I recollect little of the past hours, yet a sweet smile remains, as do the taste of nectar and the salty brine on my skin.

Standing on the balcony, I am reminded of the dance.

Looking below to the sea, fear overcomes me, but as I back away and chuckle, I now know how to overcome the fear of heights.

I picture Kaya perched against the railing, her leg raised, and the both of us inches from death but fucking with fearless abandon.

There was no fear of death then, no fear of heights, no fear of anything, but now I back off.

Yeah, I finally conquered Kaya, and now I control my destiny. I will no longer jog this way or that at the whim of others.

I am freed from that.

From a safe distance, I gaze below at the jagged cliffs and the beach.

There, I see Kaya and the Rastas in colorful costumes dancing in the gentle waves.

Suddenly, hunger overtakes me, and I smell coffee.

Breads, fruits, and juices cover the kitchen table and counter.

Famished, I tear into them and then, grabbing a pear, walk back onto the balcony to prove I have no fear.

With the pear juice dripping from my mouth, I keep my distance from the balcony's edge.

I look down at the cliff at the girls below.

I yearn to join them, so I put on my pants and shoes and walk down the cuts and switchbacks leading to the sandy white beach.

With all the Rastas looking on, and now me as well, Dahlia carefully arranges a colorful cloth on Kaya's head.

My presence at the end of the beach is soon discovered.

A virgin girl, a child unknown, runs to me and, with her hand, leads me near Kaya.

"She is so beautiful. Look at her now," says the virgin girl.

Little does she know the long history that preceded this moment; she is far too full of innocence to understand such things.

Kaya faces the sea, and while she hasn't noticed my approach, it is as if the stir of the sand alerts her, so she turns around and smiles at me.

"How do I look?"

"Wonderful," I reply.

"This place is amazing. It is so beautiful and quiet. Now I understand why you love it so."

"I'm glad you like it, but with you, every place is beautiful and exciting," I declare.

The Rasta girls are taken aback.

Delighted, Kaya moves over and kisses me, holding me in a way that signals our nature to anyone and everyone.

"Oh, Dahlia, thank you so much," says Kaya.

"It was my pleasure, Miss," responds Dahlia.

"Who taught you to wrap the cloth this way?" asked Kaya.

"Believe or not, these methods were passed from generation to generation of women from the days before our bondage on this island. One day, with the blessing of Jah, all praises to Hallie Selassie I, King of Kings, Lion of Judah, we will again put them on our girl child in the land of Ethiopia. All Praises to Jah."

Kaya looks at me and notices tears in my eyes.

"Justin, why are you crying?"

"I don't know. There is something about these people, something calming, something wise. I'm not sure… but they know something important," I reply.

Kaya turns and asks, "How did you meet Dahlia and the rest?"

I look at the girls and Kaya and reply,

"They are friends of Tosh, the fisherman. He comes on these shores. That's his boat over there."

The girls nod in agreement. I point to a small, worn skiff on the sand before us.

"Tosh is already in for the day; you must rise very early to see him.

He is Binghi, a wise man; he casts his net early and listens for Jah to speak in the morning wind."

The Rasta girls nod again and start walking up the cliff.

Dahlia looks up and loudly exclaims, almost as if in a chant, as they reach the first switchback,

"All Praises to Jah, the most high, and Halle Selassie I, King of Kings, Lion of Judah! All Praises! All Praises!"

The Rastas disappear behind the mountainside as Kaya and I turn and saunter to where the warm water meets the sand.

The blue sky and sea surround us, and the high cliff is behind us.

The gentle waves warm us as we trail our toes in the sand.

Removing my vestment, I entered the water and swam a few meters into the sea. I plunged under the clear waters, only to rise seconds later to the surface.

Kaya watched from the shore.

"Come on in; the water's great."

"I have this beautiful outfit on; I can't go in now," says Kaya.

"Come on in; no one will see. Just take it off."

Without hesitation, she pulls off her scarf and sarong, exposing her nakedness.

Kaya hasn't had enough, as her moves do not signal an innocent swim from the outset, though that is my intention.

Kaya walks a few feet into the water, displaying herself as if on a runway walk.

She gently lowers her body into the water, and ten quick strokes later, we are together.

Again, it is clear that reason has left us, though this is not my intention.

As best as I can recall, it has been barely forty-eight hours since we first met with the stranger's lack of familiarity at the Tropical in LA, and now she is by my side in her nakedness and lust.

Out of my mind, I aim to please as if it were an obligation, a chore for a bull put to pasture. Kaya demands it, and Kaya wants it!

I lift her in the water and set her down in the exact spot to a tight and perfect fit, and the water dance begins.

Currents are thrown in all directions, forming small but violent waves of passion.

Finally exhausted, we grow calm and relaxed.

Kaya and I float, then turn and look out at the Caribbean, extending as far as we can see.

In the distance, I spy Tosh tending his vessel.

"Kaya. See Tosh, the fisherman," I say, pointing towards him.

"Yes, I see him there. Shall we disturb him now? I want to meet this man of whom you speak so highly," Kaya declares.

"Perhaps later," I advise.

Again, we float, transfixed by the warm waters.

Then she says softly,

"Justin, the Rastas came to the room this morning with breakfast – fruits, breads, and so many other beautiful things – for me."

"I know. I saw the food, and I ate some," I say.

"They couldn't help but notice you asleep there, and Dahlia seemed upset. There was nothing I could say. I'm sorry," Kaya said.

"Justin, she seriously looked at me and said,

'Justin is a good man, but he is not perfect. He is full of confusion and doubt. He has given away that which is priceless. What shall he receive in exchange for pain and misfortune?'

Then she looked at me closely, separated herself from the other Rasta, and whispered in a small voice,

'You're important to him – I know that – but remember, a gift once opened cannot be returned.' Do you know what that means? She was telling me something important.

You know these people. What did she mean?" Kaya pleads.

"I'm not sure. They speak in riddles," I reply.

But in truth, I understand.

<h1 style="text-align:center">Rick's</h1>

Not long after we return to the cottage, Isaac appears at the circular drive of Villa Calm, beckoning me on the phone, which rings until I answer.

"Ya man, yuh seh yuh waan go Rick's, an mi deh yah. But why yuh waan fi go deh, dat a mystery to mi!"

"No worries. It will be fine. Stay there. We'll be right down," I say.

"Isaac is outside," I tell Kaya, sitting at a desk, jotting in her log.

"I want to take you to this great spot called Rick's—about a forty-five-minute drive from here. The road's beautiful, and the place is even better. Come on, let's go," I say.

Kaya looks up and says,

"It's so pleasant here. Can't we rest for a while? So much has happened, and this morning with Dahlia… Perhaps we should take some time and rest."

"What are you talking about? Let's go. It will be fun."

"OK, go ahead; I'll be there in a few minutes."

Downstairs, Isaac is waiting right in front of the cottage, the Caddie as shiny as ever.

Kaya soon follows.

Her spirit is uplifted, and her face is aglow. There is great energy in her step, as though whatever disturbed her before has somehow vanished. She is fully alive.

Perhaps she hit the spiff; it's hard to tell.

Is this not what I've always wanted?

Kaya has freely given herself to me, far more than in our youth.

As we entered the car, Isaac craned his head towards the back seat and us.

"Isaac, what's up? You seem angry. What's the problem, man?"

"Yuh know mi nuh like Rick's. Babylon dem an' pure trouble, always trouble a dat place, yuh done know dat!"

"Come on, Rick's is fine. It has some excellent views. I don't know what you're talking about!"

"Babylon, you say. So, it's a bad place?" asks Kaya.

"Dat place full a ball head, pure Babylon it be. Ya, missy, nuttin good deh so," Isaac confirmed.

"Don't be a killjoy, Isaac. I want Kaya to see it. Kaya, you will like it. It has a bar, and there are beautiful views. We'll have fun."

"Okay, Justin. If it's bad, we can leave."

"Absolutely, we can leave."

Leaning to the front seat, she touches Isaac and says,

"It's fine; we'll be careful."

Isaac kisses his fingers, touches the Star of David hanging from the rearview mirror, and then chants:

"To Rick's inna safety, All Praises to Jah!"

The Cadillac slowly moves out of the circular drive and up the gravel road towards Negril and Rick's Café.

The gravel road from Villa Calm to the main highway is less than a quarter mile long, and Kaya's eyes gaze out the window like a little puppy on her first trip.

I cannot help but admire her nonchalance and sophistication, a distant, captivating coolness that I adore; these moments in the car just riding with her bring the most pleasure, just being in her presence.

As we drive, Isaac sucks on a spiff and hands it to Kaya over the back seat. She inhales deeply, blowing the smoke out the open window, and hands it to me.

I pass.

Just as in our youth, there is a moment when all things seem perfect, as if you are aligned with the universe.

As the gravel road ends, we turn onto the main highway, heading toward Rick's.

Trees and shanty houses dot the road.

Our time on the island seems to have slowed our pace as if we have always been here.

The Caddie reached a tree-filled lane, and Kaya leaned toward the Styrofoam box perched on the floor.

It was restocked with a coconut and rum concoction, and she handed me a cupful.

Bob Marley blasts from a million speakers.

The rum, the Caddie's movement, and the blasting reggae end all thought and reason, blurring time and space into one.

I anticipated that time spent with Kaya would be intellectual, erudite, sophisticated, and artistic.

Still, instead, it seems we are immersed in hedonism as the pungent scent of ganja permeates the car, and somehow, this seems off;

I am not sure why.

The trip to Rick's ends in a long, steep driveway crowded with tourists' cars.

The grounds cover several acres of hillside south of Negril and offers excellent views.

It's an open space filled with well-placed bars to attract and entertain. Isaac finds a spot on the steep drive that slopes up to the café.

"Mi wi drive yuh up an' drop yuh a di entrance. No need, fi walk," Isaac says.

"This will be fine. Just leave the car here. We will walk up. Do you want to come up with us?" I ask.

"Nah, mi wi stay yah an' wait. No Babylon fi mi."

Kaya pecks Isaac on the cheek as we get out of the car.

Then, I grab Kaya by the arm before ascending the steep drive. Kaya takes a last look at Isaac and says,

"Thanks for the kaya.

Isaac smiles as Kaya continues,

"All these years, my dad told me my name means pure and pleasing in Japanese. Now, I come to Jamaica and find out that it is their word for pot. How funny."

"How did you know it meant pot?" I ask.

"Dahlia mentioned it when she gave me some yesterday; we had a good laugh."

"Well, the Japanese meaning is more beautiful. And you, you have been quite pleasing lately," I say.

Kaya does not respond but cracks a smile as we drag each other up the hill.

Affected by the smoke, she seems dazed as we walk into the crowded outdoor café overlooking the sea.

Vast crowds of mostly young people, college types from the resorts in Negril boozing it up, populate the place.

Loud music plays from the speakers. We pass tables covered with empty plastic cups and red-stripe bottles.

The ground is covered with revelers' discarded waste, and we must move slowly and carefully to avoid the trash.

As we work through the crowded space, Kaya, somewhat off balance and obviously high, bumps into some college punk trying to balance four drinks in his two hands.

"What the fuck is wrong with you!" he exclaims.

"I'm sorry. It was an accident," I say, grabbing Kaya tighter and tighter, and we move on.

"OK, then," he says and walks away.

We make it through the crowd to the edge of the cliff.

Here, divers leap from the cliff to the awe of the crowds, who cheer as they splash into the sea below.

I find a safe place behind a rock wall with a free table and an excellent view of the divers and the Caribbean Sea before us.

Kaya relaxes.

I can see that she is still somewhat shaky, maybe from the ganja or perhaps the incident with the idiot.

"Let me get you a drink. Wait here; it's a beautiful view."

"OK," she says, "but this place is terrible. Isaac was right. It's crowded, dirty, loud, and full of assholes. Why did you bring me here?"

"Look over there, by the stairs, by the cliff. See that guy climbing up the stairs to the top of the cliff? He's going to jump," I say.

Kaya turns her head and observes a diver mounting the final few steps near the edge.

He lunges off the cliff and makes a fall that seems to last forever until he finally splashes into the sea below.

"Justin, that was beautiful, very nice. So, I saw it. Can we leave now?" A hint of sarcasm in her voice resonates.

"I jumped once!" I declare.

Kaya chuckles and then says,

"Oh, you want me to believe that?

Come on!

You've always been afraid of heights. You wouldn't even look out the window on the plane ride, and the balcony doesn't count," she says with a smile.

"No, it's true. I was here last summer with Lacy and David.

Lacy kept joking with me, teasing me, telling me to jump. David heard it all. I was scared out of my wits, but David was watching.

He said,

'Daddy, go! You can do it! Daddy, go!'

Kaya, do you see how high that cliff is, the long distance to the sea below?"

"Yeah, it's a long drop for sure. There is no way I would do it but go on. What happened?"

"I couldn't let my son down. I couldn't let him believe his father was afraid, pass along my fear; it wouldn't be right, so I walked up those steps, closed my eyes, and jumped. When I hit the water, all was well."

"Nice work!" Kaya exclaims.

"I came up and treaded water, and then I looked up the cliff and couldn't believe what I saw."

"What was that?" Kaya asks.

"David was stepping off the cliff – this little seven-year-old boy.

There was nothing I could do.

People were trying to grab him but hadn't noticed him making the final climb, and it was too late.

David jumped.

I saw him falling and falling. I just continued to tread water and waited. No thoughts went through my mind; it just happened.

David landed a few feet before me, and seconds later, he rose from the depths with a huge smile.

We hugged and took a few quick strokes to the rocky cliff.

As we climbed the stairs to the top of the cliff, we could see Lacy and the others gathered on the cliffside.

They were clapping with excitement. Lacy said she'd tried to grab him but that he was too quick. My son followed me off the cliff,"

I mumble in conclusion.

In an instant, its clear Kaya's mood has changed. I am not a master of women's emotions, that's for sure, but if I were to guess, I would say that she's suddenly become somber.

"Justin, that's a wonderful story. You must be very proud- you have a brave son.

Kaya turns away and walks towards the cliff, somehow drawn to where David jumped.

She seemed lost in it, almost trance-like, as if drawn into the place itself. I called out.

"Wait here. Let me get you a drink."

She didn't answer, lost in the view—or maybe in thought—as sailboats slipped across the horizon.

The setting sun scattered multicolored daggers across the waves, a dazzling clash of dark and light, as if the sea itself were aflame.

What could be more perfect?

I knew she would like it once we got there.

Drinks in hand, I return to find Kaya with her head flat on the table, sobbing.

"Why are you crying? What happened?" I ask, nudging her gently.

She doesn't look up. She is still.

I've seen this before. Not with Kaya, but I've seen it.

My mind flashes to Dr. Levy. Lacy. Yes, Lacy.

Dread overcomes me.

The noise around me—the music, the crowds—dims as if I'm no longer at Rick's.

Finally, slowly, Kaya lifts her tear-streaked face, pale lines cutting across her brow.

She drags the back of her arm across her eyes, then looks at me—really looks at me.

Not the way she has before. Something has shifted.

Her gaze is intense, like she's seeing me for the first time.

"Don't you see, Justin?" Kaya says between her tears.

"Don't I see what?" I ask.

"This is a sign. How can you not notice this?

Your son literally followed you off a cliff without thinking, without hesitation.

He demonstrated great respect and love.

I'm Japanese. I know that having a son who loves and honors you is the highest form of filial devotion. I have been insolent. I've been reckless. I have judged wrong!

I'm ashamed and embarrassed; forgive me.

Justin, forgive me.

When she finishes speaking, she tumbles out of her chair and onto the grass, falling to my feet, crawling, crying, and begging for forgiveness.

People stare openly at us, some shocked, some amused, some looking almost menacing as I scrape up her limp form.

"Justin, please… forgive me. Please."

Rest

Trying to move her is like lifting a boulder: she will not or cannot move.

She is immobile as if struck down by some odd paralysis.

Her arms fall limp at her sides, and she digs her feet deep into the ground.

It takes all my strength to prop her up and get her headed toward the car.

Fortunately, the way back is downhill, which is good because if it were otherwise, the short trek would likely be impossible.

Even with these optimal conditions, she falls to the ground again every ten or twenty feet and commences the sickening groveling.

Her mouth foams, and tears stream down her reddening face.

Grabbing my legs as if she were begging for her life, she kisses and kneads my feet as if they were sourdough.

I am overcome with embarrassment… eyes from all sides provide plentiful, withering, spiteful gazes.

The Cadillac comes into view, and Isaac frantically runs our way as soon as he spies us.

"Justin, she tek sumting from di ballhead?" Isaac asks.

"I don't think so," I reply. "Maybe it was the ganja?"

"I an' I tell yuh nuh come yah so. Chicken merry, hawk deh near!
"Isaac declares.

"Isaac, the frickin' ballheads didn't do anything. It was about David," I reply.

"David, nah, come yah," Isaac says.

Then, looking intently and concerned at Kaya, he asks her,

"Yuh listen, di ball head dem gi yuh sumting?"

Kaya raises her head weakly as if in great pain. She looks at Justin with odd eyes and says,

"No, nothing but your son."

"David, him deh deh?"

Isaac, looking confused, questions Kaya.

"No, David wasn't there."

Kaya says in a whisper as she climbs into the backseat, throwing herself down.

A hollow look is upon her face as if all the spirit and blood have been sucked out.

"Stop this right now! Please, I mean it." I say.

I grab her by the shoulders and pull her to sit. Her red eyes are fixed in an empty stare.

"Kaya! Kaya!"

I yell while shaking her with considerable force.

Her eyes pop back. Looking at me, she says,

"Justin, I'll be OK. I'm OK. I just need to rest."

She grabs my hand, holds it tightly, straightens up, and then lays her head on my shoulder, closing her eyes.

"I'm alright; I'm fine," she says inaudibly.

"Sorry, Isaac, if I upset you. Let's go back to the villa. I'm fine, really," she says.

The forty-five-minute drive to Villa Calm is a silent one.

Kaya's head rests on my shoulder, and her hand holds mine.

Wind buffets through the open windows.

From the Father Come the Son

Wilson or no Wilson, I need to spend the night with Kaya.

So, the staff will all see – fuck it.

How can I leave her alone in this condition? There's no telling what she'll do next.

Isaac and I help her up the stairs and into the bedroom, where she collapses on the bed.

She lifts her hand when he leaves and says,

"Justin, just lie down and hold me."

I do as she asks, and she falls into a deep and immediate sleep; then I doze off.

I arise at 4 A.M., and though it's still dark outside, I am somehow invigorated.

I head into the little kitchen, which Lacy loved so much.

I can see her standing there and cutting up the fish David caught with Tosh, David looking with pride upon his catch.

I prepare an early morning coffee and milk, which I carry to the balcony to drink.

Finding a comfortable chair with an excellent view of the moon over the Caribbean, I sit in the pre-dawn peace.

Early morning calm is upon the sea as if Jamaica is asleep and has not yet awoken – a great slumbering expanse beyond the balcony, the cottage, and the villa behind.

Kaya lies fast asleep but a few feet away from me, covered with a fine sheet as thin as my understanding of her.

She lies there beautifully, at peace.

But what the hell will I be dealing with when she wakes up?

Standing near the edge of the balcony with my coffee, to the East, I spy Tosh walking over to his battered and worn boat as if he intends to go to sea.

Amazingly, he looks up and motions to me.

Putting on my shoes, I trek down the switchbacks to the base of the cliff.

As my feet touch the sand, Tosh exclaims,

"Justin! Yuh no visit I dis yah time? Yuh nuh have no time fi I?"

"Hey, Tosh. I've been busy, but here I am. How are you?"

"Mi good, all thanks an' praises to Jah, "Tosh responds.

Walking over to his skiff, he pushes it a few feet towards the deep. Then he looks back at me, carefully studying my visage, taking his time, staring.

Then, with some uncharacteristic hesitation, he speaks:

"Ah true… yuh deh yah wid anadda one?"

I hesitate but then say,

"Yes, Tosh, yes. I'm here with an old friend from Los Angeles. She came to help me."

Tosh pushes the skiff a few more feet towards the sea, then stops and looks back.

"Help yuh? Ya man, I an' I know how it go."

With one long shove, shoulder to stern, he moves his skiff a few more yards to where the water meets the sand, turning it bright and shiny gray.

"Yuh waan sail wid I an' I today?"

Tosh says as he looks back at Justin.

As Tosh makes the final thrusts of the boat into the water, I look up at the cottage on the cliff and then out to sea.

The sun has not yet risen, and there are no lights on in the cottage other than the one I left on in the kitchen.

Surely, Kaya is asleep. I walk to the other side of the boat, grab the gunwales, Tosh at the stern, and we push in unison.

"Thanks for asking. Sure, let's go."

We push the little craft over the gently rolling surf and out a few meters; the warm waters are comforting. Then, we hoist ourselves into the little craft.

Moving to the rear, I recline as Tosh carefully unfurls the tattered sail and hoists it into the wind, and, as if by the hands of Jah, we are carried out to sea.

Sailing in silence, we move slowly, with a wake so low and effortless that it's as if some magnetic rail below is carrying us forth.

Tosh looks to the sky as if gazing at the infinite as he prepares to cast his nets.

Standing high against a barely rising sun, his dreads blowing in the breeze, his dark and crevassed skin shimmering in the light reflected by the water, Tosh says,

"In di name of Jah, di Most High, blessings pon yuh, an' may Jah find wi worthy fi di fruits a di sea."

Only then does Tosh toss his nets to the wind.

Landing as a feather upon a feather, tiny droplets rise a few inches and then fall like rain, creating small, dazzling pimples on the surface.

Tosh stands over the nets, high in the boat.

I remain mute and curled up in the stern, appreciating the space, the flat sea, the wind, the air, and the warmth of the beautiful sparkling green island in the distance.

The sun throws its first rays over the earth; there is comfort and peace where we are now.

Then, Tosh looks at me as though he wants to tell me something.

He looks away, then turns to me again and, after hesitating a bit more, says,

"Justin, dere someting mi haffi know 'bout yuh."

He pauses.

"Why yuh bring dis woman yah so?"

Hesitating momentarily, I take a deep breath, knowing Tosh cannot be deceived.

"Because I love her. Is that not reason enough?

Tosh replies quietly.

"Justin, mi sure yuh love plenty people an' tings, but Jah neva give yuh leave fi lay wid anadda man's woman.

Dat nuh love, dat a someting else. Jah see all mortal deeds, yuh know.

An' in him wisdom, Jah set challenge fi every man an' woman, so dem can freely choose good ova evil.

In him mercy, Jah give yuh a sign, nuh true?

Him put di name David pon yuh tongue as a sign fi remind yuh seh even a great king cyaan hide him sins from Jah.

An' pon di mountain, just like Moses at Sinai, him show yuh di way.

Yuh nuh see it?"

"Tosh, what are you saying?"

"From di fadda come di son.

The Awakening

Returning to the cottage, I find Kaya sitting among bright tropical flowers, with a fine ink pen in hand, jotting letters in tiny blue squares on a graph paper tablet.

There is a smile on her face that I have never seen before, a smile of satisfaction and approval, the smile I've wanted to see all these years.

"Good morning," she chimes and then returns to her script.

"What are you writing?" I ask.

"It was really nice," she says.

There it is again, that smile.

"I don't understand," I say.

"This morning was nice. I am writing notes about this morning."

She began to read her notes, summarizing them for me.

"In the morning, from the balcony, I saw Tosh and you far out at sea. He was standing and casting a net, and you were sitting in the back of the boat. It was a beautiful scene in the rising sun.

I want to remember it, so I'm writing it down. There is so much I feel and have always felt that I could never tell you, and from now on, I will, that I promise.

I want you to know everything that's inside me. I have kept so much from you, and now I understand that I was so wrong."

"That's wonderful. What brought this on?" I ask.

"Justin, when I woke this morning, at dawn, it was as if a load had been lifted from my mind.

I started rearranging the flowers. I had never arranged flowers before, but I wanted to make this place beautiful for you when you returned.

I felt that everything must be in order. You must know that I have never done this sort of thing before, but I will from now on.

I will.

Let me explain.

When you told me the story of David yesterday, about how he made that leap, and on your behalf, I was ashamed, for at that moment, I understood that you had made the same leap for me all these years.

And for that belief in me, I have given you nothing.

As you have earned the respect and admiration of your son, you have earned mine, too, at long last.

Too long, I know. But at least… at least I know now."

"You are doing this because I dared to jump off that frickin' cliff?" I ask.

"It wasn't your jump off the cliff that brought me this clarity; that jump was merely a moment of courage, and even a lowly person can possess courage. Nor was it your… our passion that awoke me. Passion?

It's just flesh at the end of the day.

It says nothing about the inner person.

It was the story of your son's demonstration of devotion, his leap of faith, that opened my eyes, for he would not offer his life so freely if you had not given so freely to him.

Justin, it was then that my eyes were opened and filled with shame, for it was clear that you had done the same for me, yet I had given you nothing in return.

Throughout all the years of your undying love, I have given nothing of myself.

Yet, you have loved me without knowledge, and at that moment, I recalled the words of my Japanese grandfather,

Shiranu ga hotoke, which means, 'Not knowing is Buddha.'

Justin, when I heard about the leap, I questioned myself.

Clearly, your son respected and loved you, but why?

I knew there was something special about you, something different. That is why I allowed you to continue to contact me, yet I understood nothing, so I told you nothing.

You told me everything and said you would give me everything, yet you knew nothing.

Kaya bows as she says those words.

"So, I'm a Buddha?" I ask.

"Justin, Justin, I'm not saying you're a Buddha, but you have demonstrated a true Buddha nature.

I don't care if you don't understand that; I do.

And henceforth, I will honor that nature," she says with another bow.

"It will be hard. It will be so hard for us – we'll have to change many things and hurt so many people, I'm afraid, but Justin, I love and honor you as you love me."

"I love you, too, Kaya," I echoed on autopilot.

"I've always known that. Always. But I have one question," Kaya asks.

"Sure, what is it?" I reply.

"For my notes, I'm curious. Did you have an enjoyable time with Tosh?" she asks, smiling.

"Um, yeah, it was fine.

Sure. We fished a bit. He had a good catch; he was happy."

"Did he ask about me? What did he say?"

"Like I told you, these Rastas speak in riddles. It's hard to tell."

The Mountain Top

Whatever distance between Kaya and me now seems like an ancient memory; there is no longer angst, mistrust, and doubt on one hand, and simple sexual dynamism on the other, but rather a beautiful woman at peace and in love.

"Justin, I've planned a trip this afternoon to the Blue Mountain; Isaac has family at Hadley Gap. It will be a wonderful day in the cool, clean air at the mountaintop.

Can we go?"

"Sure, why not? "Anything you want to—"

I begin to reply, but before I can get the last word out, Kaya grabs me snugly by the waist, twirls me around with one hand, and grabs a picnic basket with the other.

Then we're out the door. Descending the stairs of the cottage, I look askance at Kaya.

For a second, I thought I was with Lacy.

Isaac pulls the Caddie in front of us and, without saying one word, picks up the basket and a small suitcase Kaya had laid at his feet.

On the backseat floor, in place of the cheap Styrofoam cooler, is a shiny new aluminum cooler crammed with soft drinks, water, Red Stripe, and a selection of tropical fruits.

This made no sense at all!

How did they plan all this so fast?

How did she, I should wonder…

Is it confusion or simply fatigue?

Perhaps it is a result of the too-early rise?

Or maybe it was the brutal, tiring walk up and down the cliff… or simply the heavy words from Tosh.

Or could it be Kaya's confession?

In any case, I'm exhausted. Confused. Overwhelmed is the word.

"Justin, lie down," Kaya said.

As I recline, Kaya sets a pillow on her lap to support my head and gently tosses a soft blanket over my torso.

The gentle back-and-forth rocking and Gregory Isaac's mellow riffs lull me into a deep and restful sleep.

When I awake, the Cadillac is parked high on a green mountaintop, surrounded by a V-shaped canyon lined by verdant hills and punctuated with piney trees.

Not far from the Cadillac is a rundown shack.

I find myself alone and call out for Isaac and Kaya, but they are nowhere to be found.

The car door opens onto a grassy meadow.

Still half-asleep, I find a soft patch of grass near the shack and recline, figuring they can't be far away.

The quiet of the mountains and the clean, cool air invigorates me.

Slowly, I grow alert and aware.

I take in the sights, scents, and sounds of the place I find myself –
perhaps following the will of others is not altogether a bad thing.

A few white clouds pass high above in the azure sky.

Does a cloud determine its own course?

No, it is driven by the wind, but without protest.

"Hey, Justin, wah yuh deh do deh so?

"Isaac calls out as he exits the tumbledown shack across from my
green patch.

"Just looking at the clouds," I say.

"Where's Kaya? I woke up in the car, and you guys were gone."

"She go batty when she see di place. She love it yah so! She tek a
walk wid di ragamuffin dem. She soon come," Tosh answered.

"Egad, man! Where's the motherfuckin' Blue Mountain Coffee?
This is the Blue Mountain, isn't it?" I say.

"Schuss, mi Auntie deh a di house. She mek wi coffee, but watch
yuhself. Madda, she nuh like no tarra warra. See her a come now!"

Auntie slowly walks out the front (and only) door of the clapboard
shack, balancing a tray of black coffee on her head.

I pull myself up and dust off some dirt and grass to make myself
more presentable.

She sets the tray of hot drinks down on a wooden picnic table
about twenty paces from the shack.

Sweet steam rises into the air.

I stroll over with as much poise as I can muster.

Auntie hollers at me even before I get to the table.

"Set yuhself down, bwoy. Mi bring yuh some coffee from di hills—di best inna di world, dem seh. Blessed by Jah, high pon di mountaintop, all praises. Set yuhself down now, Isaac. Him seh yuh crazy an' rude, but him love yuh same way."

Grabbing Isaac by the waist and turning him around, I declare,

"Dat is fe mi bredda."

Auntie looks at Isaac and asks,

"Where he learns to talk like dat?"

Isaac smiles, and we all laugh, then Auntie says.

"Isaac, yuh ah di best outta di Wilkins, seen?"

"Well, thank you," I reply,

"but I'm not a Wilkins. I just married into the family."

As soon as I finish saying this, I feel a sharp twinge of pain in my stomach.

"Dat explain it," she says with a sassy laugh.

Auntie picks up a cup of coffee from the table, hands it to me, and continues,

"An' Kaya, yuh wife, she nuh look like no Wilkins, but people mix up nowadays, an' dat a good ting. Jah mek we all wid one blood, so we all di same."

"No, Madam,"

I struggle to get the words out and to keep my voice firm.

"Kaya is just a friend; she's not my wife."

Isaac chimes in.

"Matey she be."

I look over at Isaac.

"Isaac, what is, Matey?"

"Mistress," Isaac chuckles in response.

I want to protest but can think of nothing to say.

He's telling the truth, by Jah.

Just then, Kaya appeared from around a bend in the road.

She's with two small children, carrying a fistful of wildflowers and sporting that same smile on her face that I saw for the first time yesterday – the one I always wanted to see – a restful and calm smile.

Kaya motions to Isaac as if it were a plan.

Together, they remove a basket from the Caddie and return with the scrappy kids and two gruff but friendly dogs.

Auntie and Kaya spread the goodies, and we all began to eat.

The kids truly resemble Isaac, which makes me wonder, but given current circumstances, I am in no position to ask or pass judgment here, so I make no mention of the likeness.

Kaya looks my way, and I can't help but notice that she has the same look and determination I've often seen in Lacy.

"I was looking at the map as we drove up here," Kaya says.

"Hagley Gap is at the base of the Blue Mountains.

From here, the hike to the peak isn't difficult.

Not even a hike, really, just a walk!

We can do it in less than an hour. It'll be a lovely stroll. Please, let's do it."

The last thing I want to do is trek up this fuckin' mountain, and the more I think about the entire day, the more uneasy I become.

"OK, Kaya, we can go, but we gotta be back before dark."

"Yeah, sure!" she replies, near giddy.

Bidding adieu to Auntie, Isaac, and the kids, we begin our hike. It soon becomes clear that the trail is incredibly steep.

Had I known this, I would never have agreed to the adventure, but I held my tongue.

The farther and farther we ascend, the cooler it becomes and the narrower the path.

The stream the path follows roars louder and louder as we climb— more waterfall than stream with each step higher—and the wind whips the leaves on the trees, which tower above us, forming a dark canopy blocking the sky.

Kaya seems as if in heaven as she runs to and fro, looking at this or that and alerting me to beautiful discoveries hidden amongst the brush, but the best I can do is meander up the trail and count the minutes until our return.

Exhausted by the climb, I found a quiet spot beside the rushing waters.

I sink to my knees, concentrating on the stream as it pours rapidly down the rocky slope.

Banks of low clouds, fog, and mist surround us.

An eeriness overwhelms me.

In fear, I called out, "Kaya, Kaya."

I hear her far in the distance.

I find a quiet spot beside the rushing waters.

Clouds surround us.

I hear Kaya shouting in the distance.

"It's so beautiful; it's like we're in heaven!"

I sway in the wind amongst the clouds; my mind tells me that my feet are firmly planted, but for the life of me, I cannot feel the earth.

Overcome by fear and surrounded by empty space.

Kaya is sitting high on a throne as if in a vision.

To her right, standing and observing it all, is Lacy.

Between Lacy and Kaya is David, whirling and twirling in all directions, sometimes looking up and sometimes looking down, rudderless as I and I in space.

Floating above Kaya is Dahlia, and Tosh hovers above my son.

Overcome by panic, now frozen, the rushing water churned louder and louder, and the wind and the trees let out a dreadful howl.

The riverbank is at my feet.

I am sure of this, but there is little else.

Reaching out, the cool waters cover my feet.

I sense Kaya is near; undisturbed by the fog, she reassures me,

"I am here with you," she says.

"Stay by me; lead me out, for I cannot see," I say.

"I can see," she says. "I can see. I'll find my way out."

I reach out to touch her.

I can feel her, then not.

The sounds of the leaves at her feet fade in the distance and then.

Silence…

www.ingramcontent.com/pod-product-compliance
Lightning Source LLC
Chambersburg PA
CBHW051136300726
48978CB00011B/300